KINGPIN WIFEYS
VOLUME 3

BY
K. ELLIOTT

OTHER TITLES BY K. ELLIOTT

Kingpin Wifeys Series
Season I
Kingpin Wifeys Part 1
Kingpin Wifeys Part 2
Kingpin Wifeys Part 3
Kingpin Wifeys Part 4: Jada's Story
Kingpin Wifeys Part 5: Lani's Dilemma
Kingpin Wifeys Part 6: A Starr is Born
Kingpin Wifeys Part 7: Who Do You Love?
Kingpin Wifeys Part 8: Finale for Season 1
Season II
Kingpin Wifeys 1: A Dollar Before Sunset
Kingpin Wifeys 2: The Bad Guy
Kingpin Wifeys 3: Going Hard

Dilemma

Dear Summer

Entangled

Treasure Hunter

Street Fame

Godsend Series
Godsend 1: A Necessary Evil
Godsend 2: The Search for Rochelle
Godsend 3: Pissed All The Way Off
Godsend 4: Hiding In Plain Sight
Godsend 5: Blasphemy Out West
Godsend 6: All Jokes Aside
Godsend Full Length Novel: The Weight of Echo
Godsend 7: The Halo Effect
Godsend 8: The Value of a Woman
Godsend 9: Square In The Mouth
Godsend 10: That Stupid Hooker
Godsend 11: Taken for Granite
Godsend 12: The Audacity
Godsend 13: Selling Woof Tickets
Godsend 14: Ass to Kiss
Godsend 15: Kill Somebody Else

– PART 7 –

CHAPTER 1

MIKE PASSED THE PHONE BACK TO LANI. THERE WAS AN AWKWARD silence.

Kenny-Boo saw the look on Mike face and asked, "What the hell is going on?"

Mike sat on the sofa in total shock. How in the hell did Black find out where his parents lived? Did Lani tell him? What was he going to do now? If he killed Lani and Man-Man, he would never see his mother and stepfather again. He would be without his parents and his brother.

Lani held Man-Man's hand. She spoke into the phone. "What the hell's going on?"

There was nobody on the other end of the phone, only a dial tone.

Mike ordered Kenny-Boo to get the money, count it, and give it back to Lani.

"For what?"

Mike barked, "Do what the fuck I say!"

Kenny-Boo dropped his head and made his way to the back room and re-emerged with the $249,000 from earlier. Black had been a thousand dollars short with the payment.

Kenny-Boo passed the suitcase to Lani. Then he turned to Mike and said, "So you're not going to tell me why we're giving the money back?"

Mike ignored his silly ass and asked Lani to call Black.

She dialed the number and passed the phone back to Mike. "Lani has the money. How do I know you're going to let my mom go?"

"I could've snatched your mom a long time ago. I've known where she lived for a while now. I don't want your mom. I want my son and my motherfucking money. You give the money back and you won't have no problems."

"Put my mama on the phone."

Seconds later Mike's mother said, "Hello?"

"Ma. You okay?"

"I'm fine."

"Do you believe he'll let you go?"

"I think so, son. They haven't harmed us at all."

Black snatched the phone out of her hand and said, "Listen, nigga, give me the goddamned money back and you won't have any problems."

"Lani has the money."

Kenny-Boo said, "If it were me, I wouldn't give them a goddamned thing."

Man-Man said, "Quit cursing so much."

Kenny-Boo said to the kid, "Shut the hell up!"

Lani terminated the call. She could tell that Kenny-Boo wanted to slap the fuck out of her. He gave her back the fifty thousand dollars that she'd brought over today as well.

Mike said, "Call him back one more time and tell him you have all the money."

Lani dialed the number and said, "I have the money."

Lani was scared as hell. She wondered how in the hell Black found Mike's parents house and sure as hell hoped that Mike didn't think she let Black know where they resided. There was no way in hell she would do something like that, but she was almost certain that even if Mike didn't think that, Kenny-Boo damn sure did.

Black said, "Kyrie is outside. When he is in possession of the money, I'll release his parents."

Lani terminated the call and said, "He's going to release them when I'm outside, and Kyrie has the money."

Kenny-Boo with his limited comprehension had just figured out that Mike's parents were being held. "Don't believe him."

Mike said, "Shut the fuck up! Mama is all I got."

Lani stared at Mike, she could feel his pain. This whole ordeal had gotten completely out of hand, and it was time for this bullshit to stop. Lani walked toward the door with Man-Man in front of her and Kenny-Boo behind her. As she exited into the hallway, Kenny-Boo shoved the fuck out of her and she crashed into the wall before dropping the briefcase and stumbling over the suitcase. Man-Man looked frightened as Lani rose back to her feet.

Kenny-Boo said, "Bitch, your day is coming!"

He slammed the door as Lani made her way outside where Kyrie was waiting behind the wheels of a blue Honda Accord.

CHAPTER 2

TREY SAID, "OFFICER, CAN YOU TELL ME WHY YOU PULLED ME OVER?"
The man ignored Trey and said, "License and registration."

Shantelle was awake now, wondering what in the hell they were going to do. Hell, they couldn't run. Though she was in better shape than most girls, she was wearing sandals and Trey wasn't in the best condition. Even if they did run, the police would have the car. She'd gone through this with Monte. She didn't want to get arrested. It was time for her white-girl voice.

"Honey, just do what the man tell you. I'm sure whatever you did, the officer will let you know, write your ticket, and then we'll be on our way."

Trey passed the trooper his license and registration. The trooper walked back to his patrol car and when he was out of sight, Trey said, "Remain calm as possible. Whatever he stopped us for, it's going to be okay. Think positive. Think legit. Act legit."

"Got ya," Shantelle said. Though she was a smart girl, she knew she wasn't as street smart as Trey.

Seconds later the trooper returned. He asked Trey to exit the vehicle.

Shantelle was nervous as hell. She'd been calm, she acted legit. This was not how this was supposed to go.

Trey removed his seatbelt and sprang from the car. The trooper waited for him by the rear of the car.

Trey asked, "What did I do?"

The trooper's face got a shade redder and he said, "I'm going to ask the questions. Not you. Got it?"

Trey wanted to smack the fuck out of the hillbilly cop but instead he said, "Yes sir."

"Where you coming from?"

"Texas."

"What part?"

"Houston"

"What were you doing in Houston?"

"Visiting."

"You got family down there?"

"Yeah, family and friends."

"What kind of work do you do?"

"Why you want to know that?"

"So you don't have a job?"

"I'm in the music business."

"Somehow I figured you were going to say that."

Shantelle heard the whole conversation. She scrolled through her phone looking for her friend Lori. Somebody had to know if she was going to get arrested. She spotted Trey's phone on the seat. She picked it up and decided to call Q. He picked up on the first ring.

"What's up?"

"Hey, this is Shantelle. Me and Trey just got pulled over."

"Oh yeah? Where is Trey?"

"He's outside talking to the trooper. "

"Where are ya'll?"

"About thirty minutes away from Baton Rouge."

Q hung up the phone and when Shantelle tried to call him back, she got his voicemail. Fuck! She dialed Lori from her phone and her phone went straight to voicemail as well. Fuck!

Trey said, "Why do you want to know what I do for a living? You can google me and my company if you want. I have my own record label."

The trooper laughed. "Let me guess the name of it. Hmm...Dope house records?"

"Google me if you don't believe me."

"Google you?" The trooper laughed. "I'm not on Google, Instagram, Facebook or none of that shit."

"Google is a search engine."

"A search engine? You know what else is a search engine? I'm a search engine and I'll search this whole goddamned car, including the engine, if you don't tell me where the goddamned dope is, Boy!"

"Boy?"

The man looked Trey straight in the eye and he said, "Yeah I said 'Boy'. You got a problem with that?"

With ten kilos of cocaine in the car, Trey had absolutely no problem with the redneck calling him boy, or nigga for that matter. He simply had to accept it.

"There's nothing in the car."

"So you're telling me if I search this car, I ain't going to find nothing?"

"You don't have any right to search this car. Where is your probable cause?"

"I don't need no probable cause but if you want it, you'll get it. I'll just write the goddamned report up and say you were swerving like you'd been drinking, and when I pulled you over, I smelled marijuana, and that pretty little girlfriend of yours was drunk and belligerent. Then you'll go to jail for six months while awaiting trial by a jury of your peers. If you're lucky, you'll get one black on your jury who is going to go along with the whites because he has to live in this town of thirteen thousand residents. Who do you think the courts are going to believe, a decorated officer of the law or two goddamned niggas?"

The man looked Trey straight in his eyes and there was a long silence. "You want to take your chances?"

Trey didn't respond.

"Now you can hand them drugs over and I can forget about this, or I can radio in the K9 unit. I'm trying to be nice and I'm asking you nicely."

"You call that being nice?"

"I could have cuffed your ass first then searched the car."

"What do you want from me?"

"I want the truth."

"There is nothing in here."

Trey popped his knuckles and kicked dirt.

The trooper said, "Somebody is nervous."

"Listen, I've told you the truth."

"I don't believe you," the trooper said, his handlebar mustache curled up further because he was visibly angry with Trey. "In fact, I know you're lying. I've been a trooper for over twenty years. I can smell a slick-talking drug dealer from a mile away."

Trey laughed, not because the man was funny but to keep from crying. There was no way in the hell he wanted to go to prison for possession for ten kilos of coke.

The trooper said, "Hand over the drugs and I'll drive away. You'll never hear from me again."`

"What?"

"Hand over the drugs or I'm calling K-9 and we'll find them."

Trey couldn't believe what the fuck he was hearing. Did the man say hand over the drugs and he would never hear from him again. "What if I give you money?"

"Even better, how much you got?"

"A hundred thousand, at least."

The trooper handed Trey his license and registration back and Trey retrieved the briefcase full of money from the car and passed it to the trooper.

The grinning-ass trooper said, "Have a nice day, Mr. Carter, and slow down." He winked.

CHAPTER 3

JADA REMOVED THE LAST OF SHAMARI'S BANDAGES AS HE STOOD looking at his new face in the mirror. He barely recognized himself, but that was the point. He didn't really notice a difference in his nose. Jada had warned him that it would take a few years before he'd notice a difference. He turned to Jada who stood beside him with her mouth wide open.

"So what do you think, baby?"

Her mouth was still open and she was unable to speak.

"Do you like it or not?"

"It's okay."

"What do you mean, 'it's okay'?"

"I think he did a good job. He did what he was supposed to do."

"But you don't like it?"

"I don't like it! Not at all!" She stormed out of the bathroom and made her way to the bed. She buried her face in the pillow and cried. She was not attracted to his face at all, even though it was beautiful. She liked him looking a little more rugged. That's what she was used to, not some perfect pretty boy.

Shamari came in seconds later and sat on the bed beside her.

Jada stared at Shamari, she recognized only his eyes. His chin was hideous and those cheek implants made her feel like she wanted to vomit. The tears rolled down her face and she wiped them away.

"Am I that ugly?"

"You're beautiful, but I don't like that look on you. I want the old Shamari back."

"I don't look that much different."

"I hate this new look."

Shamari removed her hands from her eyes and said, "It's not for you to like, baby. Remember, I did this to evade the police."

"But what about your ID?"

"Going to get a new one today, but we need to get the fuck up out of this hotel."

"I'm going to look at a town home today. If I like it, I'm going to give the man the money then I can move in next weekend."

Shamari noticed that she had said I instead of we so he asked, "So, I'm not welcome to your new home?"

"Of course you are, baby."

She sat up on the bed and he leaned into her and they kissed.

Shamari said, "Trust me, it's going to be okay."

"You think?"

"I sure as hell hope so."

"You're not going to turn yourself in?"

"I don't see a reason to. Do you?"

"No. Not at all. There is no way anybody is going to know it's you. I want the old Shamari back."

"You'll get used to me."

Jada kissed him again and said, "I don't think so."

●　●　●

Trey was on his way to Jessica's to see his son when he dialed Q's number and received a recording saying that the number was not in service. Trey hadn't heard from Q since the day he'd gotten pulled over. He tried to reach him with the three different phone numbers he had for him. He wished like hell Shantelle hadn't called him. Trey had dealt with Q for years and Trey knew that if Q thought he had gotten arrested, there was no way that he would ever do business with him again. Period. So he was in a really fucked up position. He would have to chill for now. Maybe this was God's way of showing him that he needed to slow down.

Jessica opened the door she said, "The world's greatest dad."

"Kill the sarcasm, Where is my son?"

"You mean my son."

Trey was annoyed with Jessica but he knew he would have to put up with her bullshit because she was his son's mother and there was no way he could see T. J. without dealing with her.

Jessica invited him in, and they made their way to the living room. Seconds later, T. J. appeared.

Trey said, "How is daddy's big boy doing?"

T. J. ignored him and took a seat beside Jessica on the love seat.

Trey was pissed the fuck off. How in the hell was his son going to ignore him?

"T. J., did you hear me?"

"I heard you."

"What's wrong?"

T. J. ignored Trey.

"Jessica, what have you done to my son?" Trey turned to Jessica.

"I haven't done anything. T. J. is a growing boy. He's old enough to know when someone cares about him or if they are full of shit."

"You been poisoning my son's goddamned mind?"

T. J. said, "Quit cursing my mommy."

"I'm your daddy!"

"You ain't my daddy!"

This made Trey furious and before he knew it, he'd said, "Boy, I will whip your lil ass in here! I brought you in this world, not the other way around!"

Jessica turned to T. J., "Trey is still your father. Go back in your room and play with your video games. Let me and your father talk for a minute."

When T. J. was gone, Trey said, "What's his goddamned problem?"

"You're his problem, Trey."

"You're turning that boy against me. I know what's happening."

"Oh my fucking god, Trey!" Jessica threw her hands up in disgust. "You really think I would do that?"

"You're capable of it."

"I don't have to. T. J. is just tired of you lying to him. You're always telling him that you're coming to pick him up and he gets his hopes up high, not only don't you show up, you don't call either."

"Well, I got things to do, money to make."

"Money is more important than your own son?"

"Never."

"Take him with you then."

Trey was hoping that she wouldn't ask that of him. Not that he didn't want to but he didn't have a place to take him besides his stash spots, his mother's house, or Shantelle's apartment. He knew Shantelle would be cool with it at first, but then she would get all emotional on him. He didn't want his son to stay at the stash house. It was too dangerous.

"Just as I thought." She laughed. "You have no idea what it's like to be a parent, Trey. How in the hell can you even call yourself a dad?"

"He can go with me."

Jessica called T. J. and he ran into the living room. He took hold of his mother's arm and stared at Trey and asked, "Are you being mean to my mom again?"

"Of course not, champ." Trey laughed.

"He acts just like you. That's the scary part," Jessica said

Trey made his way over to T. J. and said, "I'm going to take you to Cirque de Soleil."

"What's that?"

"It's like the circus but a hundred times better," Trey said.

T. J smiled but then remembered that he was supposed to be mad at his dad. He held his mother tight."

Jessica turned to T. J. and said, "Don't you want to go with your father?"

"No."

Trey said, "Why not?"

"Because you always lie to me!"

Trey said, "Give daddy a chance to make it up to you. I want to take you to see Cirque de Soleil and I'm going to take you to grandma's house. Grandma has been asking about you."

T. J.'s face lit up and said, "She called me yesterday."

Trey looked confused and Jessica said, "Yes, your mother keeps in touch, and I'm glad she does."

Trey had no idea that his mother kept in touch with them. He was barely in touch with his mom himself nowadays. He would have to do better with his priorities.

Jessica said, "Let's go to your room to pack some clothes." They disappeared into the bedroom.

Trey texted Starr.

Trey: *Hey.*

Starr: *Hey!*

Trey: *I really need my money. I had some bad luck.*

Starr: *Sorry to hear that.*

Trey: *Do you think you can meet me to give my money back?*

Starr: *Yes, I can meet you on Wed. Anytime after 7.*

Trey: *Cool. I'll meet you on Wed.*

Starr: *K.*

Jessica and T. J. entered the room carrying his backpack. T. J. said to Trey, "Can we go to grandma's first?"

"Of course."

Trey brushed T. J.'s hair as T. J. grinned.

Trey and T. J. had made their way to the door when Jessica said, "Trey, let me talk to you for a second alone. Take T. J. to the car and come back in."

"Leave him in the car alone?"

"Not with the keys, silly, and this is a nice neighborhood. He'll be okay," Jessica said. "Trey, just think how much it would mean to T. J. if I could come with you guys?"

"Huh?"

Jessica smiled and said, "We can be one big happy family. T. J. is always asking me why aren't we together."

"Yeah, I know every kid wants their parents to be together."

"T. J.'s no different."

"Bad idea. We don't get along."

Jessica said, "Look, Trey, I'm not trying to marry you. I just want a couple of days where T. J. can be with his parents. Is that too much to ask for?"

"I'm not with it."

"It's your new girlfriend, isn't it?"

"It's because you're going to be thinking that we're something that we're not."

She laughed. "I don't want to be with you."

"Okay, well let me spend time with my son."

There were tears rolling down Jessica's face. "You ruined my life!"

"How?"

"You got me pregnant and just left."

"You knew I had a woman, from day one."

"Now you're not with that woman, so why can't we be together? T. J. needs a family!"

"I knew that was what this is about."

"So what if I do want to be with you? What's wrong with me wanting to have a family for my son?"

"Leave T. J. the fuck out of it because you not going to get no sympathy from me, bitch!"

She lowered her voice. "I'll leave T. J. out of it."

"You tried to ruin my life. You ruined my relationship with the only woman that I ever loved."

"You never loved her. If you loved her, you wouldn't have fucked me and you damn sure wouldn't have fucked Shantelle."

"What did you say?"

"I said you wouldn't have fucked me or Shantelle."

"How do you know Shantelle's name?"

"I sent the pictures to Starr, remember?"

"I swear, you're the biggest stalker ever. I could never be with you."

Trey headed to the door and she took hold of his shirt and said, "Please! Don't leave! I wanna be one big happy family."

Trey shoved her and she stumbled to the floor. She took hold of his leg. He struggled to make it to the front door and she said, "Trey! Please don't go! Why can't we be one big happy family? I want a family, Trey."

When Trey made his way to the door, she was still locked on to his leg like a pit bull. Trey pried her fingers off his leg and slammed the door shut.

Jessica was still on the floor screaming, "All I want is a big happy family! All I want is my family to be together!"

CHAPTER 4

BLACK STARED AT THE SCREEN OF THE CELL PHONE AT A PICTURE OF a Blue pit bull that his daughter Tierany had sent him. He'd promised that he would get her and Man-Man a dog, but he didn't know if he wanted them to have a pit bull since they were so temperamental. He was quite surprised that Tierany wanted a pit bull since she was a girly-girl. He thought she would have wanted a Yorkie. Black was about to text her back when he noticed someone he didn't recognize creeping up his driveway. Black grabbed the Taurus nine millimeter from his waist, cocked it, and opened his front door.

"What's up, Partna!?" Black yelled out to the stranger.

"You can give me all your motherfucking money." The man smiled, but Black wasn't smiling.

"You better get the fuck away from here before I blast yo ass." Black brought up his gun.

"It's me. Mari."

"What?"

"It's Shamari."

Black looked closely and finally he recognized him. "What the fuck have you done to your face, man?"

"Changed my look, man."

"What the fuck?"

"Yeah, had to get some work done if I'm going to be on the run."

"Damn. I swear I didn't recognize you. Only a slight resemblance. I was 'bout to kill yo ass, asking for money."

Shamari laughed and Black asked, "Who did it?"

"Plastic surgeon that Jada knows."

"How much did it cost?"

"I ain't pay him shit."

"Huh?"

"It's a long story."

Black led Shamari inside the home and once they were sitting at the bar, Shamari asked, "Where's Kyrie?"

"I don't know? Why?"

"What ever happened with that case of his son taking the dope to school?"

"Nothing yet." Black eyed Shamari suspiciously, wondering why Shamari was asking all the goddamned questions about Kyrie. Black said, "Do you want something to drink?"

"What you got?"

"Henny, water or soda."

"Give me a soda. Got the taste for sugar."

Black came back with a can of Mountain Dew then he poured himself some Hennessey.

"Why all the questions about Kyrie?"

"When I was recovering from my surgery, I saw on the news that a few people had OD'd on heroin."

"What does that got to do with us? You know how many heroin dealers in Atlanta?"

"How many of them have the name Obamacare?"

Black sipped his liquor said, "We stole that name, remember?"

"I know, but now don't you think it's time that we give it back?"

"Maybe."

Black stared at Shamari's face and said, "I'm going to have to get used to this face, man. It's tripping me out."

"Freaked Jada out too."

"I bet."

"We need a new name."

"We need more product first."

"I can find us some."

"Where?"

"L.A."

"Look, I ain't into trafficking shit all the way across the country, but you get it back, I'll help you."

"I have no choice. If I'm going to be running, I gotta make some money."

"You're going to chance it going through airports and shit when you're on the run."

"I'm driving. I got a new license." Shamari flashed a license Hunch's cousin had made for him. His new alias was Ricky Stevenson.

"Driving it back is a big risk."

"I ain't got shit to lose."

Black said, "You got a point." He then downed his liquor.

• • •

Lani had been watching Netflix when someone rang her doorbell. She figured that it had to be someone at the wrong house because nobody had used the building keypad to notify her. She looked through the peephole and saw that it was Black. Lani opened the door but blocked the entrance into her home.

"I'm sorry I didn't call before I came, but I figured you didn't want to see me," Black said.

"You're smarter than I thought you were."

"Can we talk?

"About?"

"Can I come in? I'll be quick."

"I don't have time for this bullshit."

She stepped aside and let him inside. He followed her to the kitchen. They sat side by side at her bar. She offered him a drink but he declined.

"What do you want?"

"I wanna say I'm sorry. I swear to god, I didn't want to get you involved."

His eyes were sincere and she wanted to believe him, but there was no way she could believe him. She always wanted to believe what he said, and that is what has gotten her into trouble before.

"Tyrann, cut the bullshit. You know there was no way that I wasn't going to be involved. No fucking way. I'm the common denominator between you and Chris. You've been in trouble with the law before. You knew that once you killed Chris, the police were going to come see me."

"Shh. Quit saying that."

"Saying what?"

"I killed Chris because I ain't killed nobody."

"Who pulled the trigger?"

Black attempted to frisk her. Why was she asking him all these goddamned questions?

"Get your goddamned hands off me. You know I ain't wearing no wire."

"Twan pulled the trigger if you must know."

"How did Twan know Chris?"

"He didn't."

Lani and Black locked eyes. "Chris's blood is on your hands, not Twan's."

"Says who?"

It was now clear to Lani that Black was delusional as hell. In his mind, he was innocent of murder since he didn't actually pull the trigger.

Black rubbed her back. He wanted to comfort her. He knew she'd been through a lot.

"You get your motherfucking hands off me!"

Black laughed and said, "All that I've done for you, this is how you treat me?"

Lani made her way to the fridge to get some Greek yogurt. As she stood at the fridge, Black examined her body. Her ass was poking out nicely. He wished she would remove that robe but didn't think that would happen.

Lani sat at the bar and ate a spoonful of yogurt. "Look, Tyrann, you've done a lot for me and I appreciate the hell out of you, but there is no way I can be with someone like you. You showed me a different side of you."

"Like what?"

"Motherfucker, have you forgot that you murdered Chris?"

He placed his finger over his lips. "Shh."

"You got me in the middle of a bunch of bullshit."

"You have an excellent lawyer. Nothing is going to happen to you."

"You don't know that."

"I know nothing can happen to you because you didn't know about it."

"I do now."

"But I'm the only person that knows for sure that you know about it."

"Mike kidnapped Man-Man for nothing, right?"

"Mike thinks he knows."

"Now, I'm almost certain he thinks that I told you where his mother lived."

"But you didn't."

"He doesn't know that."

"Don't worry about Mike. Fuck Mike! I can handle Mike!"

"Now you see, this whole vigilante lifestyle is what I can't deal with."

Black stood up from the bar and said, "Don't say shit about my lifestyle. This same vigilante lifestyle got you living good."

"So what do I owe you? Some pussy? This is what you do, Tyrann. Ever since I've known you, it's been the same thing. You made a lot of money and spoiled a lot of women and you think the money is going to allow you to do what you want to do. Can't you see that way of thinking is fucked up?"

"I might be fucked up in the head. Just a little. I'll be the first to admit, but if I'm fucked up then that means that you're fucked up too."

"Huh?"

"You broke up with me. You went to Chris. You thought he was legitimate, but he turned out to be nothing but a dope boy too. A has-been basketball player that was no better than me."

Tear rolled down her face. Not because of what he said, but because of how he'd said it. He mentioned Chris in the past tense. He was gone.

Black said, "I got issues, but you got issues too. You ain't no better than me."

Lani took another spoonful of her yogurt and said, "You're right. We're both broken. It's time to re-evaluate my life. I'm not a young girl anymore, and you're not young anymore either."

Black grinned. "I know."

"What do you want from me? What do you want me to say? You want me to accept your apology then you'll leave. Well, I accept your apology. Now leave."

"I want you to come live with me."

She laughed and said, "You're sick."

"Look, nothing is going to happen to you. I know you're worried, but I swear to you, ain't a goddamned thing going to happen to us."

She finished her yogurt. It made no sense to go back and forth with the fool.

Black made his way over to her. He started massaging her shoulders and she liked it. She liked the way he made her feel physically and she hadn't been touched in a while. She needed sex. She wanted him inside of her. She sat the empty yogurt container on the bar and he leaned into her to kiss her.

She stopped him and said, "Get the fuck out right now."

Black stood there with a silly-ass grin on his face. He said, "It's like that?"

"It's like that, motherfucker."

He made his way to the door and she followed him. Before he left he said, "I love you, Lani."

She closed the door. She believed Black loved her—the only way he knew how to love, and at the moment, it wasn't good enough to keep putting herself at risk with him.

●   ●   ●

Lani needed a drink, so she called Starr and Jada to meet her at the W for cocktails. They sat at a table in the back of the lounge. All three ladies had strawberry margaritas. Starr paid back Jada the money that Jada had given her earlier. She told the ladies about her new showroom and business.

Jada smiled, "I gotta check it out. I'm so proud of you."

"You need to send some of your rich friends to do business with me."

"I'll send Big Papa to you."

"Who?"

"My friend, Ty. I call him Big Papa because he's a big guy, but he's a teddy bear."

Lani said, "Teddy bear translation - he'll spend his money on you."

Jada laughed and said, "Well, why wouldn't he? Ain't I worth it?"

Starr wanted to say something to Jada about that kind of behavior but who was she to judge. Besides Jada was a grown woman.

Jada said to Lani, "So, what about your love life?"

"What love life? You know I'm not with anybody? Damn sure ain't with Black."

"What's wrong with Black?"

"What's not wrong with him? He's a big juvenile."

Lani didn't want to tell them about the kidnappings. She didn't want to scare the girls because she hadn't spoken to Mike and she was almost certain that he thought she was involved.

Jada turned back to Starr. "I've always wanted to start a business, but I don't know what I would do."

"Just think about whatever you're good at and whatever there's a need for."

Jada said, "I got a few ideas. I just gotta make sure I'm ready to put in the work."

Starr sipped her drink and said, "That's important for sure. Sometimes I ask myself, do I really have the work ethic to make this thing work? Well, I'm going to have to put in the work. Trey is not supporting me anymore."

"So I'm assuming he gave you the money to start the business." Lani said.

"No, I took it." She sipped her margarita.

"You took it?" Lani asked. "What do you mean, you took it?"

"I took what I felt was mine. I took the money for the showroom and I took some money for me to live off."

"I can't believe you did that," Lani said.

"Why not?" Jada said, "She deserved it."

"I sure as hell did. I was damn near married to that man and he thinks he can just kick me out with nothing."

"You kicked him out, tho," Lani said.

"Same damn thing." Jada sipped her drink and turned to Starr. "You did the right thing."

"I think so."

"What did Trey say?"

"I haven't seen Trey, but I'm going to give him back the money I didn't spend."

"How much did you take?"

"Five hundred thousand dollars."

"Black would kill me if I took his money," Lani said. "That's a fact."

"Does he know?" Jada asked.

"Yes." Starr sipped her drink and then said, "I thought he'd sent his brother over to try to talk me into giving it back, but can you believe Trey's brother tried to hit on me?"

"I didn't know Trey had a brother," Lani said.

"Half brother. His dad was a whore, well mine was too," Starr said as she thought about Ace's infidelities.

"Sounds like Black's daddy. That man got twenty-three kids spread across Georgia, South Carolina, and Alabama."

"Damn. So Trey's brother tried to holla," Jada said.

"Yeah, girl."

Lani said, "They're obviously not close."

Starr sipped her drink and said, "He's not like Trey. First he's younger and went to college and works as a pharmacist. He's a square."

Jada said, "I've fucked with a few squares in my day."

Starr said, "He's attractive, but I can't roll like that."

"Why not?"

"He's Trey's brother."

"Let me tell you something," Jada said. "When a man decides he wants to fuck something, he's going to fuck whoever and whomever he pleases."

"Not every man is like that," Lani said.

Jada said, "Not every man, but the men we deal with do. And that's all I can speak on."

Jada turned to Starr and said, "If you like him, go out with him. You don't have to fuck him."

CHAPTER 5

STARR LAY NAKED ON A SET OF 1500 THREAD COUNT SHEETS. SHE wanted to be held, needed to be fucked, but her man was somewhere holding somebody else, fucking somebody else. She stood up, and walked to her dresser to retrieve her white rabbit. It wasn't a man that could hold her and tell her everything was going to be alright, but what it could do was aid her in getting off and right now she needed an orgasm more than anything. She rarely used toys. Most of the time when she did use them, it was with Trey. He used to love seeing her get herself off.

She dimmed the light and retrieved some lube from the bathroom, lit some candles and crawled back into the bed. She turned on the battery-operated rabbit and stimulated her clitoris as she imagined Trey's head between her legs. She loved how he would go down on her. She would often grab his head when he was down there even though he had hated it when she did that.

Her mind wandered. She thought about what she would do without Trey and what he was going to say when she handed him the money. Suddenly, Troy popped into her head. She hated to admit that she thought he was attractive, but she wondered what it would be like to be with him sexually. Would he fuck her or would he make love to her? Sometimes she liked to be held and romanced while being made loved to and sometimes she liked to be fucked. Her ass smacked. Hair pulled and just manhandled. She knew Troy could make love, but a woman like her needed to be fucked and she didn't know if she could find someone like Trey who was so in tune with her body.

The white rabbit stroked her kitty and it felt damn good, better than Trey's tongue. God she loved this. She was almost there, but she couldn't quite get there without some help from her imagination. She'd have to rely on her mental rolodex.

She remembered the time Trey had fucked her on the balcony in a Vegas hotel while the people in the suite above were looking at them. The memory was turning her the fuck on when Troy popped into her head again. In her mind, he was licking her kitty exactly how she liked it. She felt dirty for thinking about two men getting her off. Two brothers at the same time, but it was getting her off. Troy sucked her clit and now Trey bit her nipples. She exploded.

Starr was dressed up in a blue pinstriped business suit and three inch heeled Louboutins made for work, when Trey showed up at her place and though she was wearing a business suit, she looked damn good to Trey. Her three-inch heels elevated her ass and Trey smiled when he saw the pantsuit struggling to contain it. Damn he missed those hips and that tiny-ass waistline, but more importantly he missed a great woman.

"Why are you all dressed up?" Trey asked.

"Been working."

"Working?"

"Yeah, what regular people do, you know?"

"What is that supposed to mean? I'm a regular person too."

Trey sat on the sofa and Starr sat across from him. Trey said, "So what's been up? Did you miss me?"

"What do you think?"

"I think you do miss me."

"Maybe a little."

He smiled.

"You look nice."

"Just nice?" She asked.

"Well what do you want me to say? You're wearing a pantsuit. I can't say that you look sexy. I mean it's a business suit."

"You can say whatever you want—you do whatever it is you want."

"So you want to argue?"

"No, I don't, but I can't believe that you didn't ask me where I work. I tell you I've been working and you have nothing to say about it."

"That was my next question."

"I work for myself. Since you're so interested." She was very sarcastic.

"Doing what?" His tone was very demeaning, as if there was nothing she could possibly do to earn a living and needed to depend on him forever.

"Interior design."

"I didn't know that you liked doing that."

"Hmmph. That's the problem, Trey. You don't know me. Everybody that comes here talks about how I have an eye for design and how it comes natural to me, but my own man says he didn't know I like that."

He grinned and said, "So I'm your man?"

"You know what I mean."

He laughed and said, "I've always encouraged you. You forgot about the salon."

"My heart wasn't in that salon. That's why I never go and it's barely making money."

"I hate that you feel that way about me. I want the best for you."

"But you never encourage me. Even your brother complemented me on how nice the place looks."

"My brother has been here?"

"Yeah."

"What did he want?"

"Looking for you," Starr lied. She didn't know why she lied but she did. She wasn't ready to tell him that his brother had tried to hit on her. She wasn't sure it was her place to tell him since they were no longer involved.

"I wonder what he wanted."

"He didn't say."

"How did he know I lived here?"

Starr shrugged. "Maybe your baby's mother. I didn't ask."

"But he liked the place, huh? "

"Yeah."

"Look, baby, I like what you've done too."

Starr stood and they made eye contact briefly before she turned away. She had to admit that she missed him—him and his dick.

Finally, she said, "I'll go get your money."

She made her way to the bedroom where the rest of the money was as he stared at her wonderful ass. She turned and said, "Oh, there is something that I forgot to tell you."

"What?"

"I spent some."

"I figured you were going to spend some. How much did you spend?"

"Close to a hundred and forty thousand dollars."

"What did you spend that kind of money on?"

"My showroom."

"Showroom?"

"Yeah, for the business."

"Where is this place located? I mean I should at least know where my money went."

She disappeared into the bedroom and then reappeared with a gym bag containing the rest of the money. She passed it to him along with a business card.

" 'A Starr is Born.' I like that play on words."

"Thanks."

He pulled her into him until she was on his lap. Trey stared at her for a moment before leaning into her and they locked lips. They kissed passionately for five minutes; his mouth was warm and salty. Damn, she missed this man.

Finally, he said, "I missed the hell out of you."

"I missed you too."

He kissed her again and then removed her suit-jacket. He removed her shirt and bra and began sucking her tits. Her nipples sprang to life as he licked and kissed them. She was rubbing his hair as he tongue kissed her neck. Trey knew this made her hot, and this time was no different. She stood and removed her pants. She stood in front of him only wearing some pink boy shorts. Her ass was even more amazing in the flesh. Trey missed the hell out of her.

He stood and kicked off his shoes and his dick was now as hard as concrete. He dropped his pants, underwear and his dick was at full attention. The thickness and the veins were just beautiful to her. He sat back on the chair and she sat on his lap and stroked him. He continued to kiss her neck. She wanted him inside her. His hands were on her and she kept pushing him away.

"I want you," he said.

"I want you more."

"Why do you keep pushing me away?"

"I don't know."

"This is crazy. If you want me, let me have you."

"I want you, but I'm confused. I mean, this isn't right."

He kept trying to yank her boy-shorts down without results.

"What's not right about it?" Trey asked.

"You love her."

"I love you."

"Do you have a condom?"

"A what?"

"A condom."

"No."

"I can't do this. I can't fuck you knowing you been fucking somebody else. I can't take a chance with my life."

She stood and he said, "Are you fucking serious?"

She scooped her pants from the floor and he was focused on that ass and those tits. This was absolute bullshit to him.

He stood and picked up his pants and shoes. "So, you're serious?"

"Trey, I just can't trust you."

"I ain't got time for these silly-ass games," Trey said.

"I'm playing games? Motherfucker, as loyal as I was to you, and I'm the one playing games?"

He slid into his pants and he was now lacing up his sneakers. He grabbed the gym bag with the money and made his way to the door.

CHAPTER 6

IT WAS NINE P.M. AND BLACK WAS AT SASHA'S HOUSE. SHE HAD ONE of those white Martinque headboards, the third woman that Black had slept with this year with a headboard like that. Her bedding was all light colored and too damn delicate looking for a roughneck-ass nigga like Black, but it was very inviting. The smell of lit vanilla scented candles filled the room. Black kicked off his Jordans and was about to sit on her bed.

"Don't sit on my bed with your jeans on," Sasha said.

Black sat on a chair in the corner of the bedroom. He said, "You women kill me with that 'don't sit on the bed with your jeans' shit. You complain, then be eating doing your nails and all kinds of shit in a man's bed."

She smiled and said, "You're so right. I never thought about that, but I just think of my bed as a kind of sanctuary."

"A sanctuary. No way is this bed a sanctuary."

"There's more than one meaning of the word sanctuary, asshole. Sanctuary doesn't have to be like a sacred place. It can also be a place of safety."

"I'm sorry. I didn't go to college like you did."

"That's why you need a woman like me. You can be the muscle, and I can handle the money."

"What money?"

"Don't play dumb."

"So, you want me for my money?"

"No, I want you for that dick of yours, but I'm just saying that if you want someone to help you manage that money, I can invest it for you."

"How do you know if I have money?"

"Am I wrong?"

"I might have a few coins."

She stood from the bed and made her way into the bathroom. When she returned R&B was playing through the surround sound speakers. She was wearing a yellow thong that looked amazing on her. Her waistline was almost non-existent. Six-inch stripper heels made her ass sit high and round. Black couldn't take his eyes off her.

She was smiling. "I want you to do something kinky to me tonight."

Black stood, kicked his shoes off, and removed his shirt. He stood there in a pair of blue boxers that was fighting hard to contain his pulsating dick.

She said, "How did you get the scars?"

"Gunshot wounds."

"Really?"

"Yeah."

Sasha didn't know why, but Black's gunshot wounds and tats were turning her on in a weird kind of way. She was a princess and he was a bad boy. She wanted him to fuck the hell out of her and treat her like a slut.

He made his way over to her and pulled her into him. His hands were now resting on her ass.

"What did you have in mind?"

"I wanna be spanked."

"You mean like when I'm hitting you from behind?"

She laughed and said, "Hell no. I'm going to lie across your lap and you're going to spank me."

"What the fuck?"

She laughed and said, "Just do it. You'll enjoy it. I promise you."

Black sat on the bed before he sprang back up. "Is it okay to sit on the bed? You know how you be tripping about your bed."

"Of course, silly."

He sat on the edge of the bed. She disappeared and came back with a small paddle and passed it to him.

"Use this or use your hands. I'd prefer your hands," she said.

"I don't know if I can do it."

She made a sad face. "Too weird for you?"

"I've never done nothing like this before."

She sat on his lap, wrapped her legs around his, and kissed him and bit his ear. She whispered, "I want you to manhandle this pussy."

She sang along with the radio. Black closed his eyes, his dick was throbbing. He wanted to be inside her. She lay across his lap and said, "Don't think about it. Just do it."

He smacked her ass.

"Keep going."

He kept spanking her and she was squirming and gyrating on his knee.

"Keep spanking me, Daddy. I've been a bad girl."

He paddled her ass and she was getting off. She was actually getting off from a spanking. In a weird kind of way, this was turning Black the fuck on. He kept spanking her ass. He pulled her thong aside and began fingering her and spanking her at the same time.

"Oh my god! You feel so goddamned good to me," she cried as her body began to convulse and she reached multiple orgasms.

He stopped spanking her and she lay across his lap for a moment, catching her breath. Finally she stood up and removed her thong.

"I want you inside me," she said.

Black stood and dropped his boxers. He made his way over to his pants to get his Magnum.

"What are you doing?" she asked.

"Getting a condom."

"I want you inside me bareback. I want to feel that dick inside me."

"No more kids for me, I'm sorry I can't do that." Black would fuck only one person raw nowadays, and that was Lani because they had history.

She made a sad face.

"I'm sorry, baby, but I'm through having kids." He removed the Magnum and slid it on. She propped herself on the bed and he entered her doggy-style.

Two hours later they were still cuddling. "I gotta admit, I like you."

Black didn't respond. He didn't know how to respond to that. He'd told her that he wasn't ready to be in a relationship and he was wondering about her alleged boyfriend.

She laughed and said, "You don't have to be quiet. I'm not trying to make you marry me."

"I know you said you have a boyfriend. Where is this mystery man?"

"Don't worry about him. I don't ever ask you about all your women."

"Whatever."

"But seriously, I think there are a lot of things I can help you with."

"Like what?"

"You ever think about not hustling. You know, making legitimate money."

"Who said I was a hustler?"

"Come on. You don't work. I can call you anytime of the day and you're doing absolutely nothing. Besides, you told me yourself you were a bad guy. Your words, not mine."

"I did say that, didn't I?" Black grinned.

"You absolutely told me that."

"But you don't have to be the bad guy? I can help you invest your money. Just give me a little at a time if you don't trust me."

"What do you call a little?"

"Well, there is this franchise opportunity that I'm interested in that requires about a hundred thousand dollars in capital. I can come up with the money myself, but I'd rather have a partner."

Black said, "Wait a minute. Your father is the mayor. He has money."

"That's a misconception. He doesn't make that much money as mayor. He has a little bit of money, but that's his money, not mine. I'm a grown woman, what would I look like going to him? Besides, he's done so much for me. He paid my tuition in full, so while most people my age are walking around here with student loans. I don't and I'm grateful."

Black said, "I can respect that. What kind of franchise?"

"Well, there are a few I'm interested in."

"Give me the details and I'll consider it."

She scooted her ass next to his dick that was now rock solid. She reached for his dick and tried to put it inside her, but he resisted and said, "No, No, No. Not without a condom."

She grinned. "Well, you can't knock a girl for trying."

CHAPTER 7

DETECTIVE MIKE WILLIAMS HAD CONTACTED LANI AND ASKED HER IF she wanted to meet up and answer a few questions. She gave him the name of her attorney, and a few hours later, her attorney, Tom Gilliam, contacted her.

"Detective Mike Williams wants to meet and talk to you," he said.

"Do I have to talk to him?"

"You don't have to, but I think it's best."

"Why?"

"I just believe in being proactive. My job is to clear you and make sure nobody brings any charges against you. I spoke briefly with Joey Turch, and he told me the gist of what has been going on, but I can meet you at my office in a couple of hours and you can tell me your version of events. Then, I'll drive you to the detective's office."

Lani didn't want to meet with the attorney and she damn sure didn't want to meet with the police, but she kind of expected this. She knew that the police weren't just going to go away. "Okay. What's your address?"

"300 PeachTree Street NE."

Mike Williams eyeballed Lani's breasts and this brought back the memories of him rummaging through her underwear. She didn't like his perverted ass.

Thomas Kearns and Tom Gilliam exchanged pleasantries before Thomas Kearns said, "Good to see you again, Lani."

Tom Gilliam was a tall slender white man with a naturally red face and dark brown hair. He had a hook nose and wore horn-rimmed glasses. He had absolutely no sex appeal and a very matter of fact demeanor, but he was a very smart and capable attorney.

"Likewise." Lani didn't want to be there, but it was the right thing to say. She looked at Mike Williams but didn't say anything to him. Thomas Kearns sat behind his desk and Lani and her attorney sat across from him. Mike Williams stood behind Thomas Kearns occasionally stealing glances at Lani's erect nipples.

Thomas Kearns said, "Let's get down to business."

"Let's do it." Tom Gilliam said.

Mike Williams said, "We're going to take this case to the state grand jury and we're giving your client a chance to come clean about her involvement of the murder of Chris Jones."

Lani said, "Come clean? I haven't done anything."

"Do you think that the grand jury is going to believe that you had absolutely nothing to do with this man's murder? The common link between the murderer and the victim is you."

Tom Gilliam said, "So, who's been charged with this crime?"

"Kelvin Bryant."

He turned to Lani. "You know him?"

"No, I have no idea who that is."

Mike Williams said, "Her link is Tyrann Massey."

"But he hasn't been charged?"

"No, but he masterminded the whole thing."

"So you're operating off assumptions that he's going to be charged?"

"I'm almost certain that at some point he will."

"Almost is not absolute."

Mike Williams said, "Look, we wanted to give your client a chance to come clean with us. She seems like a nice girl."

Williams stared at Lani's lips wondering what it would be like to make love to a girl like her, but he could tell by her hair, expensive handbag and jewelry that it would take money to sleep with her.

Thomas Kearns said, "You know how these things go. I see it every day, young women covering up for their boyfriends. Then when we get the boyfriend, he spills the beans, tells everything, implicates the girl and then she gets more time than the boyfriend."

Lani said, "First of all, I'm nobody's girlfriend."

"But you were Chris Jones's."

"I was."

"And you were Black's."

Tom Gilliam looked confused.

"Black is Tyrann's nickname, Mr. Gilliam. Isn't that right, Lani?" Mike Williams said.

"I don't know. You tell me," Lani said.

Tom Gilliam said, "Can I have a moment alone with my client?"

Mike Williams and Thomas Kearns stepped out into the hallway.

When the door closed, Tom Gilliam said, "So you know nothing about the murder?"

Lani looked the man in the eye and said, "I didn't orchestrate the murder. I didn't order anybody to kill Chris."

"Sounds like they are trying their best to nail Tyrann and if they do, can he implicate you?"

"No." Lani felt bad because she knew about the murder, she felt like she was betraying Chris, but she knew that Black would never say that he admitted the murder to her. Hell, she knew Black wasn't going to admit shit to anybody. Besides if she cooperated with the police, there was no telling what Black would do to her.

"Well, if you are certain that you can't be implicated. We're going to end the interview."

When Mike Williams and Thomas Kearns came back into the room, Tom Gilliam said, "Gentleman, we have nothing to tell you. We'll see you in court." And they left the small office.

Lani said to Black, "So you ain't worried about getting picked up by the police?"

"Why should I worry? Whatever is going to happen, will happen. I'm not going to have a goddamned heart attack about something that may or may not happen. Besides, I'll let my lawyer worry about that bullshit. His job is to make shit go away. I pay him good."

"But the faster he makes shit go away, the more shit you get yourself into."

"Whatever, Lani. You're always so motherfuckin' negative. You know how I am, and I ain't about to change for nobody."

"Well, I can tell you right now. They're on your ass. They are trying their best to link you with the murder."

"Look, I know how the police work and what they were doing was trying to get you to flip on me. That's why I got you an attorney," Black said. "I'm a mastermind at this shit."

"That's exactly what they are calling your stupid ass—the mastermind."

"Well, they are just assuming I did some shit. How are they going to prove it?"

"Are you sure your boy is not going to flip?"

"He ain't going to say shit about me, and if he did, it will take me to implicate you and you know there is no way in the hell I'm going to say anything about you."

She believed him. She knew that if he didn't go to the police when his son was kidnapped, there was no way he would talk if he was arrested.

"I think they know for sure that you had something to do with it."

"Me too," Black smiled.

"How can you not be concerned?"

"Look, I know they know I had something to do with the murder, but proving it is different from knowing. How the hell are they going to prove it?"

Lani's phone rang. Jada was calling. "Hello?"

Her phone beeped, and she said, "My battery is dying. I'll call you back on Black's phone."

Black passed her is cell phone. "But you can't worry about that. I don't know for sure what's going to happen to me, but ain't shit going to happen to you." He put his arms around her waist and she moved away from him.

"Quit acting like that."

"Acting like what?"

"I already told you there will be no more you and me. We're friends. That's it." She took a deep breath and said, "I can't believe that I'm even your friend with as much shit as you have put me through. Yeah, I've dated hustlers most of my life and I've reaped some good benefits, but I never imagined being questioned by the police about a goddamned murder."

"You gotta take the good with the bad."

"That shit sounds comical to me. I gotta take the good with the bad."

"You're a pretty girl, Lani. You could have gotten a professional nigga, Hell, that pervert-ass police officer sniffed your goddamned panties. You could have had him too, but you know what? You chose dudes like me and Chris."

"Every time you see me, it's going to be about how flawed I am," Lani said.

"Hey, you keep telling me how fucked up I am. So I'm supposed to just sit here and put up with that?"

"I was just letting you know that there is no you and me."

"And I'm letting you know that you can't be with a regular motherfucker with a nine to five."

"What's your security code for your phone."

"1982."

When she punched in the code, a picture mail came though from a woman named Sasha. All Lani could see was a naked ass and heels propped on the edge of the bed.

"Somebody sent you a photo." She showed Black the picture of the naked-ass woman.

Black stood there with a silly ass grin.

"So you want to be with me, huh?" Lani asked.

Black shrugged and said, "What am I supposed to do? You ain't trying to give me no action."

She flung the phone at him and he ducked. It barely missed his head.

He picked up his phone and saw that the screen was shattered. "What the fuck was that all about?"

"Quit saying shit that you don't mean!"

"You just told me that we will never be together, but you get mad cuz somebody sent me a pic?"

Lani was trying to calm herself down. She said, "Look, I'm sorry."

"No, bipolar is what you are."

"Whatever."

"Seriously, why did you do that?"

" I got caught up in the moment. I'm sorry. Let me see the phone."

"The screen is cracked."

"Look, Black, I'm sorry."

"You love me, and I love you."

"I'll always love you. You'll always have my heart but not my mind, so I guess in that sense, I might be bipolar. My brain hates you, but my heart will always love you."

Black was staring at the cracked screen. Trying to decide if he could still use it to make calls.

Lani said, "Who is Sasha?"

"Why?"

"I've never heard you say anything about her."

"She's just somebody I know."

"You don't need any more baby mamas."

"Trust me, no more kids for me."

"Trust you?" Lani laughed. "You're a comedian."

"I think it's time for me to leave."

"I was thinking the same thing."

CHAPTER 8

STARR HAD HIRED BROOKE, THE GIRL WHO LIVED BESIDE TREY'S
stash house. She was enjoying her second day on the job when an irate
customer walked in. Mr. David Walker stormed in and demanded to see
the manager. Seconds later, Starr appeared and said, "Mr. Walker, what
seems to be the problem?"

"I want I full refund. I am very unsatisfied with the work you did to
my home."

Starr was calm. She didn't want to get into a verbal sparring match
with the man. He'd been her first customer when she opened up the
showroom. She earned close to eight grand decorating his home. His
wife had told her that she had another home in Florida that she wanted
decorated and would give her an even bigger commission.

"What's wrong?"

"I want my money back."

"I'll give you a full refund, but first I want to know what didn't you like."

"The furniture in the den looks tacky and cheap, and I hate the artwork
that you chose."

Starr said, "You're wife chose the artwork."

Troy entered the showroom. He stood a few feet away from Mr. Walker
and listened to the whole conversation.

"My wife didn't choose that tasteless artwork."

Starr said, "Could you hold on for a second?" She disappeared into the
office and returned with a consent form stating that all the artwork

sales were final. Starr showed Mr. Walker his wife's signature on the paperwork.

David Walker scrutinized the form before admitting that it was his wife's signature. "Okay, I'll take the loss on the artwork, but that still doesn't excuse the piss-poor job you did."

Starr wanted to curse him the fuck out, but she kept telling herself she had to be professional.

Troy approached Mr. Walker. "Sir, is there any way we can make this right?"

Mr. Walker was startled and he turned to Troy. "Who the hell are you?"

"I'm her business partner, and we're just starting out and want to make sure you are satisfied. If you're not satisfied, we'll refund your money and even the money for the artwork." He winked at Starr.

Starr didn't know if she could survive a hit on the artwork if she gave Mr. Walker a full refund.

"I get this. You just don't want to give my money back," Mr. Walker said.

"That's not it at all. We're more concerned with our reputation than your money."

Mr. Walker was silent for a long time. "Can you put this in writing? That you will refund the money for the artwork if I'm not satisfied."

"We sure will, but only if you're going to give us your input. We got your wife's input the first time, and we assumed that she would be happy, but we never considered you."

"Not only will you get my input, but I'll be there while you're working." The two men shook hands. Mr. Walker left without signing any paperwork.

When Mr. Walker was gone, Brooke said, "What an asshole."

Starr came from behind the counter and hugged Troy and said, "Thanks for handling that situation, I was about to curse his ass out." Then she turned to Brooke. "Will you fix me a cup of tea?"

"Sure," Brooke said then disappeared to the back.

When Brooke was gone, Troy said, "I'm glad you didn't curse him out. This is the business world. This is not easy money. You have to be patient with people. People are not going to just throw money away. They are going to scrutinize everything you do. This is not the drug business."

"I see. So what brings you here?" she asked.

"I wasn't doing anything, so I decided I would stop by. How is business going?" he asked.

"Mr. Walker has been my only client this far. I have another client this weekend and another the following weekend. I guess to answer your question. Very slow."

"It'll get better."

"I hope so."

He smiled and said, "Well, at least you stepped out on faith to pursue your dreams."

"But is faith going to pay the bills?"

Troy looked around the showroom. "This is a very nice place you got here."

"Thanks."

"What are you doing to market yourself?"

Starr shrugged. "It's just mostly word of mouth, but Brooke my assistant has been doing some social media stuff."

"That's what I was going to suggest and I have a couple of friends that are realtors and maybe you could pair with them, so they can give your business a boost."

"That's a good idea. If you could help me do that, I would be grateful."

"Can't believe Trey hasn't tried to help you."

"Please. Trey is only concerned with Trey. You know your brother."

Brooke reemerged with a cup of green tea and 3 packets of Stevia for Starr.

"Thanks for your help, Troy. If you will excuse me, Brooke and I need to do some organizing."

"Maybe we can meet up later for a drink. I'll text you."

"Okay, cool."

When Troy was gone, Brooke said, "I can see you have a type."

"What do you mean?"

"That man resembles Mr. Trey."

"He does, doesn't he?" Starr wanted to laugh.

Starr called Troy later that evening and they decided to meet at a little bar across from her building. She sat at a small table in the front, so she could spot Troy. She noticed him right away when he entered the room. He was wearing a blue plaid button down with a pink tie and Ray-Ban eyeglasses. His pants were a little tight but somehow he made it work. The outfit made his athletic body look even more amazing. Starr couldn't believe that she was even attracted to the metrosexual look, but maybe she was growing up. Troy sat at the table and he was smiling hard. When he sat at the table, the barmaid appeared and asked what they were going to have to drink.

"Water for me," Troy said.

"I thought you were a grown-ass man."

He laughed. "I am."

"Two Cirocs with cranberry juice."

When the barmaid returned, Starr slid one of the drinks to Troy's side.

"I'm not drinking."

"You are if you want to talk to me."

He laughed and sipped his drink. "I hope I can get up and go to work tomorrow."

"You will."

"I know I can't afford not to. Too many damn student loans."

Starr sipped her drink and said, "So, Troy, what's your deal?"

"What do you mean, 'what's my deal'?"

"Why do you want a girl like me?"

"I don't understand."

"You're a college boy, and you know I like street dudes."

Troy laughed and said, "So you're calling me a square?"

"No, I'm just trying to figure out what's your motive. Do you want to fuck me to get back at your brother or something? What is it that you want with me?"

Troy sipped his drink. "I see where you're coming from."

"Good, because I'm puzzled by this attention that you're giving me."

"Look, I'm not trying to get back at my brother, and it's not about sex. I'm not trying to press you for sex."

"If it's not about sex, tell me what is it about?"

"It's about knowing a good woman when I see one."

Starr laughed. "How do you know I'm a good woman?"

"I had a good woman before."

"What happened?"

"I wasn't ready."

"You cheated?"

"Well, not exactly."

"What the fuck does that mean?" Starr sipped her drink and said, "I'm sorry, but I'm not feeling cheaters these days, and just in case you didn't know, I have a foul mouth from time to time. You sure you want to deal with that?"

"Well, she wanted a title and I thought that was high school."

"How old were you when this happened?"

"Twenty-eight."

"Well, why wouldn't she want a title? You're the one that's high school."

"I know."

"But you cheated?"

"Well, she wanted to take a break from seeing each other. While we were away from each other, I slept with somebody else."

"Just like your brother."

"I'm nothing like him. Nothing. Ever since then, I've been keeping it real with everybody I meet. If I want to be in a relationship, I say it, and if I don't want to be in one, I say it. I don't lead nobody on."

"You're a grown-ass man, huh?"

"Exactly." He sipped his drink and said, "You're loyal to my brother and he don't deserve it."

"You know, if I fuck with you, my reputation is going to take a hit."

"Look, that dude has fucked around on you so much, you wouldn't believe it."

"You sound like a hater."

"You're right."

"Let's talk about you and me. What do you want from me? You want pussy? What?"

"I want more than that."

"Really?" She licked her lips, not to be suggestive, but he took it as that and his dick jumped.

"I want you to give me an opportunity."

"Troy, I like you a lot, but I can't be with two brothers. No matter how hard I try, I would never be able to get over the fact that Trey is your brother."

The barmaid appeared and asked if there was anything else she could get them. "No," Starr said.

Troy dug into his wallet and removed twenty-five dollars then he stood, kissed Starr on the cheek, and made his way to the door.

CHAPTER 9

BLACK HAD BEEN TRYING TO CONTACT KYRIE ALL MORNING. HE started calling him at around 10 a.m. and it was now 1 p.m., and he still hadn't answered his phone. Black felt something was wrong. Kyrie always answered his phone. He dialed Kyrie's wife, Melody, but she didn't answer either. He was just about to make a drive out to their home when someone knocked on his door. Peering through the peephole, Black realized it was Kyrie.

"Where the fuck have you been?"

"I been talking to the cops all morning."

"The cops?"

"Calm down, bruh. You know I didn't give them shit."

Black led Kyrie to the den where Kyrie sat on an armchair and Black sat across from him.

"What the fuck happened?"

"They were talking about some heroin ODs."

"No shit."

"Yeah they been ODing off the Obamacare package."

"Damn." Black remembered what Shamari had told him days earlier. "We gotta put a new stamp on the package," he said.

"I know, and the fucked up thing about it is that it may not have even been our shit that people are ODing off of," Kyrie said.

"No. The fucked up part is we gotta get a new product out there and one that everybody knows again."

"I don't want to deal with this shit no more."

Black said, "Motherfucker, don't be such a pussy. Man, we're making three times as much as we did with coke."

"So I'm a pussy now because I don't want to go to jail for life? You weren't the motherfucker getting interrogated."

Black had never heard Kyrie talk like that before. Though he believed in his heart that Kyrie hadn't given the police any information, he detected a softness in Kyrie he'd never seen before. He'd have to distance himself from him. He could crack under enough pressure.

"You're right man, I'm going to chill," Black said.

"Listen, man, I didn't say we had to chill. I still want to make money, just not with heroin."

"Too much is going on. We'll take a break then we can get back to business in a month or so."

Kyrie studied Black's face wondering if he'd said something wrong. He was concerned with Black's change of heart.

Black said, "So what did the police ask you?"

"Wanted to know where I got the heroin from."

"And you said?"

"Mexicans, but they didn't believe me."

"Why?"

"They said it came from Pakistan."

"What else did they ask you?"

"Who were my customers."

"And you said what?"

"I told them I sold mostly to business people."

"Really?" Black was skeptical as hell.

"Yeah, I had to tell them something because they held up some pictures of two white teens saying that they'd overdosed."

"That don't mean that you were responsible."

"I know. Maybe I shouldn't have said nothing at all."

"You think?"

Kyrie sensed Black's sarcasm and said, "I know you probably thinking I said something about you."

"Now that's where you're wrong. Not for one minute did I believe that you would implicate me. You and I both know that you know better than that."

"You seem pissed.

"Cuz you shouldn't have said a motherfucking THANG!"

"You're right."

Rashida rushed to the door wearing a robe. She was surprised to see that it was her brother on her doorstep. They embraced and she invited him in. He was sweating and he looked very concerned.

"What brings you here?" she asked.

"I got a lot of shit on my mind, and you're the only person I can talk too. I need to use the restroom."

He walked in the direction of the hall bathroom before she said, "Use the one on the other side of the dining room."

Black stopped and he looked confused before she said, "I have company, Tyrann."

"My bad." Black didn't know why he had assumed his sister spent her nights alone. Hell, she was a grown woman with needs and she was a lot older than he was, but he still didn't like to think of some clown humping his sister. Even though she was damn near a genius, she wasn't that smart when it came to picking men. He used the restroom and met her at the kitchen table.

"Who is he?"

"A friend I knew since college."

"Not that married clown again."

Rashida laughed and said, "No, not him, and quit judging me."

"Not judging you. I'm judging him. That nigga is exactly like me, just with a college degree."

Rashida was laughing her ass off.

"What's going on?"

"I'm afraid, sis, and you're the only person I can tell this too. You're the only person that has ever seen me afraid."

"I can't remember ever seeing you being afraid."

"Remember when I was a kid and those twins, Donald and Darnell, tried to jump me? I ran home afraid and you made me kick both of their asses."

Rashida laughed. "But you were only eight years old."

"Doesn't matter, I was afraid."

"Don't understand your point, but what are you afraid of now?"

"There was no point to the story. It's just that I don't like everybody to see me vulnerable."

"What the fuck is going on?"

"I don't know where to begin."

She rubbed his hand and said, "You can tell me anything, lil brother. I won't judge."

"I been thinking about K.B. a lot lately and I don't know if he can hold up."

"K.B.? Who the hell is that? What are you talking about?"

"K.B. is the dude that they holding for murder."

"The one that you had something to do with?"

"Yeah."

"Why did you do it?"

"You just said you wouldn't judge, so I don't wanna hear all that coulda, woulda, shoulda bullshit. Besides, I wasn't the one that pulled the trigger."

"Is that what you like to tell yourself to justify shit? We all like to tell ourselves things to make us feel good about ourselves, but, Tyrann, the bottom line is you did wrong. Admit it. Get it out. I'm not going to judge you and I damn sure ain't going to tell anybody."

Black turned from his sister's gaze. "Yeah, I did wrong, sis, and I know that I'm going to have to answer for it one day."

"Why'd you do it?"

"The man tried to kill me."

"Why did he try to murder you?"

"He was Lani's boyfriend."

"This is about Lani?"

"Not exactly." He didn't want Rashida or anybody in his family to think badly of Lani because the fact of the matter was, Lani was a good person.

"So you're afraid K.B. might rat you out?"

Black stared his sister in the eyes and said, "If he does, I'm going away for a very long time."

Rashida felt herself tearing up. She didn't even want to think about the possibility of losing her brother.

"Don't cry, sis. Now that's the exact reason I didn't want to tell you anything. I knew that you wouldn't be able to take it."

"You're my baby brother, and when I see you in pain, I can't help but cry."

Rashida stood and ripped a paper towel from the roll in front of her and dabbed her eyes.

"I need a favor," Black said.

"Anything."

"Go see K.B."

"In jail?"

"Yeah, I think he's on Wright Street. I need you to find out where his head's at. I know you don't like to visit jails, but you're one of the only people I trust besides Lani and I can't send Lani down there because she's been questioned. The police think that she had something to do with it."

"I'll do anything that you want me to." She finished drying her eyes and he stood and hugged his sister before walking to the door.

"So I'll meet you the day after tomorrow."

"That's fine, preferably in the morning."

Before she opened the door to let him out, Black said, "You tell that nigga that he better treat you right or else I'll kill his ass."

She said, "You don't need to kill anybody else. You've done enough, boy. Please go somewhere and sit yo ass down."

He laughed and gave her another hug.

The next day at 11:45 p.m., Black was standing on Rashida doorstep again ringing the hell out of her doorbell. She frowned when she saw him and stood there with her hands on her hips. He sensed that she didn't want him to come in. She looked pissed off. Her hair was messy as hell and not wrapped. He sensed that his big sister was being a victim of a brutal doggy style when he started hammering on the door again.

"Why in the hell do you keep popping up at my house like this?"

"What did K.B. say?"

"I thought the deal was that we were supposed to meet two days later, not one day?"

"That's what I said, but I needed to know what's going on now. There is no way I could get any sleep without knowing what the fuck is going on."

"Hold it down. I have company again tonight."

"I figured that was why you were looking pissed when you opened the door. Getting some dick, huh?"

"Boy, I'm not about to discuss my personal life with you. Just keep your voice down."

"Was I that loud?"

"You know how your voice carries."

"Promise not to wake your Boo."

"Will you shut up!" She knew he was teasing but she wasn't in the mood for it. She led him back into the kitchen and before they were seated, she got a Coke Zero from her fridge and handed it to him.

He popped the top and took a sip before asking, "So what'd you find out?"

"K.B. said he was offended that I'd come down there to see him."

"Why?"

"He said that he would never let anything bad happen to you. I took that as he wasn't going to talk to the police."

"But why was he offended?"

"Because two and two is four, Tyrann. He figured out that I'd come down to see if he was talking to the police. I'm your sister. I've never seen this man before, and all of a sudden, I show up to visit him. Don't have to be a genius to guess what that is all about."

Black laughed and said, "I see, but I gotta watch my ass now."

"He said to give his baby's mother some money for his attorney."

"I know I've been meaning to take her some money and also Twan's baby mother."

"Who the hell is Twan?"

"A friend of mine from Alabama."

"Is he locked up too?"

"No. He's dead."

"Was he in on the murder?"

"Yes."

Rashida stood up and made her way to the fridge to get a Coke Zero for herself. She said, "Jesus Christ, Tyrann. I don't even want to know what happened to him!"

"Good. But look, sis, don't worry. Everything is going to be fine. Don't worry about me."

"But you're worried. You told me so last night."

Black took a swig of his coke. He didn't respond because she was absolutely right.

"Look, Tyrann, I don't know what the fuck is happening. I just don't want anything to happen to Nana."

"Nothing is going to happen to Nana. Trust me, sis. I'm going to buy her a new house as soon as this blows over."

"Then what are you going to do with your life? Being a forty-year-old drug dealer is not cool."

"Forty? I'm nowhere near forty."

"You'll be surprised how fast time will creep up on you."

"I've got some things in the works."

Rashida laughed. "You've been saying that all your life."

"I know I have, but this time it's for real. I met a girl who wants to partner up with a couple of franchise opportunities."

"I hope so." Rashida stood and said, "Bro, I'd love to talk to you all night."

He finished is coke and said, "Your dick awaits you."

They both laughed their asses off.

CHAPTER 10

SHAMARI HAD JUST ARRIVED FROM CALIFORNIA. HE SCORED SOME heroin from his connection, and it took his runner three days to drive the product back from Los Angeles to Atlanta. It was nine a.m. when Shamari rang Black's doorbell. He carried a blue backpack containing the product. Black laughed when he saw him.

"What's funny?" asked Shamari.

"I still gotta get used to that Caucasian-looking face." Black chuckled and said, "You know what I was just thinking? You look like a goddamned black-white man."

"What is that supposed to mean?"

"You ever see a black person that looks like a white person?"

Shamari was getting pissed and Black sensed it.

"Have a seat."

"What's in the backpack?

"Pure shit." He removed the product and tossed it on the table.

"Where'd you get it?"

"L.A. Remember, I told you I had a friend in Cali that could get it for me? He taxed me, but it's pure."

"Black dude?"

"Yeah."

"Well it ain't pure, I can guarantee you that."

"Looks good, but since I don't do it, I'll have to get somebody to test it." Shamari said.

"You trust your connect?"

"Yeah, I've been to his mom's house before."

"Look, like I said before, I doubt that it's pure, but I hope it's decent."

"We'll soon find out. So what are you going to call it?"

"Obamacare." Black replied.

"No way in hell! Are you crazy? That shit is killing people!"

"But it's what people want and it's in demand. It's the package that people want. We gotta give them what they want."

Shamari stood and paced. "You've lost your goddamned mind, man! White kids are dropping left and right because of this. I don't want to be the one that they associate with this shit. The mayor, police chief and the DEA were on T.V today talking about how they're going to find out who is pushing this poison. It was a huge press conference with a couple of white families holding pictures of their kids that OD'd."

"I understand all of that. But understand that you're already a wanted goddamned man that needs to make money!"

Shamari sat his ass back down.

Black said calmly, "There's a million motherfuckers out here selling hamburgers but you know who the big three are—McDonald's, Burger King, and Wendy's. You know why? Because motherfuckers recognize them, that's why."

Shamari smirked, thinking was this motherfucker serious with his analogy?

Black said, "Obamacare is a brand that people recognize and they want. I don't want to have to build up another brand."

"It's also a brand that's killing motherfuckers so quit comparing dope to hamburgers."

Black said, "Okay, you're the one that needs the money, not me."

Shamari sat there and thought about everything Black had said. He weighed the risk with the rewards and said, "You know that I'm in. I don't think it can get much worse than attempted murder on an informant."

Black gave him a pound.

"Where is your boy?"

"Who?"

"Kyrie."

"Man, police picked him up, but they let him go and he came over here all shook up."

"The police picked him up for what?"

"Questioned him about that heroin he'd gotten charged for, but we knew that was going to happen."

"What did he say?"

"He said he'd gotten it from some Mexican but they didn't believe him. Police said it came from Pakistan. I told you when I first saw it that I thought it was from Afghanistan or Columbia."

"So, did he tell them anything else?"

"No. But he was scared. Kind of like you were a few minutes ago," Black laughed.

"I wasn't scared. Just being careful."

"Okay, are we going to make this money or are we going to join the army?" Shamari said, "You've got to be the craziest motherfucker I've ever known."

Black laughed then they embraced. Suddenly, there was a knock on the door.

Shamari said, "Who the fuck is that?"

There was a black nine millimeter on the end table. Black grabbed it and made his way over to the door. "Who is it?"

"It's me."

"Me who?"

"It's Kyrie. Open the door."

Black opened the door as Shamari stood behind him. Black stepped aside and let him in.

Kyrie said, "What's up, Shamari?" His eyes went straight to the product that was on the coffee table. "Just as I thought."

"What the fuck are you talking about?"

"I knew I scared you earlier. I knew you were bullshitting me about taking a break."

Black said, "Dude, you talked to the police and you come here all shook up, like you're afraid and shit. I don't like pussies. You know that."

Kyrie said, "I understand and I'm not afraid of shit. I just want to change the name and quit cutting the dope with rat poison. That shit is killing people, man."

Shamari said, "Cutting it with what?"

Black said, "Don't pay that nigga no mind."

Shamari said, "I know goddamned well you're not cutting the dope with rat poison! Please tell me that's a lie. Please tell me that you're not cutting this shit with rat poison?" Shamari glanced at Black.

Kyrie realizing that he'd said something that he shouldn't have and said, "No, we're not cutting it with rat poison. That was just a figure of speech, nigga."

Black stared at Shamari and could tell that he wasn't buying it. "You want to make your million dollars, don't you?"

"But I don't want to kill a bunch of motherfuckers in the process."

Black said, "Look, I'm not forcing them to use this shit. I've never forced nobody to snort anything. There is a risk in ODing off any drug. Quit worrying about that shit."

Kyrie said, "Black, you think I would tell on you? I've been knowing you since we were kids, nigga. I would never, ever, tell on you. I love you, man, but I'm with Shamari. I'm not feeling all these motherfuckers dying and we got to change the name of the dope."

Black stared at the two kilos of heroin and said, "I understand, but you know what happens when somebody ODs off Obamacare. It makes the news and gives us publicity. And guess what? The junkies hear about it and they want to try it. They know they can die, but they want to try it. I know it's the craziest shit you've ever heard but that's how it works."

"Change the name," Kyrie said.

"To what?"

"I don't know. Anything but Obamacare."

Black said, "Cool."

"No more rat poison," Kyrie said.

Black said, "Okay, Okay."

CHAPTER 11

JADA WAS HEADED TO HER MOM'S HOUSE TO PICK HER UP SO THEY could run a few errands when her phone rang. Craig? What the fuck did he want? She didn't know if she could trust him after she and Shamari made him operate on Shamari's face. She doubted he'd call the police but she knew that he would probably try to get even with her. She decided not to answer but at the last moment changed her mind.

"Hello?"

"Can you talk?" Craig asked.

"No. Why?"

"I need a favor."

"What?"

"I need some blow. Just a couple of grams."

"For what?"

"Jada, you know I use."

"Quit calling me about goddamned drugs on my cell phone! What the fuck is your problem?"

"Nobody is trying to get you busted."

"Get me busted? I'm no drug dealer. Look, I'm going to hang up on your stupid ass."

"Do you really think if I had the police with me, I'd be asking for a couple of grams? Get real."

She thought about what he said. There would be no way the police in Atlanta would be worried about a couple of grams. They had the Big

Papas and Treys and Blacks of the world to think about, even the Cartel.

"Look, I don't wanna talk on the phone about this."

"Let's meet up."

"I have to take my mom to a few places. I'll call you back and we can meet up."

"Look, can you get what I asked for or not? I mean if you can't, just say so. I'll see if I can get somebody else to do it."

"What about Skyy? Why don't you get Skyy to cop it for you?"

"I asked her already."

"So you're asking every black girl you've slept with to cop coke for you?"

"Jada, if you can't do it, just say you can't do it."

"I didn't say I couldn't do it. I said let's meet and talk about it."

She could hear him breathing heavy into the phone. Finally, he said, "I need it. Can you get it for me or not?"

"I'll see what I can do." She ended the call and dialed Big Papa.

"Hello?"

"Hey, baby," Jada said.

"You finally call me back?"

"Been super busy, trying to find a place to live."

"You still in that hotel?"

"No. I'm in another hotel, but I've found a place in Buckhead. I'll be moving in this weekend."

"So what's up, baby? You wanna see me?"

"Of course."

"When?"

"First, I gotta take my mom a few places then let's meet at the Atlanta Fish Market at one p.m."

"See you then."

Big Papa and Jada sat at a booth. Big Papa looked like he'd lost ten more pounds since the last time Jada had seen him. At least, he was able to fit comfortable in the booth. That was a feat in itself. She had to admit he was still big as hell but she admired his discipline and determination.

"Looking good, babe," Jada said.

"Not as good as you." Big Papa looked at her like he wanted to throw her on the table and eat her pussy right there in the restaurant. As thirsty as he looked, it actually made Jada feel good because it was a jeans and t-shirt kind of day and her hair was in a pony-tail. Nothing special, but she was sure that she looked better than every woman that he'd ever slept with.

"So what's going on, baby? Why did you want to see me?"

"I need a small favor."

He took a deep breath indicating that he was possibly tired of her using him.

"What do you need?"

"White girl"

"Huh?" Big Papa's dumb ass actually looked confused.

"Blow!" Jada said then she sniffled hoping he would get the hint.

"Coke? Who said I sold coke?" Big Papa said loudly.

"Well, why don't you just get on top of the goddamned table and yell it out and let everybody in this motherfucker know we are talking about drugs."

"You think I sell coke?" He lowered his voice.

"Nobody said you sold coke, and I'm still not saying you sell coke. Do you know where I can get some?"

"No."

Jada realized this clown was thinking that she was trying to set him up. She wanted to laugh. She knew he was no dummy, but she was no dummy either. She knew that his fat ass knew where to find coke.

"Look, I'm looking for a gram."

He laughed and said, "A gram? Who the hell wants a gram? Wait a minute, you snort?"

When he said that, the couple at the next table looked toward them.

"Will you shut the fuck up! No, I'm not a coke head."

"But, you do lines?"

"No. This is for a friend."

The waitress appeared and Jada ordered a chef salad and a margarita. Big Papa declined to order. When the waitress had gone, Big Papa said. "So you're looking for coke for your friend?"

"Yeah."

"A gram? Who is the friend?"

"You don't know everybody that I know."

"Atlanta is small."

"You don't know him."

"That dude that was at the hotel that day? That nigga told me to 'take a hike, Fat-Boy'. I've never been so humiliated in my goddamned life."

Jada reached over and massaged his hand, trying to repair his fragile little ego.

"Look, I'm sorry for that."

Papa tapped the table. "So you want a gram?"

"Look, it's for a friend of mine. A white professional man. Not a police officer. He likes to party and he doesn't know where to find it."

"I ain't gone lie. I was a little leery at first." Papa said.

Jada knew she'd read him right. She knew that his fat ass thought she was trying to set him up. Comical.

"So can you get it?"

"I can, but a gram is not going to be enough. Nobody that I know sells grams."

Jada stared at him. Now she would have to play his silly-ass game like she didn't know the coke was coming from him.

"So what is the least amount your people will sell?"

"An ounce."

"How much?"

"800 dollars."

"Are you kidding me?"

"Well if he gets a gram, they are going to tax."

"How much?"

"A hundred dollars."

Though Jada slept with her share of drug dealers, she really didn't know the ins and outs of the actual business, but she could tell that it would make more sense to buy the ounce. She just wasn't sure Craig wanted to spend 800 dollars for the ounce.

"I'll have to ask him."

The waitress dropped Jada's salad and when she was gone, Big Papa said, "I'll get you a gram for your friend."

Jada removed a hundred dollar bill from her purse and was about to pass it to Big Papa when he said, "Just keep it. Tell your friend, it's on me. Next time he's going to have to buy an ounce."

"I'll let him know."

Jada finished her salad real quick, and then she followed Big Papa to his condo. Thirty minutes later, one of Big Papa's friends arrived with the coke. He was tall, dark, and well-built with some very neat locks. Jada thought the nigga looked fine and she would definitely fuck him, but out of respect she'd have to pass. Besides, she knew from experience those kind of men didn't like to pay for shit. Big Papa sensed Jada staring at his friend and he led the man to the kitchen. Moments later, Big Papa let the man out and then he made his way back into the living room where he presented Jada with the coke.

"Thank you, baby."

"This is three grams."

"You treat me so well."

"I try my best, but I know you really don't like me."

She made a sad face. "Why do you say that?"

"I just get a sense that you don't like me."

"I love you."

"You love me? How can you love me? We've never been intimate except that one time."

"What time?" Jada was trying to jog her memory. Had she gotten drunk and fucked this disgusting motherfucker?

"You remember that time I went down on you."

"Oh yeah," Jada said, trying to block that shit out of her memory.

"But you said you loved me."

"I said I loved you, but I'm not in love with you."

He looked sad.

"Don't look like that, Daddy."

He shrugged and said, "What am I supposed to do?"

"About what?"

"My needs. You know I got needs too."

"What are you saying?"

"Just hold on a second." He disappeared into the bedroom and came back with five thousand dollars and tossed it on the table.

"What is that for?"

"It's yours?

"You giving that to me?"

"On one condition."

"And that condition is?'

"Let me taste it again."

"You think I'm a ho?"

"No, baby."

"I'm insulted, motherfucker! I let you do that to me the last time cause I liked you and I was in need. But I wouldn't have done that if I didn't really like you."

Jada was playing on him. The last time she let him perform oral sex on her was because she needed the money. "No, I'm not saying that you a ho."

"I hope not." Jada started crying fake tears, and Big Papa ran over to her. She laid her head on his shoulders and he was rubbing her head.

Jada said, "I thought you really cared about me, like I care about you. You know it took me a lot to say that I love you and now you playing me like I'm some kind of two-dollar ho."

"I didn't mean to upset you."

"I had sex with you, I trusted you, and you treat me like a low-class stripper."

"No."

"You don't respect women." Jada pulled away from him and made her way over to the door. "I'm leaving and you can just delete my number."

Big Papa ran over to the door and blocked the exit. "Please don't be mad at me. I'm sorry."

"I'm just a sex object to you. I'm more than sex, you know?"

"I know."

"I shared my body with you. I don't do that with everybody. I thought you were one of the good men and you turned out to be just like the rest."

"I'm sorry. You know I'm not like that." He eased over to the table where the money was and scooped it up. He tossed it to her and said, "Go to Phipps and go shoe shopping."

She tossed the money into her bag and said, "I forgive you." She approached him and hugged him and said, "I gave myself to you, and like I said, I love you."

"I love you too."

"Text me later and I might just come over and let you get a taste."

"You don't have to."

She gave him a peck on the lips and walked toward the door. Before she opened it to let herself out, she glanced over her shoulder; he was staring at her ass.

Jada met Craig at Starbucks on Peachtree. They sat at a table near the front window. He didn't look well at all. He looked as if he hadn't slept in a few days. His hair was disheveled and he had a three-day growth of stubble on his face. She passed him the coke under the table.

"Thanks. How much do I owe you?"

"Well that's three grams and it's a hundred dollars a gram." Though Jada had gotten it free, he didn't have to know that.

"I only got two hundred in cash on me. You can follow me to the ATM."

"You give me the two hundred. Consider the last gram on me."

"Thanks." He slid the drugs into his pocket.

"You are turning into a coke head, man."

"Hey, I like to party a little bit."

"Whatever, man. You were begging like this shit was a matter of life and death."

"I got problems. Who doesn't have problems?"

"What kind of problems? You can talk to me. I care about you."

"You care about me?" He laughed and said, "You care about me, extort me and then practically abduct me and make me perform three procedures pro bono."

"Pro bono?"

"Well not pro bono because that would mean I volunteered."

"Tell me what's going on."

"My life is going to hell, that's what's going on."

"Be specific."

"My wife has basically kicked me out."

"For what?"

"Well I guess she suspected me of cheating and she had some goddamned software hooked up to my cell phone. She was somehow able to get all my text messages and pictures."

"Pictures of women, I'm assuming."

"Yeah, but surprisingly, there wasn't a picture of you."

"But you had my goddamned name in your phone, didn't you?"

"No. I simply had J. That could be anybody. She don't know shit about you."

"So she knows about Skyy?"

"Yes. And this girl was sending pictures every goddamned day."

"Wow."

"Okay, your wife knows you've been sleeping with a black stripper, that's still no reason to go on a coke binge."

"Look, I got more problems than you'll ever know."

"Well, how will I know unless you tell me?" She reached for his hand and held it.

"Got financial problems."

"I don't believe it. "

"Well, I gotta pay the mortgage for three homes, and the judge said I have to pay spousal support until we go to court."

"Then what?"

He looked away then made eye contact with her.

"Talk to me," she said.

A tear rolled down his cheek and she squeezed his hand. "You can tell me," Jada said again.

"You already know."

"You're an addict?"

"I have a problem." He wiped the tears from his face and said, "I know you're saying, if I know I have a problem, why don't I just stop?"

"No. I'm not judging you. My sister has been battling addiction most of her adult life."

"I didn't know that."

"I never talk about her. I never see her. Though I hear she's been doing better."

"Well, that's good."

"Back to you, how can I help you?"

"Unless you've won the lottery and you want to give me a loan, there's not much you can do."

"I still have the money that you gave me. I can give it back to you."

"You mean extorted from me?"

"Whatever." Jada laughed. She had no intentions of returning money to a known addict.

"No. Keep it."

"I don't understand. Why don't you want the money?"

"If I need it, I'll ask for it back, but right now, I've been borrowing money from my business."

"How long do you think you can do that for?"

"I don't know."

She let go of his hand and said, "Well, the money will be here for you if you need it."

"Thanks."

CHAPTER 12

TREY ENTERED SHANTELLE'S APARTMENT WITH A KEY SHE'D GIVEN him. She was startled when he barged into the bathroom. She was standing in front of the mirror, butt naked.

He kissed her and she said, "Hold on a minute, babe." She laid the hair curlers down beside her Sonicare toothbrush and applied some lip balm to her upper lip then puckered up.

He laughed and said, "All of that for a kiss."

"I'm a girly-girl."

"And you know that's what I like."

"You do, don't you, Daddy?" She tried to hug him and he moved away. She frowned.

"I have a surprise," he said.

She smiled. "I love surprises."

Trey held onto something behind his back. She tried to see but he was concealing whatever it was very well.

"Guess?"

She thought hard, wondering what he could have behind his back, but she had no idea.

"I don't know, but please tell me." She tried to peek around his back again, but he kept moving."

"Take a guess?"

"Big or small?"

"Small."

"Jewelry."

"You're good."

She was smiling hard as hell. "A ring?"

"Not quite."

Trey brought the package to the front where she could see it.

"David Yurman."

"Yes." Trey passed her the bag and she removed the two boxes. Inside she found two bracelets.

She placed the boxes in front of the Sonicare toothbrush and leaped into his arms. He struggled to hold her, not because she was heavy, but because she surprised him. She planted kisses all over his face.

When he released her, she embraced him again and said, "I love them."

"I'm glad"

"Why'd you do it?"

"I appreciate you."

"Awww."

She kissed him again and said, "So, are we official?"

"What do you mean official?"

"Are we a couple?"

There was an awkward silence. Trey didn't know how to answer her question but he could see how giving her gifts could relay that message.

"So, I guess that means no?"

"No...I mean that doesn't mean no."

"So it means yes?"

"No."

"What does it mean?"

"It means we are adults. Do we really have to have labels? As long as I love you and you love me, what difference does it make?"

"It means a lot. It means I'm in a relationship, and I will have certain boundaries that I don't cross."

"I was in a relationship with Starr and I crossed boundaries with you. So saying that you're in a relationship don't mean shit."

"Can we ever have a conversation without you bringing that bitch up?"

"Look, I'm sorry."

"No you're not. I'm not stupid, Trey. That's who you really want to be with."

Trey pulled Shantelle into his arms and said, "Don't feel like that, baby. I want to be with you."

They kissed and he held her for a long time.

CHAPTER 13

BLACK AND SASHA MET AT THE ATLANTA BREAD COMPANY. SHE ordered clam chowder and a cup of water. Black had a coke and a turkey sandwich. Sasha was looking spectacular as usual. She was wearing a high-waisted pencil skirt that made her waist look extra skinny and it was shellacked on her showing her curvy figure. Her hair was in a do that highlighted her face.

Black watched her ass sway from side to side as he followed her, while carrying the food. Finally when they made it to the table he pulled her chair out. After she was seated, he said, "You are fine as a motherfucker."

"Is that a compliment?"

"Damn right it is."

She laughed. "You are too funny." She stared at him and she could tell he wanted her. She felt a little horny too, but she was pressed for time; otherwise, it would be nothing to deep throat him in the backseat of her car.

"So what's up? How you been?" Black asked.

"I made a list of the companies that I would like to seek franchise opportunities with."

"What are they, and how much is it going to cost?"

She laughed and said, "The black man always wanting to know the bottom line."

"I don't know about other black men, only this black man, and I need to know how much I'm spending."

"I feel you on that one."

Her phone rang and she said, "Excuse me, I gotta take this call." She stood up and dipped into the ladies room. Five minutes later, she was back at the table.

"Sorry about that," she said.

"Was that your boo?"

"No actually it was my dad. Man, he's getting on my nerves. He's going to have another press conference and he wants me there to support him."

"A press conference?"

"Yeah. Supposedly there's some heroin on the street that's killing people, and he, the police commissioner and the DEA are having a press conference."

"But didn't they just have a press conference about that?"

"They did. Just a few days ago and it's really pissing me off because black people are dying off drugs and killing each other all the time; now, a few white people die, and it's like we gotta do something about this. But when you're in politics, you know how it goes. You move for the people with the money."

"He's a puppet," Black said.

"Huh? Did you say my dad was a puppet?"

Black sipped his coke and said, "Look, I'm sorry."

"No, it's okay, I never thought about it like that, but I guess you're right."

Black bit into the turkey sandwich. He knew damn well that this new heroin was not the same as before, but it carried the same name, and though it was killing people, the name was branded and that's what people wanted because they believed it was the best.

"What's wrong?"

"Oh, nothing. I was just thinking about what you said."

"What part?"

"Oh, the part about how now that white kids are OD'ing off heroin, all of a sudden, drugs are a priority for the city."

Sasha said, "Drugs are paradoxical for black people."

"Para what?"

"What I mean is, black people want drugs off the streets but when we give the dealers a lot of time, we scream that it ain't fair."

"True, but the time should fit the crime. I think that's all black people want. I mean, don't give me a hundred times more time than somebody else that does the same thing or worse."

"True."

"Let's talk about something else."

"Have you ever done time?"

Now this bitch was being nosey. He really didn't want to answer the question, but hell, he was who he was.

She was staring at him, waiting on him to answer.

"Yes, I've been to school a time a two."

"School?"

"People like you got schools like Spelman and Georgia Tech, and then there is people like me that attend other schools. You know the kind of schools where niggas don't know what paradoxical mean."

She was laughing her ass off. "You are one funny dude."

"Let's discuss business," Black said.

"I have a list of the franchises that we can decide on."

"What are they?"

"Smoothie King, ColdStone and Wingstop which I think would do great in the Atlanta area."

"Okay, what will I need to come up with?"

"I will let you know in a few days. Well, after we decide which one we're going to pursue."

"One more thing, my sister will be your partner. She's totally legit. Knows what paradoxical means and everything."

"Really?" Sasha eyed him like she didn't believe a goddamned word he said.

"Yes, she's a physician's assistant."

"A physician's assistant or a medical assistant? There is a difference, you know?"

Black laughed and said, "Man, you trying to play me. I know the difference. My sister is right under a family practitioner."

"So she'll be my partner on paper."

"Absolutely."

Sasha's phone rang. It was her dad again. She stood up from the table and said, "I gotta go get ready for this damn press conference."

CHAPTER 14

CRAIG: CAN YOU GET ME THREE MORE GRAMS?
Jada: *Are you kidding me?*
Craig: *I need them like yesterday. Can you help me or not?*
Jada called him and he picked up right away.

"Why are you texting me this bullshit over my phone. I've told you this over and over. Plus, you told me your wife had some kind of tracking device on your goddamned phone. I don't want to be dragged into your divorce proceedings. I don't want my motherfucking name to come up. Is that clear?"

"Look Jada, I'm sorry, but I need to see you. Can we meet up?"

"No, I'm busy."

"Okay, you're too busy for me?"

"Look, I've just moved into my new place and I was getting everything situated. Unpacking and stuff."

"I can come over."

"No."

"Why? You don't want me to know where you live, huh?"

"Do I know where you and your wife live?"

"Look, she kicked me out of the house, so I'm living in a hotel. I told you that."

"I can't meet up with you."

"Well, you told me if I needed the money that I gave you, that you would give it back. Well, I need it back."

"Can it wait till in the morning?"

"No. I have a proposition."

"What kind of proposition? I'm not fucking you for money. I'm not a goddamned prostitute. You need to call Skyy for that."

"Not that kind of proposition."

"Why don't you just say it?"

"I would, but you get all weird about cell phones."

Jada took a deep breath. She really didn't want to leave the house and she knew Shamari would be back soon. Even though they weren't officially together, she didn't want him to be giving her the side eye.

"Look, I can meet you for thirty minutes then I gotta go. Where are you?"

"I'm at the Days Inn on Spring Street. Can you come here?"

"No. Let's meet at Cheetah's."

"Perfect."

R&B played as they sat at a table next to the stage. A scrawny-ass black girl in a neon green thong and tits that looked like they belonged to a thirteen year old, danced on stage. Craig was admiring the woman and Jada said, "You like that?"

"No, I just like the way she's dancing."

"The girl looks like a fucking adolescent teenage boy. But you will fuck anything."

Craig smirked but didn't respond. There was no time to argue with her, he had more important matters.

"So, tell me, good doctor?"

"Tell you what?"

"Tell me what the fuck was so important that I had to run out of my house?"

"I need a fix."

"But you said you wanted the money back and by the way I didn't bring it."

"It's okay, but can you get me something to snort?" He sniffled and snot was now on his upper lip.

"Clean your nose."

He scooped a napkin from the table and dabbed his nose.

"I'm not going to get you any more coke. Fuck that! You can get high, but you're going to have to get high on your own. I'm not going to be the one that helps."

"Okay."

The scrawny girl stepped off the stage and approached the table and hugged Craig.

"Hey, handsome. You want a dance?" the girl asked.

"Not right now. Come back in a few moments."

When the woman was gone, Jada said, "Why didn't you get a dance? I saw you looking at her."

"With what?"

"You want coke. Where were you going to get the money from?"

"I was hoping you could get it for me."

"Are you fucking serious?"

"Very."

"Look, I cannot believe you're that broke."

"I have a little bit, but my wife is trying to take all of my goddamned money. Can you believe she just told the judge that she can't live off eleven thousand dollars a month? She wants sixteen thousand."

"What?"

"That bitch just wants to take everything I have. She wants to leave me with nothing."

"Damn."

"I'm selling two of my cars tomorrow. I need some money."

Jada flagged the waitress, and then asked for a Ciroc and Coke.

"So what did you want with me?"

"I don't know. I was thinking I could do some more work on your boyfriend's face. Give him a brow lift maybe some fillers. To make him even more un-recognizable."

"He's not going to go for that, and I don't like the way he looks now."

"You didn't think it was good work?"

"It was great work, but I don't like him looking like that. I liked him better when he looked rugged."

"But he's friggin hiding."

"I guess."

The waitress dropped the drink and Jada took a sip and said, "I'm sorry, but I don't think we can help you with that."

"What about the rhinoplasty you wanted?"

"I decided I don't need one," Jada said. "Wait a goddamned minute! What's going on with your business? Why are you trying to get side business?"

"Well, my partner is counting every goddamned coin that comes into the account."

"So, you want to do some work under the table?"

"Exactly."

"There is nothing I can do for you," Jada sipped her drink. "Did you ask Skyy to get some of her stripper friends?"

"Most strippers are broke, you know that."

"You ain't lying."

The scrawny bitch was eyeing them from across the room, looking desperate for a dance. Jada waved her over, handed her a twenty, and said, "Give him a dance, honey."

R&B was playing. Jada's mind was racing, trying to think of someone who might need some under-the-table work. Lani's view on surgery was that she would have it after kids. Jada doubted Starr would want any surgery. She was stacked like a brick house, naturally. The skinny bitch finished dancing and asked Jada if she wanted a dance.

"Gain a few more pounds, sweetheart."

The woman frowned and thanked Craig.

Jada said, "I'm the one that paid for the dance, skinny bitch."

When the woman was gone, Jada said, "I've been thinking, and there is nobody I can think of that would need your services right now."

Craig's face got serious. "Can I help your boyfriend in some capacity?"

"Huh? What the fuck did you say?"

"Can I help Shamari?"

"Help him how? I already told you, he's not going to get any more surgery."

"No, I didn't mean like that."

"What did you have in mind?"

"I was thinking I could be a mule."

Jada spit her drink out thinking about him being a drug runner. "First of all, who uses those terms except the goddamn police?" She was laughing her ass off thinking of his corny ass trying to traffic drugs.

"No seriously, I could bring the drugs back. Look at me? Who would think of stopping me? I'm a middle aged, professional, white male. No cop is going to stop me."

She looked at him seriously and said, "This ain't Breaking Bad, white boy. This is serious and you will go directly to prison if you get caught. You need to reconsider it." She sipped her drink and said, "Actually, you need to find you a twelve-step program. Get your ass clean and then get back to being the top plastic surgeon in Atlanta." She looked at the snot crawling down his nose again. "You have fell way off."

"I hear you and I do want to get myself clean, but that doesn't take away the fact that I need some money now, Jada. I don't think I will get caught."

"But if you do?"

"It's not going to happen."

"But if it does?"

"If I get caught, I'll take my licks."

"This ain't grade school. There will be no licks. There will be time."

"I understand."

"But he's not going to go for it because you have a habit."

"What does that have to do with anything? And he doesn't have to know."

Jada passed him a napkin and said, "Wipe your nose again, please."

Craig cleaned his nose and said, "Are you saying that I would steal something from him?"

"Fuck no! I'm not saying that at all. Just saying you'll get pulled because your nose is running like a goddamn faucet."

"That's not going to happen."

"Look, I'm going to be honest with you. I don't think he's going to go for it. He don't like you. He don't trust you."

"I understand that, but he's a business man and as a business man you have to put your emotions aside."

"I'll ask him."

"That's all I'm asking. It's worth a try."

Jada stood up and was about to leave when he asked, "Can you bring me a gram back?"

Jada said, "You need to stop your nose from bleeding."

He dabbed his nose with the napkin as Jada made her way to the exit. When she looked back, the skinny bitch was on his lap rubbing his back.

• • •

Shamari had unpacked most of the boxes, set up the bed, and hung the bedroom TV when Jada arrived home. Jada sensed that Shamari thought he would be moving in. While she didn't mind him staying for a while, she would have to make it clear that this was not his home. She would do anything she could to help him, but he was wanted by the Feds. When she entered the bedroom, he looked up.

"Hey, baby," he said.

They kissed briefly.

Jada said, "Have a seat. I need to ask you something."

He looked at her and said, "I think I know what it is and I don't plan on being here long. I love you, Jada and I always will, but I know that the Feds are after me and that's not your problem. Even though I have a new face, my fingerprints are the same and I still have tattoos that they can identify me with."

Jada smiled and said, "Well, I'm glad to know you love me and that you're thinking about me."

"Is that what you wanted to talk about? Me leaving?"

"Well, I was going to have that talk eventually."

"Look, you don't have to explain. You've done enough for me."

"Thanks."

"Plus, I don't want you to get a harboring a fugitive charge on you. You were my girlfriend. It's just a matter of time before they come here."

"Ok, but that's not what I wanted to talk about."

He looked confused.

"I wanted to ask you how you were transporting your work."

"Huh?"

"I know you went to Cali a few weeks ago to pick up something. How did you get it back?"

"A girl name Erica, a friend of my sister's boyfriend, brought it back."

"Is she black or white?"

"Black. Why?"

"What if I tell you I could get a middle aged, white man to bring it back?"

"What are you talking about? How do you know him?"

"You know him too."

"Who is he?"

"The surgeon."

"No way."

"Yeah, he wants to do it."

"Why do he want to do it? I don't believe it. Why would a man like that want to be involved with something like this? He's making legitimate money."

"He has a problem," Jada said.

"What kind of problem?""

Though Jada was more loyal to Shamari, she still didn't feel good about telling him Craig's business. But she had to, if she expected him to want to help him out.

Shamari pressed, "What kind of problem?"

"A habit."

"What kind of habit?"

"Coke."

"He's a coke head?" Shamari laughed. "But he doesn't look like a coke head."

"I know."

"He needs money?"

"Well, things are going really bad for him. His wife is divorcing him and he has to pay her a lot of money per month."

"And he has to get the nose candy."

"Cut it out, Shamari."

"You defending this motherfucker?"

"Not defending anybody. He told me to ask if you can use him, and so I'm asking."

"Why should I help that motherfucker?" Then he thought about Craig fucking Jada, getting head from Jada ,and fucking Jada in the ass. "Tell me why should I help this motherfucker, Jada?"

Jada sensed that Shamari was getting upset and she said, "Now would you really be helping him or would you be helping yourself?"

"What the fuck are you talking about?"

"It's a matter of perspective."

"Perspective?"

"It's all about how you look at shit, Shamari. You would really be helping yourself. I mean, look at this motherfucker? No cop is going to stop him."

"You're right." Shamari thought maybe this wasn't a bad idea after all.

"I mean, he's not going to go through all the bullshit a black male or female will go through."

"True. What does he want for doing this?"

"I don't know."

"He's gonna want a lot more money than what I'm willing to pay."

"Maybe. Maybe not."

Shamari said, "Think about it. You think this man is going to risk his personal life and freedom for three thousand dollars?"

"Three thousand dollars?"

"Yeah, that's the most I'm paying a runner."

"You're right. He's not going to want to do this for so little. It just won't make sense."

"Exactly!"

CHAPTER 15

TREY WAS LYING ON SHANTELLE'S SOFA ABOUT TO DOZE WHEN THE phone rang. It was his son, T. J.

"T. J., my main man, what's going on?"

"Daddy, what are you doing?"

"I'm lying on the sofa. Why? What's up?"

"Can you come and play with me?"

"Sure," Trey said. There was nothing else he was doing, so there was no reason for him not to meet up and play with his son for a few hours.

"Can we go to the park and then to grandma's house?"

"We can do anything you want."

"I want a Mountain Dew too. Mommy won't let me drink sodas like you do."

"Where is your mother?"

"She's in the other room."

"Don't let her hear you say that."

"I know, Daddy. That's our secret. Remember we pinky promised."

"That's right." Trey sat up and looked at his watch. "I'll be there to pick you up in about an hour okay?"

"Ok. Yay!" T. J. yelled.

When Trey terminated the call, he glanced over his shoulder to see Shantelle staring at him with her hands on her hips.

"Who was that?"

"My son. I'm going to pick him up and play with him for awhile."

"That's nice."

"Yeah, I figured I wasn't doing anything else."

Shantelle sat on the edge of the sofa and said, "Baby, when am I going to get to meet your son and your baby's mother?"

"In due time."

"Why can't I meet them now?"

"Now is not the right time."

"When will be the right time?"

"I don't know."

"Trey, give me an answer instead of saying it's not the right time."

Trey looked her straight in the eye. He wanted to tell her to shut the fuck up, but he knew how super sensitive she was and he didn't like being verbally abusive. He never had to say anything to Starr. She just followed his lead, but she could hold her own. Damn he missed that woman.

"Why is this important to you?"

"T. J. is a part of you and I want to see him."

"I'll tell you what, I'll let you meet T. J. I'll bring him by, but now is not the time to meet his mother. She'll make it hard on me."

Shantelle smiled and said, "At some point, I'd like to meet your mother."

"Slow down. One thing at a time."

"Okay, baby."

Trey stood up from the sofa and made his way to the door. Shantelle's insecurities were beginning to get on his goddamned nerves.

Trey had spent the whole day with T. J. They had gone to the movies. He'd taken him to see his grandma. He played catch with him at the park and he had taken him shopping to buy him some new shoes. Then they met Shantelle, who had baked T. J. some cookies. He was exhausted and though he liked spending time with his son, he was happy to be bringing him back home so he could go home and get some rest. When Trey approached Jessica's driveway, T. J. became sad.

Trey said, "What's wrong, champ?"

"I don't want you to go."

Trey said, "I'll come back and get you next weekend."

"I don't want to go in there. I don't like being home."

"Why not?"

"Because it's lonely in there. It's just me and mom all the time. I don't have any brothers or sisters like the other kids."

Trey knew exactly how T. J. felt. He grew up in a house where he was the only child. Although he had a half brother, he hardly ever saw him growing up and Trey knew it could be lonely. He didn't know what to do right now, he didn't want to try and gain custody of T. J. until he was through with the drug business. Right now was not a good time. Trey kissed his son's forehead and said, "I tell you what, champ, I'll come to your school to eat lunch with you tomorrow."

T. J. was smiling hard. "Would you?"

"I love you, son. Don't ever forget that. Be good and take care of your mother, okay?"

"Okay."

"You're the man of the house. Okay?"

"I know that, Dad. Mom tells me that all the time."

Trey and T. J. got out of the car and made their way to the front door. They stepped inside the house. Jessica was waiting for T. J. and she looked amazing. Her hair was down, she was wearing a black fitted dress, and her legs looked absolutely delicious. Trey noticed her right away.

T. J. said, "Mom, I had so much fun. Dad and I went and saw grandma and we went to the park, the movies and this nice lady, named Ms. Shantelle, baked me some cookies."

"Ms. Shantelle, huh?"

"Yeah, she's nice and pretty too. She's gonna be my girlfriend."

The fact that her son had said some other woman was pretty infuriated the hell out of Jessica.

"So she's going to be your girlfriend?"

T. J. smiled revealing the missing teeth that most six year olds have. "Yeah."

"I don't think your daddy would like that." Then she kissed T. J. again and said, "Go to your room. Let me talk to your daddy for a moment."

T. J. high-fived his father then disappeared into his bedroom. When he was gone, Jessica said, "So you have my son around women I've never met."

"It's not what you think."

"You know, Trey, the grownup thing to do would be to introduce me to your new girlfriend. But that's what a grownup would do and I'm giving you too much credit for being grown. You hid me and T. J. from Starr for years."

"Could you chill? Damn, you're getting on my nerves."

"Look, I'm not going to let you upset me, I'm in a good mood and I'm going on a date, so there is no way I'm letting you get me down."

"Look, can't we get along for T. J.'s sake?' "

"Of course."

"So where are you going? You're all dressed up."

"Catching a movie with a friend. Mom is going to watch T. J."

"Good, you need to get out more."

"I think so."

"You looking damn good."

"So, I was right."

"Right about what?"

"I thought I saw you admiring me."

Trey smiled. "I was checking you out a little bit"

She smiled and walked toward him. "You know you still want me."

"I never said you weren't fine as hell."

She leaned toward him and kissed him. He tried to resist for a moment but then he found himself kissing her back. His hand was on her ass then around her tiny-ass waist. She kneeled and placed her mouth on his dick through his jeans and his dick sprang to life. He wanted to fuck her badly but he knew that it would ultimately lead to destruction. He resisted and pulled away.

"What's wrong?"

"We don't need to go down that path."

"Why? I know you have a woman. I mean women."

"I need to be going."

"Whatever, Trey. You know you wanna fuck me."

Trey made his way to the door. He looked back at her and said, "Tell T. J. to remember I'm coming to his school tomorrow for lunch."

"Fuck you, Trey!"

CHAPTER 16

TWO WHITE MEN WERE KNOCKING AT LANI'S DOOR. THERE WAS A doorbell outside but they were knocking. How did they get into the building? They didn't know the code. They never buzzed her and she never let them in. They had to be the police on official business, not like those clowns, Williams and Kearns. They were wearing nice suits, clean shaven, and looked very serious. She did not want to let them in but she had a feeling they knew she was inside, and they were not going to leave until she answered. Besides, she didn't want the neighbors to be alarmed. She tip-toed over to the peephole so they knew that she was there.

One of them said, "Open the door, Ms. Miller."

"Who are you?"

"Department of Homeland Security."

"What?"

"Homeland Security."

"Just a second," she called out.

Lani disappeared into the back room thinking this was some bullshit. What the fuck did the Department of Homeland Security want with her? She hadn't done anything and as far as she knew, Black didn't do anything to warrant the Department of Homeland Security to want him. He wasn't a terrorist. The Department of Homeland Security went after motherfuckers like Bin Laden. Motherfuckers who are trying to take over the country, overthrow the government and hijackers who ran planes into buildings, not an Atlanta D-Boy that rides around listening to Trap music.

She knew that they had better shit to do than to fuck with her and Black. She slipped on a pair of tight jeans. She wasn't concerned about either of them lusting after her ass. They seemed to be more professional than that Williams clown who'd been in her house before.

She opened the door and the two men presented their badges. They looked to be in their mid-thirties. They were very handsome white men. One was kind of short. He had dark hair and was clean shaven. The other man had movie star good looks. Tall, blonde and very well built. The type of guy she would fuck if she were into white men.

The movie star said, "Scott Chandler."

The brunette said, "I'm agent David Carroll."

"What do you want with me?"

"Can we come in?"

"Please do."

She led them into the living room.

Once they were seated, David Carroll said, "I know you have no idea why we are here."

"I don't."

"You're part of an ongoing investigation."

"Me? Wait a minute, you're homeland security, I'm no terrorist."

The men laughed and said, "That's a common misconception that all we investigate is terrorism."

"Okay, what do you want from me?"

"Not here to ask you anything. We know you had an interview with the APD about a week ago."

"Yeah, I did."

"I'm here to tell you that this case is bigger than you think, bigger than even what the APD thinks."

"What case? And what do I have to do with it?

"You have a lot to do with it, but you don't have to."

"What are you saying?" Lani was racking her brain. Wondering what the fuck they were talking about and what the hell did they want from her? She'd never killed anyone or sold drugs. This had to be a mistake.

"I'm saying Tyrann is a major drug trafficker and has been for a long time. We know you haven't been with him for a long time."

"So why are you here?"

"Because when he first came to our attention, you were together. Remember the House at 2121 Alpine Circle?"

"Yeah. That house was in my name."

"But financed by Tyrann."

"Wait a minute, I was working at the time."

The movie star said, "So we're supposed to believe that you paid the rent with a hotel front desk salary?"

Lani realized that they had been investigating her thoroughly because she had been a front desk clerk at the Marriott at the time. "What do you want with me?"

"We're here to give you an opportunity."

"What kind of opportunity?"

"To walk away from all of this unscathed."

"In exchange for information, right?"

"Right."

Lani looked at the two white men. Both of them were very serious and devoid of any personality. She knew they weren't playing and they were in fact on Black's ass. As much as she hated that son of a bitch Black, she loved his black ass at the same time. He'd done too much for her and her family for her to say anything about him to the authorities.

"Am I being charged?" she asked.

"No, not right now."

"Listen, I would like for you to leave my house right now."

The two men stood up and made their way to the door. They didn't argue or try to persuade her. They left without saying another word.

Lani drove to Black's home in Alpharetta. Black was surprised to see her. He attempted to hug her and invited her in when he noticed that she looked worried.

"What the fuck is wrong, babe?" he asked.

"I had some visitors today."

"Visitors? What kind of visitors?"

"Department of Homeland Security."

"What? What did they want with you?" He laughed and said, "So, you're a part of the Taliban?"

"No, they came to my house asking about your black ass."

"What?"

"Yeah it was two white men with the Department of Homeland Security asking for information about you!"

"What did they ask, and why in the fuck did you talk to them?"

Lani looked puzzled and confused. "That's just it. They didn't ask anything."

Black stood up and made his way to the bar. He poured himself a glass of Hennessy.

"And you didn't tell them anything?"

"Are you listening, motherfucker? They didn't ask me anything."

Black sipped his drink and said, "But you said they were looking for me."

"They said they were there because of an ongoing investigation that I was a part of along with you."

Black was laughing his ass off. "Wait a minute, so you trying to tell me the same people that are trying to stop terrorism are investigating me? Yeah, right. What the fuck is wrong with you, Lani? Who put you up to this bullshit? Is this some kind of sick joke? Nobody is looking for me. I went to my lawyer's office. He checked to see if I had any warrants and

I didn't."

"Look, I'm not here to argue with you. I'm just telling you what happened at my house. Two white men showed up and said they had been investigating us since we lived on Alpine Circle."

Black finished his liquor.

Lani said, "I know this sounds crazy, and it sounded crazy to me to. I thought it would have been the DEA or ATF, not the goddamned Department of Homeland Security. I thought it was a joke too."

Black's face got serious and he said, "So what did they want with you?"

"They said they wanted to give me an opportunity."

"What kind of opportunity?"

"To walk away unscathed."

"And what did you say?"

"I asked them to leave my house."

Black said, "I don't believe it."

"I can tell you don't believe it."

"What in the fuck would they want with me?"

"Have I ever lied to you?"

"No." He was now quiet and reflective.

"Haven't I always been loyal to you?"

"Even when I didn't deserve it."

"You don't believe me."

"I just don't want to believe it, I guess."

CHAPTER 17

BIG PAPA CALLED JADA AND ASKED TO MEET UP FOR DRINKS. SHE asked him to bring one of his friends with him for Lani.

"As a matter of fact, bring that fine-ass nigga that came over to your house the other day." Jada said, then realized that she just called one of his friends attractive.

"You like my boy?"

"Well he's good looking, but you baby—you have substance. You are a man of character. I couldn't date a man like that. He probably spends more time in the mirror than I do, but he'd be perfect for Lani."

"Ok I'll call Shakur and we can meet at the W on 16th Street at eight o'clock."

"Perfect."

•   •   •

Lani and Jada sat at a table in the middle of the lounge and they'd already started a tab that Big Papa would have to pick up. The ladies drank mojitos while they waited on the men.

Jada said, "I'm telling you, this man is drop dead gorgeous."

Lani was smiling but she said, "You know I'm not into pretty boys."

"I'm not into pretty boys either, but when you see this man, you're going to be like 'that motherfucker is perfection'. I mean tall with long, well maintained locs, perfect skin, and perfect teeth. Gorgeous, I'm telling you."

"What does he do?"

"What do you think he do?"

"Another D boy?"

"Quit being concerned about that. All you need to know is that the motherfucker has money."

"I'm so tired of this lifestyle."

Jada looked at Lani like she'd lost her motherfucking mind. "So what are you going to do? Date a regular nigga with a nine to five?"

"What's so bad about that?"

"Just do it and you'll see. Dudes out there now be wanting to go Dutch with you on a damn forty dollar meal. I ain't got time for that."

Big Papa and Shakur approached the table and Jada introduced Big Papa to Lani. They shook hands and Big Papa said, "Everybody, this is Shakur."

Lani thought this was the finest goddamned man she'd seen in her life as she marveled at his beautiful locs, his wide shoulders, and tiny waist. And that goddamned 'I will fuck you to death' smile made her pussy wet. Those damn teeth were sparkling white and just perfect. The genetic gods had been good to him.

"How are you, Lani?"

Lani thought she'd be fine once he put his dick inside her, but she had to act like a lady. "I'm doing okay."

Shakur sat beside her and he was wearing Aventis by Creed. It was mesmerizing. Everything about him was on point. Hair? Check. Teeth? Check. Body? Check. Style? Check. He was the complete package until she spotted a beaded necklace around his neck. That shit was gay but she'd give him the benefit of the doubt for now.

He sat beside her, still smiling like he'd fuck her into a coma and then eat her out of it.

The waitress came and Lani and Jada order two more mojitos. Shakur ordered a Red Bull, and Big Papa ordered a diet coke.

Lani said to Shakur, "You don't drink?"

"I do. Been up since five a.m. so I'm a little tired."

Jada said, "And this nigga ordered a diet coke. How are ya'll going to ask us out for drinks and not even drink?"

Big Papa was grinning with his yellow ass teeth. "Gotta get this weight off me. Liquor equals calories."

Jada rubbed his back. "I'm so proud of you, baby. You've really been doing a good job."

Lani said to Shakur, "Why don't you have a woman?"

Shakur said, "Who said I didn't?"

Lani laughed and said, "My bad. So why are you here?"

Shakur said, "I don't have a woman. I was just fucking with you."

"You look like a player."

"I've heard that all my life."

"Are you?"

"I've played women but I've also been played. That's life, but right now you looking at a grown man. If I died today, I've had my share of pussy."

Lani sipped her drink thinking he must have gotten a lot of pussy with those sexy-ass lips.

Shakur said, "What about you? Who is the lucky man?"

"No man. He was murdered a few months ago."

"Sorry to hear that."

"It's okay."

"What happened? I mean, if you want to talk about it."

"I don't know exactly what happened, but his body was found in the trunk of a Lincoln...."

"Chris Jones?"

"You knew Chris?"

"Didn't really know him, but I know Mike."

Lani shook her head and said, "It's a small world."

Shakur called out to Big Papa, "Ty, this is Mike's brother's girlfriend."

Big Papa said, "No way."

"Yep," Lani said.

Shakur said to Lani, "That just happened. Are you ready to move on?"

"Depends."

"On what?"

"If I meet somebody that is good to me. Not just financially and sexually, but faithfully. God knows I dealt with my share of dogs."

He laughed and said, "I want to take your mind off all those losers."

"You do?"

"It's my mission."

"Is that so?"

"If you let me in."

With that body and that pussy-eating grin, she wanted to let him in. Damn did she want to let him in.

Later that night Lani followed Shakur to his home in Riverdale, Georgia. It was a very modest two-story home, very surprising for a big drug dealer. Once they were inside and seated in the den, Shakur made them drinks. He handed one to Lani.

"No thanks."

"So, you're not drinking now?"

"I would but I have to drive and besides I didn't see you fix the drink."

He laughed and said, "Oh, so you think I would spike your drink?"

"I'm not saying you would or you wouldn't. I just said I didn't see you fix it."

"You didn't see them fix the drinks at the hotel."

"You didn't drink at the hotel."

"Now that I'm home, I want to have a drink."

"But you said that you had to be up early in the morning."

Shakur laughed. "Look, we're arguing about nothing. You don't have to have the drink." He set her drink on the table then sat beside her. He put his arm around her shoulder and said, "I like you a lot. What do you think of me?"

Was he seriously asking her what she thought of him? She thought his tall chocolate ass was delicious, but she couldn't say that since it wasn't appropriate. "I think you're a nice guy."

"Nice guys finish last. I don't want to be a nice guy."

She blushed and said, "So what do you want me to say?"

"Say what you want to say."

She was blushing hard as hell. She would not say what she wanted to say and she would try her damndest not to do what she wanted to do.

"I like you."

"I don't think you trust me."

"We just met."

"But I let you come to my house."

"I guess that means you trust me."

"Of course. Why would you be here?"

Lani saw where this was going. Not only was Shakur fine, but he was an arrogant-ass motherfucker and in a weird way it was turning her the fuck on.

He rubbed her knee and said, "I can tell you ain't been touched in a while."

She avoided looking at those sexy-ass lips of his. She didn't want this night to end up with her face down and her ass in the air. He was making it hard as fuck.

He stood with the drink in hand and walked over and dimmed the lights then turned on his surround sound. Kanye West singing "Say You Will" came through the speakers. He removed his shirt and she couldn't keep her eyes off the tats decorating that sexy, wide-ass back or his eight pack, but damn why did he still have that gay ass beaded necklace on? Yuck!! But she wanted him inside her.

He sat beside her and placed his hands on her legs. Then he sipped his drink and leaned forward and kissed her. Before she knew it, they were tongue wrestling. His hand was now on her ass and her left hand was on his dick. He tried to remove her jeans but she resisted.

"What's wrong?"

"Nothing's wrong."

He leaned into her and kissed her again. His hands gripped her ass and he tried to remove her jeans again but she still resisted.

"Come on, you know you want to do it," he said.

"I do."

'Well what's wrong?"

"I'm a little too old for this bullshit. What happens when you don't call me and I'm somewhere pissed the fuck off at myself because I allowed it to happen?"

"I like you a lot, Lani." He made his way over and scooped up his shirt and put it back on. "I don't think you like me."

"So 'like' for you, is me face down and ass up?"

"I thought we were feeling each other."

"Me too."

Shakur said, "I get it. You think I'm going to tell Mike if we have sex?"

"Actually that hadn't crossed my mind until now. You're a grown man. I would hope you wouldn't do something like that."

"I get good vibes about you, Lani. Regardless of what people have been saying about you in the street, I think you're a good person."

"Lani said, "What did you just say?"

"About what?"

"What have people been saying about me in the street?"

"Mike and his friends are saying that you set his brother up to get killed and then had some niggas come to his parents' house and hold them hostage."

"What?"

"I'm just telling you what they are saying."

"Nobody is saying that."

"I don't know you. Why would I make some shit up like that? I don't believe them, so what difference does it make?"

"The reason why you don't believe them is because it never happened." Lani stood up, gathered her things and said, "I gotta go."

"I'll walk you out to the car."

When they were in his driveway, he gave her a kiss on the cheek and said, "I'll be in touch."

When Lani drove away from Shakur's home, she dialed Mike's number. He didn't pick up. She dialed it again and again until finally he picked up.

"Hello?"

"Mike, I need to talk to you."

"I'm listening."

"People are telling me that you think that I set your brother up, and I had your parents held hostage."

"Oh, really?"

"Mike, tell me you don't think that?"

"Look, Lani. All I know is those motherfuckers were at my parents house and you're the only person that knows where my mom lives."

"Mike, you don't believe that. You know I wouldn't do nothing like that."

"I don't know, Lani."

"Mike, that's not the part that even hurt me the most. The part that really hurts me is that you're saying I had Chris set up. I loved your brother."

"Whatever."

"Look, you don't have to believe me."

"Good because I don't believe you." He ended the call.

CHAPTER 18

JADA MET CRAIG IN THE PARKING DECK OF HIS OFFICE AFTER WORK. SHE sat in the passenger side of a rental car. She said, "You're looking well."

"Thanks."

"Have you been using?"

"No, not in a few days. Why?"

"Oh, I can just tell."

"So are we here for you to tell me how much of a junkie I am, or do you have some news about what I asked you?"

"He doesn't want to do it."

"Why?"

"He's only paying three thousand dollars for drug runs."

"Three thousand dollars? Not worth the risk."

"I know."

He took a deep breath. "Does he need any partners?"

"What do you mean, partners?"

"Well I've sold the two Maseratis. I have cash."

"You want to be a drug dealer?"

"No. You know I don't know the first thing about drug dealing. But I can invest some money."

Jada laughed and said, "You want to invest some money? Like what kind of money."

"I need to know the return first. Ask him if I invest a hundred thousand dollars. How much can I get back? I would want you to be in charge of it, of course."

"If you have money from selling your cars, why do you need to sell drugs? It doesn't make sense."

"Jada, I'm not selling, I'm investing."

"But it's not making sense."

"I have a lot going on. I told you, my wife is trying to take everything."

"Okay, but you know you can go to prison?"

"I don't have a choice."

"You do."

He turned away and said, "Look, I'm embarrassed to tell you this but I have a few malpractice suits and my insurance is going through the roof. I need money."

"Malpractice? You're the best."

"Hey, it happens to the best of us."

"I don't think Shamari wants any partners."

"Ask him."

"Okay."

She was about to get out of the car and he stopped her. They stared into each other eyes for a long time and he said, "Thank you."

Later that night she texted him.

Jada: *For a hundred thousand, he said you'll get a fifty thousand dollar return in a month but you're going to have to bring it back for him.*

Craig: *No Problem.*

The rooftop pool at the SLS hotel in Beverly Hills was just fabulous. And Jada's body looked just as spectacular as she wore a white thong and a very fitting bathing suit top that was struggling very hard to contain her tits. She'd thought about a yellow conservative one piece but decided at the last moment to wear the thong, after all this was Beverly Hills so she figured what the hell. Jada and Shamari stood next to the pool sipping drinks. Shamari was drinking a Hennessy and Coke and Jada had a white wine when Craig approached with a woman that looked like a black Barbie doll. The woman introduced herself as Imani. Imani had a very long weave and Jada could tell she'd had several nose jobs as well as cheek implants, chin implants, an eyebrow raise, veneers, and a breast augmentation.

Shamari whispered to Jada, "This woman looks like a goddamn robot."

Jada said, "Hell, I hope I don't look like that. Everything on this bitch is artificial."

Craig and Shamari shook hands without smiling and Jada suggested they go to the hotel room to discuss business. Though she loved the ambiance, she knew that nosey-ass people could still overhear their conversation.

Once they were in their room, Jada said, "So why did you bring her?" Jada pointed to Imani.

"She's going to help me get it back to Atlanta."

"How is she going to get back to Atlanta?"

"Drive." Craig said.

Shamari looked at her. She looked so goddamned fake, he figured she didn't have the brains to get back to Atlanta. Could she read a map? Hell, could she even follow a GPS navigation system.

Craig said, "Relax. I'm going to take care of her. Don't worry, I'll handle her."

Shamari said, "What do you want for doing this?"

Jada said, "Yeah, what's in it for you?"

Craig said, "I'll take care of her. We worked out a deal."

"I just want the perfect nose," replied Imani.

"This is crazy. I've never heard of anything like this in my life," Jada said. She wanted to tell Imani she looked like a goddamned cat already. This woman did not need any more surgery.

Shamari said, "Who the fuck are we to judge anybody as long as she gets what she wants?"

Jada said, "Imani does not need any more surgery. She looks..."

Imani smiled and said, "I look fake. I know. You can say it. I won't be offended. When people say I look fake, it's a compliment."

Shamari just stared at the crazy-ass bitch. What the fuck? He wondered how this happened. What had taken place in her life to get her to this point?

Jada wanted to say something, but clearly the bitch was delusional and they were there for business, not to give this ho a psychological evaluation.

Shamari said, "Where's the money?"

Craig presented him with a briefcase.

"You'll get your profit back in a month."

"Don't worry about it. I'll handle it," Craig said.

"Okay, meet us back in the hotel lobby at seven. I'll have the product."

The two men shook hands.

Shamari tossed the two kilos on Black's table and Black said, "What the fuck? Why is the dope in these balloons? This shit has probably been cut a thousand goddamned times."

"No. I gave it to the courier and he thought that it was a good idea to take it out of the original wrapping."

"He? What the fuck do you mean he?"

"Yeah, bruh, it's a white dude. I'm talking about a nerd-looking motherfucker who the police will never suspect."

Black was visibly upset. His eyes were red and he stared at Shamari and then back at the balloons on the table. "And what make you think this motherfucker won't run his goddamned mouth, man?"

Shamari turned from Black's gaze and said, "He's not just a runner. He invested with us."

"Who? We don't need no investor."

"Look, all we gotta give him is fifty thousand dollars for a hundred thousand dollars."

"Motherfucker, that's a fifty percent return. No wonder you ain't got no goddamned money."

"It's a fifty percent return if we give him the money right after we use the hundred thousand but I told him I would see him in a month. But you know how the game goes. That month might turn into two months. By the time I pay his ass, we'll have made about three hundred thousand off his hundred."

"We don't need him."

"He is the reason we got the heroin back to Atlanta. What's the goddamned big deal? We are talking about pure heroin. We can afford to give him fifty thousand dollars."

"I don't know why you keep saying pure. If you get it from niggas, it is not pure."

"Okay, but the last product was a good product right."

"It was, but why do we need him?"

"Transportation."

"Fifty thousand dollars for transportation?"

"No, he invested a hundred thousand. What part of that don't you understand?"

"I don't want to meet him."

"I never said you had to meet him. I will deal with him."

Black scooped up the packages of dope off the table and examined them.

"My contact said it's better than before."

"Perfect."

Shamari said, "One thing, before I leave we need to change the goddamn name. This is getting out of hand. I don't want to be associated with that Obamacare name. Its killing people and I don't care if it's not our package that's killing people. I don't want that name."

"Look, Shamari, I handle distribution, you handle everything else."

Shamari snatched the product from the table and said, "I will take this somewhere else. I don't want you to use that name."

Black stepped in front of Shamari. "You want to take a step back! I sent money with you, so this is partly mine."

Shamari said, "I'll give you your goddamned money back, but I'm not going to let you use that name."

"Let me use? I'm confused. You are talking to me like you are my goddamned daddy! I'm a grown-ass man. I will do what the fuck I want to do."

"Look, Black." Shamari lowered his tone. "I want to keep working with you. I really do. I think we make a good team. Can't you see motherfuckers are dying off that Obamacare heroin?"

"But it's not our package."

"You don't know if it's ours. I didn't know you were cutting our shit with rat poison."

"Look, everybody cuts their shit with deadly shit."

"I guess you're right. It doesn't matter what you name the shit if it's deadly."

"All heroin is deadly—if they OD."

"But why rat poison?"

"Look, man, when we started this shit, I didn't know shit about this business, just like you didn't. This is what the OGs said to cut it with and they showed me how to do it. I had to cut it, otherwise I wouldn't have made shit."

"What are you talking about? You gave me a hundred and fifty thousand dollars. I know you made at least that much."

"I don't know what world you living in, but you cannot make three hundred thousand dollars off a kilo of heroin."

"Really?"

"Who told you that dumb shit? Like I said, I gave you damn near all the profits the first time because you needed the money more than I did. Did I make money? Yes. But the first one was pure, but we still didn't make three hundred thousand dollars. That isn't possible. Notice the second time we made about seventy-five thousand each."

"I thought that was because it wasn't as pure as the first."

"You are right. It wasn't as pure as the first kilo and guess what? If it wasn't for the goddamned rat poison, we wouldn't have made what we made."

"Well, why do it then? Why don't we just get some coke, something that we both know about?"

"Because coke is not going to sell this goddamned fast. These heroin junkies, they need this shit, man, and I'm going to give them what they need."

"We gotta change the name."

"I've been giving it some thought. I think I got a new name even better than Obamacare."

"And that name is?"

"Pretty Hurts."

"Like Beyonce's song?"

"Exactly. I mean who don't like Beyonce? Whites. Blacks. Mexicans. Asians. Hispanics."

Shamari wanted to tell Black that Mexicans were Hispanics but he knew Black didn't give a fuck. Shamari laughed. As crazy as Black was, he was a shrewd-ass businessman.

"I actually like the name," Shamari said.

He hugged Black and Black whispered into Shamari's ear, "This partner of yours better not run his motherfuckin' mouth."

"I'll handle him."

"If he runs his goddamn mouth, I'll handle him."

CHAPTER 19

BLACK CHANGED THE NAME OF THE PRODUCT AND IT WAS A HIT IN THE streets. The two kilos were gone in a week's time and Shamari and Jada met Craig in California again. This time, Shamari purchased three kilos of heroin. Craig called Jada as soon as they made it back to Atlanta. It was a little after six p.m. and he told her to meet him at his office. The other surgeon and receptionist and all the assistants were gone for the day. As soon as Jada stepped in the office, Jada saw a woman that she recognized, but she didn't know from where. A really cute, skinny, black girl.

"Hi, I'm Jada."

The girl said, "Hi." But she didn't offer her name.

Craig said to Jada, "Just wait out here in the reception area."

Jada said, "Can you just give me what I came for so I can go see Shamari?"

"It will be just a few minutes." Craig disappeared into the back.

Jada skimmed through a People magazine but then turned to the black girl who was sitting in the lobby holding her breasts. Maybe she'd just gotten implants and they were bothering her, Jada thought. She looked really uncomfortable.

Jada said, "Where do I know you from?"

The woman said, "I don't know. Do you dance?"

"Hell no," Jada said. "Not that I have anything against dancers, but it's just not my thing." Jada sat the magazine down and said, "You dance?"

"Yeah."

"Where?"

"Mostly Cheetah's. I dance at the white clubs."

Then it occurred to Jada that the girl was the skinny bitch that had been dancing for Craig that night that he'd asked her to buy him some coke.

Jada said, "Oh yeah, I remember you. I was with him at Cheetah's the night that he met you."

"Oh yeah, I remember," the woman said.

"You got a name?"

"Rain."

"So you fuckin' for tits, Rain?"

"Excuse me?"

"Never mind," Jada said, as she scooped up a Time magazine and skimmed through it. She thought that not only was Craig addicted to coke, he was a sex addict as well. Fucking all these low-class, black, stripper girls, but that wasn't her problem. She was over his trifling ass.

Jada said, "How long have you been waiting for him, Rain?"

Rain was still holding her chest like she was in excruciating pain and Jada noticed that her boobs were leaking blood. She had a gauze that she was using to try and slow the blood."

"I was out here an hour before you came."

Jada glanced at her watch and said, "Well, this is getting ridiculous."

Jada set the magazine down and marched to the back and burst into the operating room. Craig stood over Imani who was lying naked on the operating table. When he realized Jada was standing over him, he turned to her and said, "Get the hell out of here!"

"Can you give me the dope, so I can go? I don't have time to wait for you to perform surgery on this bitch."

Craig held Imani's hand. He said, "Jada, get out of here!"

Jada was about to shut the door when she noticed two blood drenched balloons on the counter. She stepped back inside the operating room and said, "What the fuck is that, Craig?"

"Nothing. Get out of here!"

"No, I ain't going no motherfucking where! What the fuck? I can't believe you, Craig!"

Craig let go of Imani's hand and made eye contact with Jada.

"Are you out of your mind? You implanted the heroin in this woman's body? What the fuck were you thinking?" Jada yelled.

"It's not like that."

Imani looked very faint. She said, "Daddy, am I going to be alright?"

Craig said, "Jada, please get out of here."

He turned to the woman and said, "Yes, you're going to be okay."

Imani smiled and said, "Good. I want to be perfect for you, Daddy, and when I get rhinoplasty, I'll be perfect."

Her breasts were leaking blood and it was disgusting as fuck to Jada. It suddenly occurred to Jada why Rain's breasts were leaking. She'd been transporting heroin in hers as well.

"I feel so tired, Daddy."

Jada said, "What happened? What the fuck happened in here?"

"Relax. Everything is going to be okay," Craig said.

Imani faded in and out of consciousness.

"What the fuck is going on in here?"

"Everything is going to be fine, Jada," Craig assured her.

Jada grabbed Craig by his scrubs. "There's dope in this woman's blood isn't there?"

"No."

"You're a goddamn liar!" Jada said. She stared at the two blood drenched balloons. One of them was ruptured and dope leaked from it. "We gotta get her to a hospital."

Craig said, "We're going to go to prison if we do. It's going to be okay."

"Hold my hand, Daddy."

Craig held Imani's hand and she said, "I love you, and I want to be perfect for you." She took a breath and closed her eyes.

He held her hand, his thumb on her wrist and he felt her pulse getting weaker.

She looked up at him again, smiled and said, "I'm going to be perfect for you." She closed her eyes again and her pulse stopped.

He placed his lips on hers and breathed into her mouth three times then with the heel of his hands between her bloody breasts he began to apply pressure expecting her heart to jumpstart. There was no result.

"Goddamn it!" Craig said.

Jada said, "What the fuck is going on, Craig?"

Craig smacked Imani on the face three times. "Open your eyes, damn it! Open your eyes! Goddamn it, don't you die on me! No you can't go! Don't go! You can't die on me!"

He placed his mouth over hers again and tried to resuscitate her but he couldn't.

"No. No. No," he whispered, tears cascading his face.

Jada said, "I fucking hate you! I hate you so goddamned much!"

She called Shamari.

"Hey, babe," Shamari answered.

"Get over here right away!" She was crying and screaming into the phone.

"Over where?"

"The surgeon's office!"

"Why? What's going on?"

"Just come and come fast!"

Twenty minutes later, Shamari was banging on the office door. Rain opened the door and Jada was sitting in the lobby with her head between her legs crying like hell.

Shamari said, "Jada, what's wrong with you?"

She looked up at Shamari and hugged him, but kept crying

Shamari had to calm her ass down. "What's wrong, babe?"

She kept sniffling, trying to talk but couldn't get her words out.

Shamari looked at Rain. "Who the fuck are you? And what is going on?"

"Imani is dead," Jada said.

"What? How did this happen?"

Jada stood and led him to the operating room where he found Craig wearing latex gloves as he mopped up a small pool of blood. Then Shamari saw Imani's corpse on the operating table. There were speckles of blood on Craig's scrubs and his surgeon's mask.

"What the fuck happened?"

Jada said, "This goddamned clown placed the dope in this woman's implants and the heroin leaked into her blood and killed her."

Shamari grabbed him by his scrubs. "Motherfucker, I will kill your bitch ass in here! Now you got me in more bullshit!"

Shamari punched Craig in his goddamned mouth. He stumbled over the body and his head crashed into the counter.

"What the fuck have you done, you dumb motherfucker?" said Shamari.

There was a scalpel lying on the counter. Shamari picked it up and was about to stick Craig in his goddamned throat when Jada grabbed him.

"Don't kill him. He ain't worth it, Bae."

"You defending this motherfucking idiot?"

"No. Not at all, babe. You are in all kinds of shit. You don't need to kill him. If you kill him, you're fucked for real."

"I'm fucked anyway."

Jada tried to pry the scalpel from Shamari's hands. "Gimme the knife, babe."

Shamari released it. Craig rose to his feet and Shamari punched him in his motherfucking mouth again, and knocked out one of his front teeth.

Craig nursed his mouth.

Shamari said, "I can't go down for this."

"What are we doing to do?" Jada asked.

"Where is the dope?"

Jada pointed to the four medical balloons on the table. There had been only two before. Jada realized that Craig must have removed the other two balloons from Imani's chest.

"Who is the other chick?" Shamari asked Craig.

"The other courier," Craig said.

Shamari turned to Jada. "Did you know about her? Tell her to bring her skinny ass in here."

When Rain entered the operating room, Shamari said, "We're all going to have to take this secret to our grave."

Everybody nodded except Rain, and Shamari said, "Do you understand, skinny bitch?"

"Yeah."

"What are we going to do?" asked Jada.

"We got to get rid of the body," Shamari said. "That's the only thing that we can do." He turned to Craig. "Does her family know she was with you?"

"She was raised in an orphanage."

Shamari slapped the fuck out of Craig for taking advantage of the clearly emotionally damaged woman.

CHAPTER 20

TREY SAT IN THE PARKING DECK, HIS CAR PARKED DIRECTLY ACROSS from Starr's BMW.

Trey had found out from Brooke that Starr usually went home about six o'clock in the evening. He'd wanted to surprise her and show up at the showroom, but he'd peeked inside earlier to find her talking to a white gentleman. It looked as if they were discussing business and he didn't want to impose. He decided he'd let her handle her business and then speak to her later.

Trey glanced at his watch. It was 7:45 p.m. He watched Brooke leave five minutes ago so he decided now was the perfect time to surprise her. He'd observed Starr through the window of the showroom talking to someone. A black man seated in one of the sofas on display. He couldn't see the man's face since his back was turned. Trey wondered if he was an employee or a customer. If it was a customer, he'd soon be leaving. He entered the showroom. A bell rang indicating that someone was entering the building. Starr was behind the counter organizing a desk while talking to the man who was seated with his back turned. When she heard the bell ring, her eyes darted toward the door.

"Trey. What are you doing here?"

"I thought I would come by and check you out."

The man stood up and turned toward Trey. Trey recognized him immediately. His brother, Troy. What the fuck was he doing here?

Troy said. "Bruh, what's up?"

"You tell me what's up?"

Troy stood and was making his way toward Trey smiling. "Good to see you."

"Really?" Trey said.

Trey glanced at Starr. Trey was trying to figure out what the fuck was going on between the two. Troy was standing there in some tight-ass pin stripped suit with a pink shirt.

Now Trey knew goddamned well Starr was not trying to fuck with this corny-ass dude. But why was he here and why hadn't he been in touch with him? This was the second time he'd been around her without checking in with him. Well, the second time that he knew of.

Troy offered Trey his hand but Trey refused. He stared at Starr.

"Somebody tell me what the fuck is going on? Why is he here? Sitting down all relaxed and shit."

Starr said, "He was just visiting."

Trey turned to Troy. "Why are you visiting my girl, brother?"

Starr said, "Trey, we are not together."

Trey said, "We are together until I say we are not together."

Starr said, "See, that's why we aren't together. Because of an attitude like that. You think you can do whatever the fuck you want to do and I have to obey you. Really, Trey, is that how this works? You go out and fuck whoever you want to fuck but I can't talk to anyone?"

Starr made her way from behind the counter and was walking toward Trey.

"You tell me how it works! You get to fuck my brother?" Trey said.

Starr made her way to Trey and slapped the fuck out of him.

"You think I'm that kind of woman," she said.

"You may not be that kind of woman, but I know my brother and I know how dudes are. This nigga wants to fuck you."

Troy said, "I'm going to leave now."

He tried to make his way past Trey and Starr but Trey stopped him. His hand now on Troy's chest.

"It's like that, huh, bruh?" Trey said.

"What are you talking about, man?"

"Look me in my eye and tell me that you ain't trying to fuck my girl?"

"I gotta go, man."

Trey took hold of his arm and Starr said, "Trey, don't start no bullshit up in here."

"I just want this nigga to tell me why the fuck he hanging around you."

Troy said, "Look, you got a good woman. You need to learn how to treat--"

Before he could finish talking, Trey punched him in his goddamned mouth. Blood shot from his lip and he broke two teeth before falling onto one of the living room display tables.

Starr tried to get in between the two of them but Trey shoved her out of the way.

Troy tried to stand up but Trey kicked him in his ribs then pinned his arms to the floor. Though Troy was younger, Trey was stronger and had more experience with fighting. He held Troy down as blood spilled from Troy's mouth.

Trey said, "Motherfucker, I will kill you over this woman! The only reason I don't shoot your punk ass is because of our daddy!"

Trey kicked Troy in his ribs once more and said, "You get the fuck out of here, and don't never come back in here!"

Starr said, "You can't tell who to come in here."

Troy made his way to the door and let himself out.

Trey said, "I need you to answer me truthfully. Did you fuck my brother?"

•   •   •

Shamari called Black but he didn't answer. He called him three more times back to back. Finally he decided to text him, and Black was not going to like the news he had for him.

– PART 8 –

CHAPTER 21

BLACK RECEIVED A TEXT FROM SHAMARI: MEET ME IN MIDTOWN.

Black: *Hell NO! Come to my house. I'm not coming anywhere not knowing what the fuck is going on.*

Black paced inside his home. What the fuck was Shamari so excited about? What could have possibly gone wrong? Shamari had demanded that he see him right away, but there was no way Black would meet him in Midtown. Not that he believed Shamari would set him up, but regardless of Shamari's new face, he was still wanted by the Feds. He was formally charged and on the run. Black had his own investigation to worry about and didn't want to get caught up in Shamari's bullshit. Black started to second-guess himself; maybe he shouldn't have helped Shamari. Maybe it had been a bad idea.

A baggie filled with Sour Diesel lay on the kitchen counter. Black rolled himself a blunt then sat on the sofa and thought about all that had transpired in the last few months. He had been shot and his son had been kidnapped. Maybe everyone was right, maybe it was time for him to sit his ass down, invest in the franchises with Sasha, and give up the streets. There was simply too much shit going on. It had been cool when he was younger, but this was getting to be too much for even him to handle. One of his soldiers was dead, another was in jail, and Kyrie was acting like a bitch. He heard a knock at the door and Black set the blunt down.

Black wondered why the person didn't ring the bell. Black peeked through the blinds and spotted Jada's Benz in the driveway. He picked up the blunt again and took a puff before looking through the peephole again. It was Shamari. Black opened the door. He wanted to invite Shamari in but the weed was making Black cough so much that all he could manage to do was wave Shamari in.

Shamari was standing on the front porch, looking nervous as hell.

Black coughed again, the weed smoke still lingering in the air. "Why didn't you ring the goddamned bell? Knocking like you're the motherfuckin' sheriff or something!"

Shamari marched past Black without answering his silly-ass question.

"What the fuck is going on?" Black asked as he closed the door.

"You don't even wanna know."

"You called me and got me all fuckin' nervous and shit."

Shamari sat on the sofa. The smoke from the blunt was annoying the hell out of him. He looked at Black and said, "Could you put that out while we talk?"

Black deaded the blunt.

"Who got arrested?"

"Nobody."

"Okay, if nobody's locked up and nobody's been busted, what can be so wrong?"

"It's worse than being locked up." Shamari was trying to think of the right words to tell Black about the dead body.

"What the fuck is going on?"

"One of the runners died."

"Died? What the fuck you mean, died?"

"Remember the partner I told you about? He's the plastic surgeon that gave me the new face."

"He died?"

"No."

"Who then?"

Somebody had died and Shamari was looking nervous as hell but he was taking forever to get to the point of the story. Black lit the blunt again. He really needed to calm his goddamned nerves.

He puffed the blunt and said, "So the plastic surgeon is the partner?"

"Yeah."

"Okay, how did the runner die?"

"Man, this dude was fucking putting the heroin inside of women's breast implants."

"What do you mean inside breast implants?"

"He stuffed the goddamned dope inside their titties, bruh."

Black took another hit. He couldn't believe what he was hearing.

Shamari stood up from the sofa and paced before finally turning to Black and said, "The dope got into the woman's bloodstream and stopped her heart."

"Where is the dope?"

Shamari couldn't believe it. Somebody had just died and all Black could think about was whether the dope was okay. Shamari removed the balloons from the backpack and tossed them on the table.

Black said, "Ok, now this shit is making sense to me. That explains the balloons from the last time. So, what's the problem? I thought something was really fucked up."

Shamari stared Black in the face and said, "A girl lost her life! You don't think that's fucked up enough?"

"The dope is here and there is a need. It's our job to supply it."

"What about the dead body?"

Black puffed on the blunt, his eyes low from the weed. He blew out a cloud of smoke and said, "Not my problem. You got a dead body on your hand. I don't know this partner of yours or the dead bitch."

Shamari approached Black until they were nose to nose and Black said, "That's your problem, not mine."

Shamari stepped back and said, "You know what? You're right."

"Get rid of the body and you'll be okay."

"Okay, that's sounds really simple," Shamari said sarcastically. "Look, you act like I get rid of dead bodies every day!"

"Go get the body and I'll help you get rid of it."

"Okay." Shamari was about to head out of the door but Black stopped him. A cloud of smoke hung in the air from the blunt that still dangled from Black's mouth. Shamari coughed and fanned the smoke away.

Black said, "Who else knows about this?"

"Jada, the doctor and some skinny bitch that I ain't never seen before."

"Some skinny bitch you ain't never seen before?"

"One of the runners."

"She was getting her titties stuffed too?"

"Yeah."

"We might have to kill her and the doctor."

"Look, there are too many cameras at his office building. It's not smart for us to do that right now."

"Cameras." Black thought about Twan and K.B. The two idiots had been captured on camera taking Chris from the car. "You're right. As a matter of fact, don't go back there. Let the partner bring you the body. You bring it to me and we'll get rid of it."

CHAPTER 22

IT WAS EIGHT O'CLOCK ON A MONDAY NIGHT AND LANI WAS BORED AS hell, lying in the bed. She'd contemplated getting her vibrator from the top of the closet before deciding to watch Netflix. Suddenly, her phone rang: *Unknown number.* She decided to answer it at the very last minute.

"Hello?"

"Can I come over?"

"Who the hell is this?"

"Your baby daddy."

"I don't have no babies."

"Your future baby daddy."

Lani knew the voice but couldn't place it.

"Okay, baby daddy. You better quit playing on my goddamned phone or I'm going to hang up."

"It's Shakur." He laughed.

She sat up on the bed and paused the show. "I'm surprised to hear from you."

"Really?"

"Yes. I thought since I didn't give you what you wanted, I wouldn't ever hear from you again."

"You think all I want is pussy?"

"That's what most dudes want nowadays. What makes you any different?"

"Because I've had my share of pussy. Most dudes haven't, I guess."

"I don't like that answer."

"It wasn't for you to like. It's the truth. I deal in truths."

"Who wants to sleep with a man-whore? No woman wants a man that's done fucked half of the city."

"Look, Lani. I'm thirty-four. I did all my dirt when I was in my twenties. I'm over that."

"What's the longest relationship you've been in? I'm a relationship type of girl."

"Let's meet and talk. I wanna see you. I don't wanna be phone buddies."

"No. I have a lot of shit on my mind. "

"Is it about that little situation with Mike?"

"You don't know the half."

"I won't know unless you tell me. Let's meet up."

"Where you want to meet?"

"Have you eaten?"

"No."

"STK at nine o'clock."

"Ok."

* * *

Lani's ass looked sensational in her skinny jeans. She wore a wife beater and her hair was pulled back in a ponytail. It was a very simple look but her flawless skin made her look amazing. Shakur hugged her then kissed her on the cheek. He gave her a once over and his eyes landing right on her thighs. He licked his lips and she wanted him to eat her pussy right there on the spot. Shakur approached the hostess station and the hostess told him there would be an hour-long wait. He offered a hundred dollar bill to the young woman at the hostess station. The woman grinned, stuffed the money in her bra, and said, "You're next."

A minute later they were led to a table in the back of the restaurant. Seconds later, the waitress appeared and Shakur said, "We're both drinking tonight."

Lani laughed.

The waitress asked, "What can I get you to drink?"

"Two P-Diddys."

Lani said, "I've heard of that before but what the hell is a P-Diddy?"

Shakur said, "Tell her what a P-Diddy is."

The waitress smiled and said. "Its Ciroc and Lemonade."

"Two P-Diddys then."

The woman disappeared then came back with the drinks. Lani ordered the roasted chicken and Shakur ordered a salad. The waitress disappeared.

"You're drinking but not eating?"

"I had a big lunch."

"So you're not one of those healthy eaters that's going to be all judgmental and shit, are you? Cuz I'm a girl that likes to eat."

"Hell no. Do I watch what I eat? Hell, yeah, but I will not be judgmental of what somebody else eats. But if you tell me that you want to lose weight, I'll help."

"Do I look like I need to lose weight? What are you trying to say?"

Shakur laughed. "Calm down, ma. I'm just simply saying that if you ask me for my help, I would help."

"And I asked you if I needed help?"

"I like my women thick and you fit the bill."

Lani smiled but thought that she would like to lose at least five pounds, although, the last thing she needed was a motherfucker telling her what the fuck she could and couldn't eat.

Shakur sipped his drink and said, "So, what's on your mind?"

"Too much." She sipped her drink, but she was looking at him from the corner of her eye, trying to decide what she should tell him. She knew that he knew Mike and she didn't want to divulge too much to a stranger. It didn't matter how good he looked.

"Are you worried about Mike trying to get revenge?"

"Maybe. There is so much going on."

Shakur grabbed her hand and held it. He stared right into her eyes and said, "You can tell me."

"I've just met you. I don't know you."

"I told you what they were saying in the streets, didn't I?"

"You did."

"I want to help you."

"Why?"

"I think you're cool peeps."

"How do you know?"

"Ty said so."

"Ty don't know me."

"Jada told him. Jada speaks highly of you and some girl named Starr. She says that you are too good for the men that you deal with and that you are the wife type. She says she wants to be like you and Starr."

Lani hated that Jada was running her mouth but at least she didn't speak badly of her. The waitress came and dropped both plates of food on the table. They ordered another round of P-Diddys. Shakur massaged Lani's hand and stared into her eyes. For that moment, all she could think about was him licking on her clit.

"Look, tell me whatever you want to tell me," he said.

"Why are you so interested in my business?"

"I'm interested in you. I want to know everything about you."

Lani looked down at her hands. He was still massaging them and she said, "Can I have my hand back? I need it to eat."

He laughed and released her hand.

He dug into his salad and said, "Lani, it's about Mike's brother, right?"

"Maybe. Maybe not."

There was an awkward silence and she said, "I don't wanna get you involved."

"I want to be involved. I think I can help."

"Why do you want to help?"

He took possession of her hand again and said, "You ever see somebody and you think there is a connection right away? That there is instant chemistry?"

She looked him in eyes and said, "Yes."

"I feel that right now."

She smiled and said, "Come on, eat your food. You ain't one of those slow eaters are you?"

"Quit trying to get off the subject."

A tear trickled down her face into her mouth. She began to cry. He rushed to her side and held her.

"What's wrong?" he asked.

She tried not to cry but couldn't hold back the tears. She picked up the napkin from the table and wiped her eyes then she looked at him still sitting by her side patting her back. There was so much she wanted to tell him. She stood up from the table and excused herself then disappeared into the bathroom for a few moments to get herself together. When she reappeared, she apologized to him.

"No need for that."

"Can we leave?"

Shakur flagged the waitress and gave her a hundred dollar bill.

The waitress said, "Do you want me to box up the food?"

"No, that won't be necessary." he said.

He paid the valet for her car and as they stood waiting for her car to arrive, he said, "Look, I meant what I said in there. I haven't met somebody like you in a long time."

"You're laying it on thick."

"Now what I'm about to say is going to sound conceited. I used to be conceited, but I'm humble now."

She laughed, dying to know what he was going to say. She couldn't believe he said he was humble. Maybe that was his opinion of himself, but to her, he was quite arrogant.

"Say what you're going to say. I won't judge. I promise."

"I've got at least ten women in my phone that would fuck me on command."

"Command? What the fuck are you, a general?"

"I meant demand."

"You're an overseer?"

"You know what I mean."

The valet pulled Lani's BMW to the curb. Shakur gave the young man a ten dollar tip.

The man opened the door for Lani. Shakur kissed Lani and forced his tongue down her throat.

At one o'clock a.m., Lani texted him: *Thanks for giving me a shoulder to cry on.*

Shakur: *No problem. Are you okay?*

Lani: *No, not really, but I'm a big girl.*

Shakur: *Let me come over.*

Fifteen seconds had gone by and Lani still hadn't responded.

Shakur: *Are you there?*

Shakur: *Look, I promise not to try anything.*

Lani: *430 Peach Tree Street NE. Call me when you get here. I will give you the building code.*

When Shakur entered the condo, Lani stepped into the hallway and scanned the area.

"What the fuck you doing?" he asked.

"Making sure nobody's following you."

"Followed? By who?"

She led him into the living room. She sat on the sofa and he sat across from her in an armchair. She offered him some water but he declined.

"I'm surprised you invited me over."

"Me too. Well I didn't invite you, you invited yourself. I just agreed that you should be here."

"I should be here. I like the sound of that."

"I bet." She stood and paced nervously as he watched her. Then she asked, "You sure you don't want anything to drink?"

"You know what? I think I will have a glass of water or a bottle. Whichever is easiest for you."

"I can make you a P-Diddy. I got lemonade so I can make you one."

"No. Water for right now and besides you didn't even know what it was a few hours ago."

She made a sad face before disappearing into the kitchen. She came back with two bottled waters and passed him one.

He sipped his water and said, "I'm trying to get inside your head. Tell me what's up, Lani."

"First of all, I got daddy issues. I think the fact that I didn't grow up with my daddy made me pick the wrong men to get involved with," she paused, "and maybe that's why I'm attracted to you."

"Damn! You really know how to hurt a brother, don't you?"

She sat down Indian style on the sofa and said, "So where was I?"

"Daddy issues."

"Yeah, I have daddy issues and I pick the wrong men."

"So Chris was the wrong man?"

"Yes. And so was Black."

"Black? Who is Black?"

"He's from the Westside. His name is Tyrann. You know him?"

"Never heard of him. I know a few dudes named Black but none from Atlanta. I'm originally from Detroit."

"No, he's not a celebrity or anything. Just most people in the street know him."

"Is he the one that killed Chris?"

Lani didn't answer him.

He made eye contact with her and said, "Look, I'm not the police. You can ask Jada."

"How would she know?"'

"I brought her some coke."

"Coke? I don't believe it."

"I think it was for a friend. At least that's what she told Ty, but the point is, your friend has seen me with drugs. Call her and ask her."

"A drug dealer?"

"Well, I don't like to consider myself a drug dealer. That's so low level. I'm what they call a supplier. A plug."

"Like I said, I always pick the wrong men."

"Look, I understand where you're coming from and trust me this is something I'm not proud of. I'm going to leave this shit alone as soon—"

She cut him off. "I know. You're going to go legit as soon as you get your money up. That's what they all say."

"But how many of them have investments? How many of them have gone to college? How many of them have real estate?"

"The Feds can take all that shit."

"True. But I have a plan and it's going to work."

She smiled. "Confidence. I like that."

He looked at her and said, "So, what is your plan?"

He'd caught her totally off guard. "What do you mean?"

"You dated Chris and you dated Black and both of them are obviously something that you all of a sudden despise. What are you going to do with yourself?"

"I don't know." she said, mad that he'd called her on her bullshit.

"Look, I'm not here to judge you, but don't judge me either. Especially, since I have a plan."

"You're right."

"So Black pays your rent?"

"Yeah."

He dug into his pants and presented a nine millimeter. "This is exactly why I brought my tool."

"He can't get into this apartment without me letting him in. He don't have a key."

He put the gun back on his waist and said, "So you wanna tell me what's going on?"

"All I can say is that I'm caught up in the middle of a murder that I really didn't have anything to do with. Yeah, I was with both Black and Chris, but it was really just a case of male egos that just got out of hand."

He made his way over to her and she put her head on his shoulder.

"I'll protect you, Lani." He stared into her eyes then leaned in and kissed her. "Believe that."

And she did believe him.

CHAPTER 23

SHAMARI CALLED BLACK AND EXPLAINED THAT THERE WAS NO WAY he could move the body by himself. He needed Black to bring a pickup truck to Craig's office and they'd have to try to avoid the cameras. The rain was coming down in buckets. It was 9:45 p.m. when Black pulled into the parking lot near Craig's office. Imani's body had been stuffed inside a barrel and loaded onto a dolly, which Craig then rolled out to the pickup truck. Black was behind the wheel of the vehicle wearing a mask, so he couldn't be identified by Craig. Gangsta rap was blasting through the speakers. The music helped calm his nerves as did the weed. He'd been smoking a lot and was pretty fucked up. The truck didn't smell like weed though because he'd freshened it with Febreze. Shamari and Craig secured the barrel in the back of the truck with ratchet straps. Shamari hopped in the passenger side of the pickup and they drove to a junkyard. The junkyard sat on about twenty acres of land and was an hour outside of Atlanta in Newnan.

"Where the fuck are we?" Shamari said.

"Newnan."

"I know we're in Newnan, but this is a junkyard."

Black stared at Shamari for a long time, trying to decide what to tell him about the junkyard.

Suddenly there was a knock on the window. A black man about sixty with a graying beard said, "You going to get out of the goddamned car or are you going to sit your black ass in there all night?"

The man was wearing overalls and had a pint of Crown Royal in the front pocket. He also resembled Black to some extent. Black lowered the window.

"You scared the fuck out of me."

"Because you a pussy!"

Black said, "I'll whip yo' old ass out here!"

The old man removed a pistol from his pocket and shot out the front tire.

"What the fuck did you do that for?"

"You lucky I didn't do that to you."

Shamari was getting nervous before Black turned to him and said, "This is my old man."

"That's right, motherfucker! I brought you into this goddamned world and don't forget that!" He put his pistol back in his pocket then removed the bottle of Crown Royal. "Get out the car, pussies!"

Then he looked at Shamari and said, "That's right, red boy! You a pussy too, if you hang with this nigga!"

Shamari laughed, now he understood why Black was so goddamned crazy.

Black got out of the car and Shamari got out right after him.

In the pitch black dark, Black suggested that they go into a small house that sat atop of the hill.

Once they were inside Black's dad said, "I'm Bo, known in Atlanta as Bankhead Bo." Bo shook Shamari's hands and said, "I can tell you're a dope dealer."

"Why you say that?"

"Hands too soft, like you ain't never did a day of work in your life."

"How do you know I don't have an office job?"

"Nothing about you says office job. Nothing about you says job, for that matter. You a dope boy."

Black said, "Quit ragging on my friend."

"Did I hurt your feelings, red boy?"

"No."

Bo said to Black, "Will you shut the fuck up?" Then he turned to Shamari. "I used to sell that shit in the eighties, all up and down Bankhead. But I keep telling my son that the game is over. Ya'll need to get a new hustle. Them white people ain't allowing ya'll niggas to get rich no more."

"Quit and do what?" Black said.

"Help me run this junkyard. That's why I hustled so hard to make sure you didn't have to do this shit. I was smart. Yeah, I made time but how many niggas you know that did eight years and still come out with something?"

"I don't know many niggas that made eight years and still had time to make twenty-three kids." Black said.

Bo said, "Twenty-four. You keep forgetting about Damon."

"How old is he now?"

"Three."

"Damn." Black said.

Bo said to Shamari, "How many you got?"

"Zero"

"You ain't fucking?"

Black said to Shamari, "Don't pay him no mind."

"But he has a point about the junkyard. Why don't you help him run it?" Shamari asked.

Bo said, "Because he's a goddamned fool, that's why! He'd rather be riding around Atlanta and everybody saying that he's the man."

Black looked at Bo. "I'm not running no damn junkyard! You can get somebody else to do that."

"Okay, you laughing, but I made close to two hundred thousand dollars last year." He took a swig of his liquor and said, "Well, that's what I reported."

"Look, man, I done told you. I don't wanna run no damn junk yard. I'm not Lamont Sanford. Besides you got other kids besides me. One of them will run it."

"Only seven in Georgia tho' and five of them are girls and Malik is only six and Damon ain't old enough either."

"I ain't got time."

"So what's going on? Why are you here?"

"Need your help."

"I'm listening."

"I have to get rid of a body."

Bo took another drink of his liquor and said, "What the fuck?! Are you crazy, man? What the hell do you mean, a body?"

Black stared at Bo with serious eyes. "Pops, I know you don't want to do this, but I need your help."

"What happened? Did you kill somebody?"

"No."

"Tyrann, don't tell me no goddamned lies! I heard about all that bullshit you had going on at Nana's house and how Man-Man got kidnapped because of your bullshit!"

Black sighed and said, "This don't have shit to do with that."

Bo looked at Shamari and said, "What the fuck is going on? This idiot don't want to tell me!"

"Sir, with all due respect—"

"Kill that sir bullshit, and tell me what the fuck is going on!"

"Tyrann is doing me a favor. This is all on me."

Bo turned to Tyrann. "So your goddamned friend kills somebody, and you come to me to help you get rid of the body? Are you out of yo' goddamned mind?"

"He didn't kill anybody. She OD'd." Black lied because he knew this was the only way he could get Bo to understand. Also, he hoped it would make Bo shut the fuck up.

Bo said, "So you sold her the dope she got high with?"

"Yeah."

"Okay, it must be that Pretty Hurts shit that they've been talking about all over the news lately."

Black interrupted and said, "So you're going to help us or not?"

Bo turned to Shamari then back at Black. "I'm too motherfuckin' old to go back to prison, Tyrann!"

Black said. "Pop, I'll take the rap for this if it comes down to it."

Shamari said, "Sir, I know you don't know me."

Bo said, "What did I tell you about that sir bullshit?"

"I'm a man. I've done my time before. I met your son in prison."

"Okay, you went to prison once. That just prove you're a dumb-ass criminal. That don't mean shit to me," Bo said.

Black said, "I need your help, Pops. Are you going to help us or not?"

Bo made eye contact with Black. "So, the body is in the back of the truck?"

"Yeah."

"What did you have in mind?"

"I was thinking you could crush it with the car and then we can set it on fire."

"No! Absolutely not!" Bo said, "If we are going to do it, we gotta be professional about this shit. We're going to need to decompose this body."

Bo grabbed a flashlight and led them back to the pickup truck where they unloaded the barrel and brought it back into a house that sat atop a hill. They carried the barrel into the bathroom and Bo used his pocket knife to pry the top of the barrel open. A strong stench hit them making Shamari feel nauseous. He sat down on the toilet.

Bo laughed and said, "Stand yo' ass up, boy! We in for a long night."

Bo took hold of Imani's hair and struggled to remove her body from the barrel. Bo looked at the dried blood on the side of her stomach.

Black stared at her thinking that she was an attractive woman. A little weird looking from multiple surgeries but he could tell that she'd been beautiful at one time. Her nose looked awful and her cheeks had implants but she had beautiful hair underneath the weave and Black liked real hair. She was the kind of woman he wished he'd met before she started going all artificial. He'd be willing to bet she was a natural beauty.

Bo said to Black, "You want to tell me the truth?"

"What do you mean?"

"This woman is drenched in blood. She didn't OD."

Shamari said, "Tell him the truth."

Imani's head fell limp over the barrel and the barrel fell to the floor.

Bo looked at Shamari and said, "What happened?"

"We used her to bring dope back from California. We placed it inside her breast implants."

Bo said to Black, "Nigga, you are dumber than I thought you were!"

Black said, "Look, it wasn't my idea or Shamari's!"

"Who put the dope in her titties?"

"A doctor."

"So somebody else knows about this shit?"

"Yeah. Look, Pop, are you going to help me or not?"

Bo said, "The only reason I'm helping ya'll dumbasses is cuz I've already touched this woman's body." He turned to Shamari. "Go in the next room. You'll see an electric saw. It's laying beside a black tool belt and a yellow extension cord. Plug the cord in the wall and drag it in here. We got work to do."

"What kind of work?" Black asked.

"Going to disfigure the body."

"You mean dismember?"

"You know what the fuck I mean, English teacher!"

Shamari returned with the saw. Bo and Black removed Imani's body from the barrel and placed it into the tub.

Bo said, "What was she? A stripper or something?"

"I don't really know her. I don't know what she did," Shamari said.

"If you got a weak-ass stomach, leave the room now. I'm telling you." Bo plugged the saw into the extension cord. Shamari turned is head and held his nose. The body reeked.

Bo said, "Oh, you think it STANKS in here now, just wait. It's gonna smell like shit, guts and everything else, pretty boy." He turned to Black. "Hold her arm."

Black held her arm and Bo ripped into her arm right above her rotator cuff. Blood splattered his coveralls.

Shamari stepped outside. The sight of Bo dismembering the body was just too much for him to take.

CHAPTER 24

STARR WAS UPSET AT TREY FOR BARGING INTO HER PLACE OF business and at the same time, she was glad that he was jealous. But she didn't like the fact that he was standing in her face questioning her loyalty and her morals.

Starr said, "First of all, who the fuck do you think you are talking to?"

"I asked you a goddamned question and all you have to do is answer!"

"I don't have to answer shit!"

Trey took a step back and said, "I can't believe this shit!"

"Believe what?"

"You fucked my brother!"

Starr rolled her eyes at his silly ass and thought about all the shit he'd done to her. The havoc he'd wreaked in her life. The baby that he'd hid from her for years. And now he was fucking with this bodybuilder-assed ho' and these were just the women she knew about. And now this clown was standing in front of her questioning her morals? Challenging her integrity? Boy bye!

"Out of all the dudes in Georgia, why my brother?"

Starr stepped forward and slapped the fuck out of Trey. He grabbed her hand and said, "Don't you hit me again. Or—"

"Or what? You gonna beat a woman? You hit women?"

Trey held her hands as she struggled to gain her freedom. He was too strong.

They stared at each other and she squirmed trying to get free of his tight grip.

"I would have never thought you could do me so fucking wrong. You like to walk around acting like yo' shit don't stank, but you just like all these other ho's out here."

She kneed him right in the balls and he released her. She slapped him again, and he rolled around on the floor in agony.

"Trey, I want you out of here! Or I'm calling the police!"

"Call the goddamned police! I don't give a fuck about going to jail!"

He regained his stance and made his way to her again. They started wrestling again. She tried to kick him in the balls again, but he caught her leg and scooped her up. He carried her to one of the showroom sofas and pinned her arms again.

"Why, Starr?"

"Why what?"

"Why did you hurt me like this?"

She was on her back as she stared up at him. It was obvious to her that he was in pain, but she was old enough to know that the source of his pain was pride. Though she knew that he loved her, she also knew that he was only putting on this charade because of his pride. He didn't want her enough to man-up and be faithful, but he didn't want another man to have her.

"You could've slept with anybody. Why my goddamned brother?"

"Trey get off me. I never slept with your brother or no other man for that matter. I'm not a slut, Trey. I have more respect for myself than to sleep with any man that only wants some pussy."

Her hands were sweating and his body was getting heavy. She said, "Trey, please get the fuck off me! I need to breathe."

He stood up and she got up off the sofa, although, he was still in her personal space.

"You don't know me at all, Trey."

He stood there, looking stupid as hell. He wanted to apologize for being an ass but he knew what his brother's intentions were. Any man would want a woman like her.

"So, are you going to say you're sorry?" She straightened her clothes and said, "Fine, I'll say it. You're sorry, Trey. One sorry-ass nigga. I never thought that I would say that."

"Look, Starr. I'm sorry that I got emotional."

She laughed. "Emotional? I'm the woman. I'm the one supposed to be emotional."

"I can't help but get emotional over you. I love you, Starr. Nothing will ever change that. I know you'll never be with me again, but I can't help but love you."

"And you don't want me to be with nobody else!"

"Not without my approval."

"Trey, you ain't my daddy."

He approached her and slid his hand around her waist, just above her ass and pulled her into him.

He said, "You're right, I don't want you to be with nobody else. I can't let you go. I can't let you go, Starr."

A tear rolled down his face and he dried his face with his arm.

She smiled and said, "You're getting emotional again."

"You have that effect on me."

"And I feel the same way about you, Trey."

"Why can't we be together?"

"I don't trust you, Trey. I can't allow you to break my heart again."

"I feel you."

His eyes were misty. She hadn't seen Trey cry very many times. She had seen a tear here and there, but now there was a river rolling down his face into his mouth. He sat back on the sofa. His face in his hands, he realized that what he had with Starr was over forever. He had to accept it and move on with his life. It wouldn't be easy.

She sat beside him and patted his back. He raised his head, made eye contact with her, and leaned into him. They kissed. Her heart was racing and she felt herself getting turned on.

She said to him, "Trey, I think you better leave."

He stood and made his way to the front door. She followed him to the door. "Goodbye, Trey."

He said bye without looking back and she watched him walk until he was out of sight. She locked the door and fell to the floor sobbing. She knew that even though they loved each other, she couldn't be with him. The risk was simply too high. She would always love him, but he wasn't the man for her and that was tough for her to fathom.

CHAPTER 25

LATER THAT NIGHT, TREY STEPPED INTO SHANTELLE'S PLACE. HE noticed that his things were packed in suitcases and boxes. Two big boxes, three suitcases, twenty-one boxes of tennis shoes and his MacBook Air sat near the door. Shantelle sat on the sofa talking on a cell phone to her friend Lori. As soon as she noticed Trey standing by the door staring at his possessions, she began to talk louder. She wanted Trey to hear the conversation.

"Yeah, girl, ain't nobody going to think that they can fuck me and still be chasing the next chick! I'm a grown-ass woman. I don't play those types of games. What makes him think that he can do what he pleases?"

Trey was ignoring her, looking at his things. Even the David Yurman jewelry that he'd bought her sat atop one of the boxes.

Shantelle kept talking. "I mean, he can't leave this woman alone. It's like she has diamonds in her pussy or something. I saw her once, and to me she looks real basic. You know, one of those hood girls with a cute shape but who's gonna be fat when she have a kid? Her and her ghetto friends showed up at a restaurant one night when we were out eating. None of them was cute, but if he wants her borderline fat ass he can have her."

Trey said, "Get off the phone!"

Shantelle cut her eyes at him.

"I said get off the motherfuckin' phone!"

"Let me talk to Trey. I'mma need you to call back over here and check on me just in case he gets out of line."

Trey could hear Lori's voice say "I'll call the police on his ass if he hits you."

"He's not going to put his hands on me, I'll talk to you later." She ended the call.

"What the fuck is going on?" Trey said.

"What do you mean, what the fuck is going on?"

"I mean you packed my shit up. You obviously want to send some kind of message."

"You don't love me. You love her. Go be with her."

"I can't deal with your insecurities. I'm tired of trying to convince you that I want to be with you."

Shantelle stood and said, "Now you don't have to. You can take your things and move on with your life...with Starr."

"I'll never be with Starr."

"She doesn't want you?"

"No."

"But if she did, you would be with her."

"I don't deal with what ifs. I deal with reality."

"And I deal with reality too, and the reality of it all is that you don't want me."

"I do want you."

"Trey, I've never been a second choice and I'm not about to start being somebody's second choice now."

"You tripping."

"Am I?" She made her way over to Trey and wedged herself between him and his things. They were now face to face.

"Trey, look me in the eyes and tell me that you don't love her."

"This is stupid. Come on, I'm not feeding your insecurities."

"You're always giving me reasons to be insecure."

"You're insecure because that's one of your characteristics. No matter what I say, I'll never make you happy."

"Whatever, Trey!"

"But if you want me to leave, I'll leave. It's not like I don't have the money to go somewhere else."

She slid her arms around his waist and said, "Tell me that you want to be with me and not Starr."

"This is high school and I'll tell you what else is high school, talking on the phone with your friends about what goes on in this house."

"Trey, when was the last time you spoke with Starr?"

"Why does that matter? You've made up your mind and I'm leaving."

She removed her hand from his waist and said, "You spoke with her today."

"You think you know everything."

"No, but my gut is telling me that you've at least seen her."

"Your gut, huh?"

"Women's intuition."

"Look, I'm going to get my things and leave."

"I think it's best."

•   •   •

Imani's dismembered body was stuffed into 20 gallon trash bags. The smell was overpowering. Blood was splattered all over Black and Bo's clothing. There was some on Shamari's shoe, but other than that, he was clean.

Bo told Black, "I'm going to give you some clothes to wear."

"I'll change when I get back to Atlanta."

"Hell no, you aren't! I can't take a chance of you going back to Atlanta and getting pulled over having this girl's DNA all over you."

"But you know if I get caught, I wouldn't implicate you, Pops."

"What the fuck you wanna take that chance for? Just let me give you some clothes and we won't have that shit to worry about."

Shamari said, "Bo is right."

"You goddamned right I'm right!" Bo turned to Shamari. "What's your shoe size?"

"Ten."

"I got a size ten and a half Pro Keds."

"Pro Keds?" Black said. Shamari and Black started to laugh.

Bo said, "Motherfucker, this ain't no fashion show! As a matter of fact, I want my shit back!"

Bo disappeared and came back with two pair of overalls and two pairs of Pro Keds."

Black said, "You know I can't wear these small-ass shoes."

Bo said, "Stuff yo' goddamned feet in them!"

"I wanna wear my own shoes."

Bo said, "Look, nigga, you done made me a necessity to the crime!"

"You mean accessory," Shamari said.

Bo said, "This nigga here is too smart to be a drug-dealer. You know what the fuck I meant!"

Black and Shamari changed into the overalls and handed Bo their clothes.

Black said, "I'm going to get rid of the body."

Bo said, "Wrong. I'm going to get rid of it and I'm going to be the only one that knows where the fuck it is!"

Black said, "What?"

"You heard me. Ain't nobody gonna know where this body is but me and God. I'm too damn old to go back to prison fucking with you clowns and I'm going to burn these clothes."

Black looked at Shamari and shrugged, "Let him handle it. Hell, we got enough to worry about as it is."

CHAPTER 26

THE DIGITAL CLOCK ON THE DRESSER SAID IT WAS 4:35 A.M. WHEN Shamari entered Jada's home. He called out her name but she didn't answer, so he figured that she was asleep. When he peeked inside the room, she was sprawled across the bed. He attempted to tip-toe to the bathroom without waking her but he startled her and she sat up.

She rubbed her eyes and focused. "Hey."

"Hey, I didn't mean to wake you."

"I wasn't asleep. How could I with Imani dead? This shit has been heavy on my mind, Shamari." She noticed the overalls and the Pro Ked shoes. "Why are you dressed like that? Where are your clothes?"

"Long story."

"So what did ya'll do with the body?"

"I told you it's a long story."

"I wanna know."

Jada looked at him and she could tell he'd had a lot on his mind too and she said, "Shamari, I want you to know that I didn't have shit to do with this."

"Huh?"

"Just in case you thinking that I knew what he was doing."

"I don't believe you knew that. If you knew, you would have told me, right?"

"Shamari, you don't have to ask that. You know that I would have told you."

"I know you would have." He sat on the bed and she massaged his shoulders. "Baby I know you got a lot on your mind."

"I just don't know how I fucked up my life so bad, Jada."

"Your life ain't over."

"It might as well be. I don't even recognize myself. I don't know who I am anymore."

"It's not your fault that happened to Imani. It's my fault."

Shamari stared at Jada and said, "No, it's my fault. I should have gone with my gut and not brought anybody else in our business. Especially some goddamned plastic surgeon. What the fuck was I thinking?"

"So, are you going to tell me what happened to Imani's body?"

"Why do you want to know so bad?"

"If there is anybody you can trust with a secret, it's me."

"I know. You're my best friend. Not perfect lovers, but we are best friends to the end."

"What happened?"

"We took the body to Newnan. I met Black's pops. A dude named Bankhead Bo."

"Wait a minute! Bankhead Bo is Black's dad?"

"You know him?"

"No, but his name is legendary. When I was growing up, he was supposed to be like one of Atlanta's biggest dope boys."

"He's an old man now, but with a lot of spunk and obviously a lot of sperm too. He has twenty-four kids."

"Well the Lord said, be fruitful and multiply. It looks like he got that part right."

"That's for damn sure."

"Okay, you met up with Black's pops in Newnan and you gave it to him?"

"Yeah."

"Why do I have the feeling you are leaving something out?"

"Look, Jada, we dismembered the body and then left it with Bo."

"Damn, babe." She massaged him again and said, "I know you have a weak stomach. How was that for you?"

"After Bo cut her arm off, I left the room."

"I would have too."

"Jada, that was the worse shit I've seen in my life. I've never gone through anything like that."

"Well at least it's over."

"It's not over. I still got to run and hide for the rest of my life. This whole thing made me realize that I'm probably making a mistake by running. I think I need to turn myself in."

"Don't do it. I don't want you to go away for a long time."

"Jada, I'm going to get life. You can go on with your life with somebody else. My fate is probably life in prison."

"Don't say that."

"That girl didn't deserve to die, and nobody seems to care about that. "

"I know."

"Jada, maybe I'm not cut out for this anymore. Maybe I should just turn myself in."

CHAPTER 27

IT WAS 1:43 IN THE AFTERNOON AND 2 CHAINZ WAS BLASTING FROM the Beats speakers on Black's kitchen counter. Shamari couldn't stand the loud-ass music. It made him nervous, but Black loved it, especially when he was high. He was on his third blunt, but it was currently unlit resting in the ashtray. Shamari and Black sat at Black's kitchen table. Two balloons of heroin sat in the center of the table. Four cell phones were on the side of the table. Two belonged to Black and the others were Shamari's. Black counted out two thousand plastic baggies with "Pretty Hurts" stamped on them.

Shamari said, "Look, I'm going to take my kilo with me. I mean you can do what the fuck you want to do with yours, but I can't do this no more."

"You don't want to be partners?"

"Look, Black, I said I wanted to make some money to pay my attorneys and leave a little something to Jada and my sister. I'll be able to do that now."

"So you turning yourself in?"

"No, but I ain't running. If they catch me, they catch me. I can't do this no more."

"So you're done dealing with me?"

"Black, we will always be cool. You one of the realest people I know, and I appreciate you."

"You tripping right now, bruh. I know you're thinking about what happened to that broad. That ain't on you. That's on that doctor. You didn't know he was going to do that dumb shit."

"I know."

"Don't feel guilty about that shit."

"Easy for you to say since you never met her."

"From the look of her body, it looks like she already had a lot of issues."

"She did. She grew up in an orphanage."

"I don't get it, man. I like you a lot, but you might be a little too soft for this."

"What don't you get?"

"Okay, you put a hit on a snitch. Which meant you wanted him dead."

"I did. I wanted him dead because he betrayed me. I'm never one for killing just to be killing."

"You robbed Mexicans for dope."

"Look, I didn't have any money. I was broke and desperate. I'd just gotten out of jail. I'm not a robber. I'm not a killer."

"But this girl was a mistake?"

"That could have been avoided. Just like cutting that dope with poison could have been avoided."

Black stood up and said, "What are you going to do, Shamari, once you sell your share? Get a job? Dude, whether you like it or not, this is what our life has led us to do. And as soon as you accept the reality that this is your fate, the better."

"You can't tell me what the fuck to do! Nobody is going to tell me to do something I don't want to do!"

"I helped you get rid of a body. I helped pay your lawyer for a case I had nothing to do with and I sold all your dope now all of a sudden you don't want to be around me?"

"I never said that."

"You didn't have to say that. I'm not stupid, dude."

Shamari made eye contact with Black, "I might go to prison for a very long time. I just want to make sure my family is okay." He paused and then said, "Your whole family is doing okay."

"We ain't loaded."

"Your sister and grandma own homes."

"I'm not understanding."

"I don't have nobody that has my back. I have to look out for Jada and my sister, but my family don't have shit."

"I've never met your sister and I don't know Jada that well, but I can tell you that Jada is a survivor."

"There are a lot of bodies out there and now with Imani dead, that's one more."

"One that, if anything, they're going be investigating your partner for. That body ain't on us. It's on his silly ass."

"He knows me and Jada. Don't you see, I don't want to get you caught up in my bullshit. I think we need to separate."

Black said, "We need each other more than ever."

———————

"Why?"

Black glanced at the work on the table and said, "This shit ain't gonna last long at all. We're going to need more product."

"You're a mad man."

"I'm on a mission, but really, I'm just like you. I don't wanna do this shit forever, but when I retire, I wanna make sure I've made enough motherfucking money where I can stay retired. You feel me?"

"I'm not feeling you."

Shamari tried to make his way to the living room but Black stepped in front of him and said, "Look, Mari, I need you, man."

Shamari took a deep breath.

Black said, "Wasn't I there for you?"

"Wait a goddamned minute, man! One thing I hate is when a motherfucker do something for me and then keep throwing the shit back up in my face. What the fuck do you think I owe you? Okay, you gave Jada some money. You paid my lawyer for me. And I gave you the goddamned money back."

"What about the body? How many people do you know will help you get rid of a body?"

There was an awkward silence as Shamari thought about what Black had said. It was true not many people would help him get rid of a body. Black had proven his friendship to him and he knew that if he needed something if he got locked up, that Black would come through for him.

Black said, "It's not about what I've done for you, bruh. I can care less about that. I need you, man. I've been hustling ever since I was a kid and you are probably the realest nigga I've ever worked with. We don't fall out about money and I know that you're a soldier. But you're right, you don't owe me shit. I'm asking you, man to man, help me out a little longer."

"How much longer?"

"One more score and we can walk away from it. You can go your way and I go my way, but if I was you I would not turn myself in."

"It's just got to a point where you get tired of running, you know. I can't live the way I want to."

"The hell you can't. Dude, you don't look nothing like yourself and you have a new ID. I would leave Atlanta. Hell, go down to South Beach."

"That's a thought."

Black hugged Shamari and said, "I'm your friend to the end."

"Same here."

"One more score, nigga? You down?"

"Fo-sho!"

• • •

Black and Kyrie cut the dope and put it in pink and green specialized bags that would add even more allure to the brand. Pretty Hurts was buzzing on the street. They'd scored another hit. The junkies wanted it and Black intended to give them what they wanted. Black put the baggies into a Ziploc bag and passed it to Kyrie. Kyrie didn't know that Imani had died bringing the heroin back to Atlanta and Black wanted to keep it that way.

Kyrie said, "We're going to have to find another stash spot."

"What?"

"I can't keep it, bruh. I mean I can hold on to some of it. I can hold the shit that I'm going to get rid of, but I can't keep it all with me. Remember, the police is on my ass and my son even brought some to school. Social Services is investigating me and my wife."

Black wanted to slap the fuck out of Kyrie. But he was right, there was no way he should stash anything at his house. Black was trying to think where he could stash the dope. He couldn't stash it at Nana's house. She'd cursed his ass out a few years ago when she'd found out that he'd buried a million dollars in her backyard. None of his baby mamas would let him stash anything at their houses. He dialed Lani's number but didn't get an answer. After Kyrie left, he drove to her house, punched in the building code and took the elevator to her apartment.

She opened the door and let him in.

"Why didn't you answer the phone?"

"Didn't know you called."

"Check your phone."

"What do you want?"

"What's your problem?"

"I don't answer the phone for you and I have a problem?"

She wore some tight ass Victoria Secrets shorts that were squeezing the life out of her fantastic ass. This would have usually aroused him but she had an attitude, and he was there for business.

"Look, Lani, something is wrong. I know you."

"Seriously, I want to know what the fuck you want?"

"I need a favor?"

"What?"

"Can you stash something for me? For a couple of days?"

"Absolutely not! We have so many goddamned people investigating us; the APD and Homeland Security. Next, we're going to have the Secret Service after our ass."

"Calm down. How many people came here with a search warrant?"

"Nobody, but have you forgotten those two clowns who were looking around the house?"

"That's because you let them."

"No, that's because you left that blunt out in the open."

"If you can do this favor for me, I'll give you a couple of thousand dollars."

"No."

"How the fuck are you going to tell me no?"

Lani knew she had to stand firm with Black. Black had a way of trying to make her feel guilty for shit he'd done for her in the past and she'd usually cave in. She'd come to realize that Black hardly ever helped anyone if there wasn't something in it for him.

"I can't do it, Black. I'm sorry."

"Who's going to pay your rent next month?"

"I don't know. I'll make it somehow or I'll go back to my mama's house."

Black tried to grab her hand and she pushed him away. "I'm sorry, Tyrann. We're in enough trouble."

"You haven't been charged with shit."

"Not yet, but you don't know if I'm going to be or not."

"Nothing is going to happen to you."

"You are very delusional." Lani made her way over to the door and opened it. "Now, if you don't mind."

Black reluctantly made his way to the door. His eye followed Lani's eyes and when their eyes locked he said, "Can you just hold it for one night? I'll get it from you in the morning."

"I can't help you."

Black left her place and drove to Nana's house. He decided to leave the stash outside in his car while he slept on Nana's couch.

CHAPTER 28

THE LUNCH CROWD HAD THINNED AT HOUSTON'S. IT WAS 2:13 P.M. when Black met Sasha for lunch. They sat in a booth near the entrance. Black ordered a double shot of Hennessy and Sasha ordered a grilled chicken salad. Sasha noticed that Black wasn't his usual jovial self. Usually, he would have said something funny or he'd comment on her looks. She felt she looked extra cute today. She wore a blue high-waisted skirt which made her ass look unbelievable and a white blouse that accentuated her cleavage perfectly, but Black hadn't even noticed.

The food and drinks came twenty minutes later. Black downed his drink in one swig and ordered another one.

Sasha bit into her salad. "What's wrong?"

Black took a deep breath and said, "I got a lot of shit on my mind."

"Tell me."

"I don't want to ruin your day with my bullshit."

"We're friends."

"I know, but I'll be okay. It's nothing that I can't handle."

"You sure?"

"Positive."

"Okay. Well I thought you were going to set up the meeting with me and your sister. We need to get moving on this business opportunity."

"But we haven't even decided which franchise we're going to buy into."

"I'm thinking Wing King."

"Yeah, I like that one. Thing about black people, they love some wings."

"Everybody loves wings. We're not going to serve just black people."

"I feel ya." Black said. He sipped his drink and relaxed a bit. He noticed her titties staring at him. He could see her nipples through her blouse. Damn, she was one sexy motherfucker.

"I'm worried about you."

"Don't be."

"But you're not yourself and I don't like that."

"You think you know me?"

"A little bit." She sipped her water and said, "I just noticed that you're usually more social."

"I'm sorry."

"No need to be."

Black stole another look at her breasts and said, "Maybe I should come over tonight."

She smiled and slid to his side of the booth, reached under the table and unzipped his pants and stroked his dick. He wrestled his manhood away from her and zipped his pants.

"Not now," he said.

"I was just going to jerk you off."

"You're an animal."

"You like it."

"You're goddamned right."

CHAPTER 29

TREY HAD BEEN STAYING AT ONE OF HIS STASH HOUSES FOR THE PAST
six days since Shantelle had kicked him out. Rather than looking for a
place, he'd simply had a bed and a plasma TV delivered to the house,
bought himself some groceries, and got comfortable. He'd find a place
to stay sooner or later. He was relaxing in his new bed. Not quite asleep.
He knew he needed to hop his ass out of the bed and get his day started,
but he was feeling very lazy. His phone rang. The caller ID said. *Mama.* He
answered on the first ring.

"Hey, Ma."

"Baby, I hate to bother you."

"What's wrong, Mama?"

"My air conditioning unit has gone out and I wanted a little help."

"How much is the AC unit, Mama?"

"They range between four and seven thousand."

"What's the difference?"

"I don't know. You know, I don't know about that kind of stuff. The
serviceman was saying something about a rebate. I'll give you the number
and you can talk to him."

"Text me the number."

"Thank you, baby! I don't know what I would do without you."

"Mama, you took care of me when I couldn't do for myself, and I owe it
to you to make your life easier."

"I love you, son."

"I love you too." Trey ended the call and entered the room with the safe. He punched the combination and was surprised to see the safe was empty. Zilch. Zero. He hoped Starr wasn't up to her bullshit again. He dialed her number right away.

"Hello?"

"Hey, did you take my money?"

"I gave the money back, remember?"

"I'm talking about different money. Did you take it again? At the house in Alpharetta?"

"No. You know I would have told you if I did. I haven't been at that house in ages."

"Starr, don't play with me! If you need money, just ask me for it."

"I didn't take shit, Trey!"

He believed her. He knew there was no way she would have taken over a million in cash from him.

"How much are you missing?"

"A lot."

"A lot like how much?"

"All of its gone."

"Have you checked your little girlfriend?"

"She didn't have the safe combination."

"Who the fuck could have took it?"

"I don't know."

"Look, I didn't take the money, Trey. I would never do nothing like that without letting you know."

"I believe you."

Trey thought about Shantelle. She had put him out, but there was no way that she could have stolen the money. She didn't have the safe's combination, and besides, he had never taken her to this particular stash house.

"I'll call you back later."

"Please do. Let me know what happened. I'm not going to be able to sleep tonight knowing this has happened to you."

"I will."

He ended the call and dialed Shantelle's number and but there was no answer.

He called her again and again there was no answer. This wasn't like her, she always answered.

After he showered and brushed his teeth, he headed to her home. He was about half way there when she called.

"You called me?" Shantelle asked.

"Yeah. You home?"

"Yes, why?"

"I need to talk to you."

"Okay, I'm listening."

"I would prefer to say it face to face."

"Okay, I'll be here for the next thirty minutes then I'm headed to the gym."

"I will be there in five minutes."

When Shantelle opened the door to her apartment, Trey marched right past her without saying a word.

Shantelle stood there with her hands on her hips, waiting on his silly ass to say something. Finally, she slammed the door hard and said, "Trey, you want to tell me what this is all about?"

"Money is missing."

"Starr has struck again. I supposed you need a shoulder to lean on and so you come running over here. Trey, you need to leave."

"What?"

"Leave!"

"I'm not going anywhere until I know if you have my money or not!"

"What?"

"Did you take my money?"

"How would I take your money, Trey?"

"You been with me to my stash houses!"

"I think you need to go ask the chick with the combinations to the safes. We never got that far."

"Starr didn't take it."

"How do you know?"

"Because she said she didn't, and she's never lied to me."

"How much money are we talking about?"

"Over a million dollars."

Shantelle looked Trey straight in his eyes and said, "Seriously, Trey, you think if I took a million dollars, I would still be in this tiny-ass apartment? Do you think I would have the nerve to even be in Atlanta?"

"Somebody took the money, that's for damn sure."

"It wasn't me. How would I have taken it? One fact that you're overlooking, Trey, I didn't have the combination to the safe."

And that was an absolute fact. Nobody had the combinations except himself, Starr and his mother. He knew for a fact that his mother had not taken the money and he believed Starr, so who had taken the money.

Trey walked past Shantelle into the hallway.

Shantelle said, "Well, aren't you going to say goodbye?"

"I ain't got shit to say."

Lani and Shakur had been talking every day since the last time he'd visited her, and she'd decided that she liked him and felt very comfortable talking to him. She asked him to come over. When she opened the door before he knew it, he'd uttered the words. "Goddamn." She was wearing tight-ass Nike running spandex pants and a pink sports bra that made her tits look amazing. She also wore Nikes to match.

"I didn't know you work out?"

"I don't." She laughed. "Sometimes I'll do exercises watching *Fitness on Demand* on TV but I'm actually kind of lazy when it comes to that kind of stuff. Are you're willing to be my trainer?"

"I don't think I could handle training you."

"Why not?"

His eyes zoomed in on those nice-ass thighs and when she caught him staring, she blushed, showing her cute dimples.

"I see why they were going crazy over you."

"How about them niggas were already crazy?"

"But you turned them into complete lunatics."

She led him into the living room. "Let me get you something to drink."

"Not right now."

"How you been?"

"Okay."

"You seem to be doing a lot better."

"I feel better."

He made eye contact with her and said, "Lani, you deserve the best."

"I've heard that before."

"It's true."

"Man, you got that game."

"Game?"

"You know how to spit it."

"This ain't game. This is how I feel. A woman like you deserves to be a wife."

She blushed then she caught herself and said, "I need to get my shit together."

"You heard from Mike?"

"No. Why?

"Just asking. I don't want you to be worried about him."

"Black stopped by."

"The ex?"

"Yeah."

"What did he want?"

"A favor. I told him that I couldn't do it and he said he was going to cut me off."

"Cut you off? I don't understand."

"No more support."

"Tell him he ain't the only one in Atlanta with money. As a matter of fact, call him and I'll tell him."

Lani thought about the beef between Mike and Black and how it had started with Chris and Black. She said to Shakur, "No, let it go. I don't want any more problems."

Shakur made his way over to Lani and put his hand behind her head then he pulled her hair.

"Ouch! What the hell are you doing?"

"Seeing if it was yours." He smiled with those sexy-ass lips.

She reached up and pulled his neat dreadlocks.

"Ow!" Shakur cried.

"I was just seeing if this was yours." Lani said. "Hell, this is Atlanta. You know dudes on some other shit, perms and weaves and extensions."

"Not me."

She looked at his neck. The beaded necklace that he'd worn the first time he'd met her was gone. Thank you, Jesus.

He leaned into her and kissed her. "I want you to be safe, and I don't want you worrying about anything."

Lani said, "Please, don't confront Black. The last thing I need is more drama."

"I don't even know him."

"I know, but it's not hard to find out who he is. Most of the D boys in Atlanta know him."

"I promise. I just don't want nothing to happen to you."

She leaned into him and kissed him.

•   •   •

Trey knew this was a long shot but he had to find out what happened to his money. He didn't think Jessica had his money but anything was possible with this bitch. It was five p.m. when he drove into her driveway. Jessica came to the door wearing some amazingly tight-ass jeans and a wife beater that exposed a lot of cleavage. She blocked the entrance and those delicious-looking titties were staring right at him.

"T. J. is not here, and why didn't you call before you came?"

"I didn't come to see T. J."

"I have company. What do you want?"

"I need to ask you something. Something I need you to be serious about."

"I'm always serious. You're the one that's always playing the little, silly-ass games."

"Can I come inside?"

"I told you I have company."

"A guy?"

"Why?"

"I have a right to know who's around my son."

"T. J.'s not here."

"Look, I didn't come here to argue with you. I need to ask you a serious question."

"Ask me the damn question."

"Did you take my money?"

Jessica looked very confused. "What the hell are you talking about?"

"Did you steal my money?"

"How in the hell can I steal your money? I don't know where your money is! Get real."

She stepped outside and closed the door behind her so her company couldn't hear what she was talking about.

"Somebody took my motherfuckin' money and I'm going to get to the bottom of it!" Trey said.

"And you think I had something to do with it? How could I have something to do with it?"

"You're a goddamned stalker who don't want me to be happy and you called the police on me. I wouldn't put shit past you!" Trey said.

Jessica looked around to make sure Mrs. Walker, the nosey-ass bitch next door, wasn't peeking through her blinds. The last thing she needed was for her neighbor to call the police, especially since she had company waiting on her. Otherwise she would have let her neighbor call the police and let them haul Trey's ass off to jail.

Jessica said, "You're going to have to lower your voice."

"I need to know yes or no! Did you take my goddamned money?"

The neighbor to the right of her, Mr. Hemsley, a retired Social Studies teacher, was now on his porch sipping a glass of ice tea. He was trying to be discreet as he looked over to find out what was going on.

Jessica waved at him. "Hey, Mr. Hemsley."

He waved back and said, "Hey, how are you? I didn't even see you."

Jessica said to Trey, "Ask yourself, why would I take your money? Taking your money is like stealing from my son."

"Our son."

"Our son," Jessica said. "Now would you get the fuck away from here before I call the goddamned police on your ass!"

CHAPTER 30

JADA ASKED LANI AND STARR TO MEET HER AT PROHIBITION FOR drinks. The ladies sat upfront. Today marked the first time in a few weeks that they'd seen each other. They all had strawberry martinis.

Jada said, "Look, you girls are the only people I can tell what's been going on with me. Well, except my mama. You're the only ones that would understand."

"What's wrong?" Starr asked.

Jada looked very worried and she looked as if she was thinking what she would tell them and what she would leave out, but she couldn't get her words out.

Lani said, "What's wrong?"

"Shamari told me not to say anything, but I feel like I can tell you anything," Lani said. Then she turned to Starr and said, "While I don't know you as well, you've been nothing but a good friend to me."

Starr said, "I'm glad you feel like that. We got off to a rocky start, but I feel like we just had to get to know each other."

"Exactly," Jada said.

"Now, tell us what the fuck is going on."

"Man, so much." She sipped her drink and said, "Promise not to tell anybody?"

"I swear," Starr said.

"No one will hear a word from me." Lani said

"Dr. Handsome invested some money with Shamari hoping to get a return on his investment."

"Okay," Starr said, "Why is this prominent surgeon investing with a drug dealer? This shit doesn't make sense."

"Well, he has secrets and skeletons in his closet. He loves black women and he loves cocaine. He has a habit and now that his wife is suing him, he needed extra money."

"He invested with Shamari? That's not juicy."

"I know but what I really want to tell you is that he used two girls as mules. He placed heroin inside their breast implants."

"What?"

"Yeah, but we never knew he was doing that until one of the balloons burst and filled one of the girl's bloodstream with heroin. The poor girl died."

"Then what happened?"

"I had to tell Shamari what he'd been doing and he came over and whipped Craig's ass. Then he and Black had to get rid of the body."

"Black?" Lani said.

"Yeah, Black."

"What in the hell did he have to do with it?"

"Nothing, but he and Shamari are partners."

Starr drank her drink in one swallow and then called to the barmaid and said, "We're going to need another round of drinks."

The barmaid came back with another round of drinks and Starr said, "Damn!"

Jada said, "I know. I feel so bad that I brought this man to Shamari."

Lani said, "I saw Black and he didn't tell me shit about this."

"He probably didn't want you to worry."

"I'm finished with Black and I suggest you stay away from Shamari and the doctor," Lani said.

Jada became sad. While she didn't have a problem staying away from Craig, she loved Shamari and she knew he needed her more than ever now. "That's easy to say, but I just can't turn off my feelings."

"Okay, that way of thinking will have yo' ass in a jail cell."

Starr said, "I know what Jada means. Someone stole some of Trey's money and I can tell he's so hurt by it. I just want to be there for him. I still love him though I can't be with him."

Jada said, "That's how I feel, and I also feel that it's my fault this happened to him."

"Shamari is already in trouble with the Feds. It's not your fault." Lani said.

"But if I hadn't asked him to let Craig invest, none of this shit would have happened."

Starr hugged Jada and said, "You can't blame yourself for what happened."

"I feel so bad for the girl. I guess if I hadn't met her before I wouldn't feel the way I do, but I did and I just feel terrible."

"It's going to be okay."

CHAPTER 31

AFTER BLACK KILLED CHRIS AND TOOK ALL THE DRUGS FROM HIM,
Mike was left indebted to the Mexicans. Mike had been paying them off
a little at a time, but they had refused to consign him any more work
and Mike had to get consignments from Shakur and Big Papa. The
work was coming from Shakur but Shakur was getting it from Big Papa
who had a Mexican connection of his own. The difference between Big
Papa's connection and the others was that Big Papa was partners with
his connections. He and his Mexican friend had purchased fields of
marijuana down in Mexico and they bought the cocaine directly from the
Columbians at below wholesale prices. Shakur called Mike and said he
wanted to meet with him. They met at BLT steak. It was just after lunch
and the crowd was pretty thin. Shakur had just left the gym so he just
wanted water. Mike had a Cobb salad and an iced tea.

After the waitress dropped the food at the table, Mike said, "So what's up?"

"I met Lani."

"Ok." Mike looked confused wondering how in the hell they met, but he
knew this was Atlanta. While it was a decent size, it was not uncommon
for people to meet and even less uncommon for people to run their
motherfucking mouths.

"She told me what happened."

"Her version?"

"Black told her he'd known where your mother lived since the day he
followed Chris."

"So now she's admitting that Black killed Chris?"

"I don't think she ever denied that."

Mike studied Shakur's face for a long time trying to figure out why he was putting himself in the middle of shit he didn't have anything to do with. "You fucking her or something? Why would she tell you all of this? This shit sounds like pillow talk."

"Maybe."

"Ok, fuck who you want to fuck, but that doesn't change anything between me and Lani. When I see her, she's going to have to be dealt with!"

"Is that a threat?"

"Take it how you want."

"I believe her."

"And my son believes in Santa Claus. What the fuck do I care about you believing Lani? Just like I'm sure you don't give a damn that my son believes in Santa Claus. So what's the point of this meeting? Why did you call me here?"

"Look, man, I miss your brother, too. I only met him a couple of times, but he seemed like a real cool dude. I hate that happened to him."

"Do you really?" Mike stared at Shakur, knowing damn well that he didn't give two fucks about what happened to Chris. If he did, he wasn't really showing that he did by fucking his woman.

"I lost my first cousin. Not quite the same. But you and I both know these streets don't love nobody."

"That's for damn sure." Mike sipped his iced tea.

"I don't know how to say this nicely, but don't fuck with Lani!"

Mike dropped his fork on his plate. "Or what?"

"I don't like your tone of voice. You might wanna lower it," Shakur said.

Mike looked Shakur straight in the eye and said, "My brother is dead and you're going to tell me I can't get even with the motherfuckers responsible for killing him. I hope you don't think I need you."

Shakur stood and said, "Just in case you think I'm ASKING you not to fuck with her, you think again. I'm not asking you shit. I'm telling you. If you do something to Lani, there is going to be consequences. The kind that you might not be ready for."

He turned and was about to walk away when Mike yelled out, "Fuck you, nigga!"

Shakur turned and made eye contact with Mike and said, "No, fuck with me, and I swear to you, it will be the worst mistake you ever make in your life!"

CHAPTER 32

JADA WORE A LIGHT BLUE DOO-RAG TO KEEP HER HAIR IN PLACE AND she didn't feel particularly sexy. She was about to doze off when she felt Shamari's hand inside her panties. He rubbed her ass and seconds later she felt his finger slide inside her. She hadn't thought about sex in a very long time, but his finger felt so goddamn good. She turned and faced him. They stared at each other before he leaned into her. He yanked her panties down to her knees. He tossed the covers on the floor and slid down until he was between her legs. He spread them like a field goal post. Her pussy was bald as usual and beautiful to him. Her clit hung, just ready for him to taste it and that's exactly what he did. He licked her clit until she squirmed. She grabbed the back of his head and closed her eyes. "Yes, daddy! Yes!"

He inserted his finger and gnawed on her clit. He flipped her over on her stomach, and licked her from behind. She was trying her best not to have an orgasm, but she couldn't help it. This man knew exactly what to do with her body, and she loved that he knew that.

"I need you inside me, Mari."

He ignored her and continued licking and kissing her pussy. Her cum tasted sweet, and he wanted to savor it. Although she'd done him wrong, he loved her. Deep down, he knew that Jada was just like most women— she couldn't be faithful, but she'd proven to be loyal. More loyal than anyone had ever been in his life, even his own mother. There was nothing he wouldn't do for her.

"Don't make me beg."

"I just want to please you."

"Put it in!"

With her ass still in the air, unable to see him because he was behind her, she reached for his shaft. She grabbed his balls instead but she quickly released them and found what she was looking for. It was hard as hell. She put him inside. He slid out before inserting it himself and thrusting his hips.

"Yes!" she screamed.

He removed the doo-rag and her hair cascaded down her back beautifully. Her face lay sideways on the pillow and he admired her. Damn this woman was gorgeous and for a split second he could only think about what could have been. If he had been a legitimate businessman, they could be raising a family right now.

Jada said, "Harder!"

He thrust harder, snapping himself out of his dream. Then, he lay her down on her side and spooned and kissed her at the same time. She broke free and forced him on his back then took him deep inside her mouth.

He was really too big for her tiny mouth and she gagged a little and in a weird kind of way, this turned him on. She sucked his balls and hummed on them as she looked up at him. Shamari felt like a goddamned king.

"What do you want me to do?" she asked, his balls still in her hand.

"I really want to please you."

"By pleasing you, it pleases me."

"I'm good, baby."

"Put it in my ass."

"I'm too big."

She stood from the bed and disappeared into the bathroom. She came back with some KY Jelly and tossed it to him.

He looked at the KY Jelly like he was in an Algebra class—confused as hell.

"You know I ain't into that gay shit."

"How is it gay when I'm a girl?"

"Exactly, I want to fuck your pussy."

"It'll be extra tight. You'll like it."

"So you've done this before?"

"Not with a real dick." She laid on her back with her ass in the air. "Lube my asshole and put it in."

"Quit talking. You're killing my goddamned mood." He did exactly what she'd told him to do and he entered her tight asshole with ease.

"Damn, this feels good," Jada moaned. "How does it feel to you, baby?"

It was tight to him. It was different for sure. He pushed it further into her ass.

"Slow down." She reached back and shoved him just a little. "This ain't the same as my coochie."

"My bad."

"You're doing fine."

He gripped her cheeks with both hands and he was really starting to get into it. She had to tell him to take it easy every once in a while, but she had been right. He was enjoying himself.

He thrust until he erupted in her ass. She stood up from the bed and made her way into the bathroom to clean herself up. She came back with a warm wet towel and tossed it to him.

He cleaned up and said, "I needed that."

"Me too. I've had so much on my mind."

"What have you been stressed about?"

"What do you think, Mari? That girl died. That blood is on our hands, and if it gets out, we are done. I didn't mean to get myself in no shit like this. I never wanted to be an accessory to murder."

"Why do you think it's going to get out?"

"Look, I'm hoping like hell it doesn't get out, but you know someone is going to realize sooner or later that she is missing."

"I know."

"I've been thinking about that a lot lately." She avoided his eyes and he noticed.

"What are you thinking about? I can tell your mind is somewhere else."

"Lani was saying that she ain't fucking with Black anymore and that I should stay away from you."

"She said that?"

"Yeah, baby. I know I told you to leave, but I want to be there for you, Shamari. No matter what happens, I want to be there for you. I know we ain't as close as we were before, but you're my best friend and that will never change."

"But Lani is right."

"She's wrong."

"No, she's right. You can't risk getting yourself in trouble for me. And I'm going to be gone in two weeks because it's just a matter of time before the Feds come busting up in here and if they get you for harboring a fugitive, I just couldn't live with myself."

"Don't worry about me."

"I can't help it. We're best friends, remember?"

She leaned into him and kissed him. "No matter what, I'm going to always be there for you."

"So what's up with Starr?"

"Not much, just running her business. You know that girl has a good business head. Trey lost a good one."

"Huh?"

"Oh, I didn't tell you. Trey has been fucking with this other chick and tried to come back to Starr, but she wasn't having it."

"No, you never told me that. Damn."

"Things haven't been going that well for him."

"I can't say that I'm sorry to hear that. Fuck him."

"Somebody just stole a bunch of money from him."

"But he has lots of bread."

"You know me and Starr are not best friends, but we've grown close over the last few months. She told Lani that it was over a million dollars."

"What?"

"Yes."

"Damn.

CHAPTER 33

SASHA HAD BEEN CALLING BLACK FOR THE LAST TWO DAYS AND HE'D been letting her go to voicemail. When he saw her name on the caller ID, he was hesitant to answer the phone, but he answered on the second ring. "Hello?"

"Hey, baby. You forget all about me?"

"No. Been busy."

"I want to get with you, so I can meet your sister. We need to make a move on the investment."

"I know, but I have bigger problems right now."

"Anything I can help you with?"

"No, not really! On second thought, maybe you can. Where can we meet?"

"You can come to my place. I'm home today."

"You took the day off?"

"Working from home today."

"Okay. Give me fifteen minutes. I'll be right over."

"See you then."

When Black stepped into Sasha's apartment, she saw the concerned look on his face and asked, "What's wrong, my love?"

"Nothing that you need to worry about."

"You don't seem the same. As a matter of fact, you didn't seem the same the last time I saw you either."

He asked, "Can I have a seat?"

"Sure." She pointed to an armchair and she sat right across from him.

He said, "Look, I know that you want to talk about the franchise, and I'll get around to that, but I got bigger concerns right now."

"Like what?"

They locked eyes. "You know I'm a bad guy."

"You told me that."

"Well, I'm having a problem right now. I'm going to need an apartment. Kind of like a stash apartment. Do you understand?"

"I think so, but what can I do to help?"

"Can you get an apartment in your name?"

"Sure."

He smiled and said, "You don't know how much this means to me. I mean, I would let my sister get it, but she's gotten a couple of houses in her name for me already." The truth was that after the police questioned Rashida about the cell phone being in her name after Chris's murder, she told Black that she wouldn't get anything else for him in her name. She would still partner up with him in a legitimate business, but that was it.

"When do you want to do it? Do you have a place in mind?"

"Haven't found one yet."

"What will you be keeping in the house?"

"You really don't want to know that."

"I was going to say that I have an extra room here. I can give you the key and building FOB and you can leave your stuff here."

"That would be great because I won't be ready to look for the apartment until next week. Would you do that for me?"

"Absolutely!" She stood up and made her way to the bedroom. Black watched those tight gym shorts grip her ass so wonderfully. When she came back with the key and FOB, Black's dick was out of his pants and he was stroking it. She tossed him the key and FOB and then dropped to her knees and took him deep inside her mouth.

CHAPTER 34

BLACK AND SHAMARI SAT IN THE FLOOR OF BLACK'S DEN WITH A BOX of KFC and two cups of Pepsi as they counted a pile of money. There was a pile of fifties and a stack of hundreds as well as a huge pile of twenties in the floor. They threw all the one dollar bills and fives in a brown box. They would count that later and split it. Rap blasted from the speakers.

"Why don't you have a money counter?" He picked up a breast from the box. Shamari really didn't care for chicken but he loved to eat the skin. He removed the skin from the breast and chomped it down. Then he wiped his mouth because it was greasy.

"I'm old school. I want to make sure the money is correct. And besides, you get more time if you get caught with one."

"That's just some shit you heard in the street."

"I don't know, but I ain't trying to find out."

Shamari counted a pile of twenties as he was chewing on the chicken skin.

"So you don't know?"

"I don't know. Maybe I'll get one for the next time."

"The next time? I thought we were done."

"My business with you is done, but I'm not done."

Shamari grabbed a handful of taters. "Bruh, you need to do something else before you end up like me, running from the Feds."

"Who says I'm not like you already?"

"I don't understand."

"They trying to pin a murder on me."

"Not the same." Shamari stuffed the taters into his mouth.

"Look, I'm about to buy into a Wing King franchise."

"A Wing King? Why a Wing King?"

"Something that I know about. One thing is for sure, people love chicken. Look at you with your greasy-ass lips." Black passed him a napkin and said, "Wipe yo' goddamned mouth."

"You're going to buy it in your name?"

"Well, I have a partner, actually two partners. A girl I've been fuckin' and my sister."

"You trust the girl?"

"I trust my sister."

"Good. Trey left Starr for some chick and Starr told Jada that she thinks the girl hit Trey for over a million dollars."

"Damn! Trey had it like that? I didn't know he had it like that."

"Trey is kind of quiet with his, but he has bread."

"Trey alright, but I get the sense that he thinks he's better than me. I speak to him when I see him, but I don't really fuck with him like that."

"Yeah, he's wishy-washy. He gave me some money when I was down and out and we were supposed to do some business, but when he found out I might be in a little trouble, he flipped. But you know, it is what it is."

"Damn."

"If I were you, I wouldn't give that chick nothing. Keep it family. Let your sister buy the Wing King." He paused and washed the taters down with some Pepsi. Then he said, "You can't trust a motherfucking soul."

•   •   •

Brooke came running back to Starr's office and whispered, "Mr. Trey is outside." Starr signaled with her hands that she would be out in five minutes. She was finishing up a phone conversation with a potential client. When she was done, she made her way into the showroom. Trey was looking around, admiring the place as he sat on a display sofa.

She startled him when she approached. She had to admit he was looking good as hell. He looked like he'd lost some weight from the stress of losing so much money, as he stood there in True Religion jeans, Pumas and a very nice watch with a huge face. If only this man would keep his dick in his pants she thought.

"Very nice place," Trey said when he saw her.

"Trey, you been here before."

"I know, but I really didn't get a chance to check it out."

"Too busy trying to fuck people up."

"You know how I feel about you."

"I know you want to do whatever it is that you want to do, but you want me to stay loyal."

"Doesn't every man?"

"Seems that way from my father on down."

"Look, the world was like this before we came here, and it's going to be like this when we're gone."

"So, I know you're not here to talk about how trifling men are."

"No."

"What brings you here?"

"Can we talk in private?"

"Sure."

She led him into the office. She sat behind her desk and he sat in the chair in front of her. There was a picture of Starr and both of their mothers on the desk.

"You still have that picture?"

"Yeah."

"Where is the picture with me and Ace?"

"I don't want to look at a picture of you right now." Then she pointed to the file cabinet. "There's a picture of me, Daddy, and Meeka."

"So, I'm the only one left out of your office pics?"

"Trey, get to the point."

"Look, I don't know who has my money."

"What do you mean, you don't know who has it? Shantelle has it."

"Why hasn't she moved? And she didn't have the combination to the safe. Only you, mama, and me had the combination."

"Don't be that naïve. You know she has it. The question is, what are you willing to do about it?"

"I don't think she has it."

"Trey, you're one of the smartest men I know, but you're too weak when it comes to women. Women can be manipulative. But you'll never understand that. She has the money Trey and if she don't have the money, somebody she knows has the money. It's an inside job, Trey."

"How can it be an inside job when only three people knew the combination to the safes?"

"Trey, you should have never taken Shantelle to your stash houses."

"I even thought Jessica might know something about it."

"Jessica is off her rocker, but I don't think she has it."

Trey thought about it and what Starr was saying made sense. Now the question was, what was he prepared to do about it?

"Do you need to borrow some money?"

"Huh? You doing that well?"

"No. But I'm doing okay. I have a big job coming up that's going to net me fifty thousand dollars in commission."

"House decorating pays that well?"

"Interior decorating and design, you mean?"

"It pays that much?"

"No, this is four homes for the same man. Two of the homes he owns and one is for his son and one is for a friend. I think she's a mistress but whatever."

"And you're going to make fifty thousand?"

"Well, all of it's not profit. I have to pay rent here and I have to pay Brooke. There are plenty of expenses, but he's seen my work and agreed to pay upfront since I'm a small business."

"Damn. I'm impressed."

"But I can give it to you."

"No. I still have money. You know the house in Cobb has money there."

"Okay. Well, I know there's at least a million dollars there." Starr said. "Has Shantelle ever visited there?"

"Yes."

"How do you know the money is there?"

"I've been there already and it was still there and I changed the combination to it." He grabbed a pen from her desk and scribbled the combination down and passed it to her.

"You trust me?"

"With my life."

She smiled.

He stood up and said, "I just need one more chance, Starr. I want to be the man that you know that I can be. I fucked up again. But I want to make you my wife. You are the woman for me, and I've never been so sure of something in my whole life. You are what I get up in the morning for. You and T. J. is what I live for. I want us to get married, and I want to give you a daughter."

"I want a son."

"I'll give you both."

"Trey, it's time for you to go." She stood and folded the paper up and stuffed it into her purse. "I will take care of this for you." She stepped around the desk.

He starred into her eyes for a long time before pulling her into him, his hands on her ass. Her mind wanted to resist but her heart couldn't. She closed her eyes and kissed him—the man that she loved.

•   •   •

Trey rang Shantelle's doorbell and banged on her door. He called the phone and it went straight to voicemail. He kept banging until a neighbor appeared. A skinny white guy with dreadlocks and a tie-dye shirt.

"Dude, I saw her moving out in the middle of the night."

"What?" Trey said.

"Yeah, I think she's dodging rent or something. Usually when people move out like that, they don't have the rent money."

"Did she say where she was going?"

"She said something about being from Miami and she was going to go back there."

"She's not from Miami, she's from Seattle."

"Dude, I'm just telling you what she told me."

"Ok, thanks, brother."

"Hey, I know it's none of my business but she was with some Latin dude that was ripped as shit. He looked like he could run a goddamned marathon or something."

"Really?" Trey thought the nerve of this stinking bitch to move on with her life so fast. And it was now obvious to Trey that Shantelle was the one responsible for taking his money.

"Yeah, I'm just telling you because I've seen you around here before and I thought you were her boyfriend."

"Well, you know how it is with women."

"I don't trust 'em."

Trey shook the man's hand and said, "I have to be going."

"Take it easy, bro."

As soon as Trey got into his car he called Starr.

"Hello?"

"You were right. Shantelle has the money."

"I knew it. What are you going to do?"

"I don't know. I have to find her."

"Find her?"

"She moved."

"Damn. Where is she from?"

"She told me Seattle but she told her neighbors that she was from Miami."

"Why don't you go see Monte and see what he knows about her?"

"I can't go see Monte."

"I'll go see him."

"You would do that for me?"

"Of course I would do that for you."

"I'll text you his mother's phone number and you can tell her to have Monte send you a visitation form or maybe there's a way for you to download the form online."

CHAPTER 35

CRAIG MET WITH JADA AT WHISKEY BLUE INSIDE THE W. BOTH OF them had water to drink. No food. He looked disheveled and had three-day's worth of stubble growing on his face.

"So what's up?" asked Jada.

"The police asked me when was the last time I saw Imani?"

"And you said what?"

"A few weeks before she went missing."

"Did they believe you?"

"No because there was a text message of me asking her to meet me at the Westin on Peachtree."

"And what did you say."

"I told them that she didn't show up. They seemed to believe me but you know them."

"Them?"

"The police. They never stop 'til they get what they want."

"Or 'til somebody tells them what they want. You haven't been running your goddamned mouth have you?" said Jada.

"Why would I do that and implicate myself."

Jada thought what he said made sense, but she didn't like his cheerleader attitude in regards to the police. She hated the goddamned cops.

"So you asked me to meet so we could talk about Imani?" Jada asked.

"No not exactly." They locked eyes for a long time and she could tell that he was trying to figure out what he was going to say.

"I don't have all day. What did you come to talk about?"

"I need money."

"For coke?"

"What difference does it make? I need some of my money. If I choose to snort it all up, so what? It's mine."

"I'll have to talk to Shamari. You know you're not his favorite person. Especially since he had to get rid of a dead body for you."

"I didn't want her to die."

"You're fucking crazy. You had that girl's goddamned self-esteem in the dumps."

"I don't know what you're talking about."

"Making somebody traffic drugs for a fuckin nose job. That was crazy."

"Look, that's what she wanted."

"She wanted to be perfect for you. She thought she was a goddamned Barbie doll."

"So you're going to make me feel worse than I already feel?"

"You know what, Craig? I don't give a fuck about you, and I hope you rot in hell. And as soon as Shamari gives you your fucking money, you can kiss the blackest part of my ass."

"I'd like that."

"I know you would."

"So when do you think you're going to have my money?"

"Like I said, I have to talk to Shamari."

CHAPTER 36

"DUDE, YOU NEED TO BURN SOME INCENSE OR CANDLES OR SOMETHING in this motherfucker. As soon as I came through the door, all I could smell was Loud."

There was a blunt of OG Kush dangling from Black's lips. He picked up a can of Febreze and sprayed it in a futile attempt to mask the weed smoke.

It didn't work and Shamari said, "How about putting it out for a few moments and opening the goddamned windows? You need incense, bruh." He marched right past Black and sat on an armchair.

Black asked. "What brings you over?"

Shamari coughed and fanned away the smoke. Black stubbed the blunt out.

"Dude wants his money. Well some of his money."

There was another blunt of OG Kush lying on the table and Black picked it up. He lit it and took a long pull.

"Let me get this straight. This dude kills somebody. We have to get rid of the body and he still thinks he's entitled to some goddamned money?" Black said.

"Yeah, he says he wants part of it. I was thinking of giving him what he invested."

"You can't be serious, bruh," Black said.

"Look, man, we don't need this dude running his goddamned mouth," said Shamari.

"So we kill him."

"What?"

"We should have killed his ass that night. Him and that bitch."

"Neither one of them knows you."

"It wouldn't matter if they did know me if we killed them." Black had a sinister look on his face. "Now would it?"

"Look, it's too late for all of that."

"It's never too late."

"Look, I'm not killing him."

"And I'm not giving him no money. Zilch. Fuck him. You can pay him out of your money if you want, but he ain't getting shit from me."

There was a long silence. Shamari thought about what Black was saying. The fact of the matter was that Craig had murdered a woman and Shamari and Black had to dispose of the body. He didn't deserve a goddamned dime.

"You're right."

Black gave Shamari a pound. "You are finally getting it," Black inhaled the Kush again and said, "I still say we kill that motherfucker."

•   •   •

Monte was confined in Jessup, Georgia about three and a half hours away from Atlanta. It was 12:30 p.m. before Starr arrived inside the prison. She would have been there sooner but some hating-ass prison guard said her jeans were too tight and she had to go to the local Wal-Mart to buy some pants. Her ass was as equally pronounced in the Wal-Mart pants but she wasn't as fashionable. It was almost one o'clock when Monte stepped in the visitation room. The guard pointed to the table where Starr sat.

Two inmates called out, "Goddamned, Monte. Is that your girl?"

"One of them," Monte lied. He'd been there for months and he had only gotten visits from his mother, but he would be the talk of the prison yard for a couple of weeks until everyone realized that Starr wasn't coming back to visit him. Then he'd lied to them and tell them that *he* told *her* not to wait on him and that *he* broke up with *her* and told her to go on with her life.

Monte approached the table and he gave Starr a hug and she half embraced him back. He'd totally caught her off guard. She had only seen him twice and he was hugging her like they were best friends.

Monte was dressed in khaki pants and shirt and a pair of black boots. He sat across from her.

"I was surprised to hear that you wanted to come see me."

Starr was thinking, she hoped this clown didn't get the idea that she liked him.

"Trey sent me."

"Oh yeah, how's he doing?"

"Not too good."

"Well, he has to be doing better than me. At least he's free."

"That's true."

"Do you have any money on you?"

"Excuse me?"

"For the vending machine."

"Yeah, I got a few dollars."

"Well, I might as well get a couple of bags of chips and some sodas out of you since its obvious you came to talk to me about Trey, someone that I could give a flying fuck about at this point in my life."

"It's not Trey's fault you are in here."

"I'm not blaming Trey, but Trey hasn't checked up on me once since I been here. He took mama the money but what about a letter? Hell, you can email nowadays. The nigga ain't sent me one message and I've been here for months."

Starr was silent then she dug into her purse and handed Monte the eight dollar bills in change that she'd gotten from Wal-Mart.

Monte said, "Thanks." Then made his way over to the vending machine.

Starr watched him as several inmates gave him a thumbs up symbol. They clearly thought that Starr was Monte's girlfriend. He'd been walking around the yard saying that he'd been caught with a shitload of cocaine and that he was rich on the streets. Since he had the arrest paperwork to prove that he had, in fact, been caught with a lot of coke, people believed him. Now the gorgeous girl in the visitation room would further reaffirm Monte's lies.

Monte returned with two cokes and a pack of crackers. He offered a drink to Starr but she declined.

"So what's going on with Trey?"

"He needs your help."

"For what?"

"The girl."

"What girl?"

"The girl you got caught with."

"What about her?"

"Trey started fucking her."

"What? He started fucking around on you for *her.* Is he out of his goddamned mind?" Monte bit into a cracker. He was smacking loudly and enjoying the crackers like he was famished.

"Yes, as hard as this is to believe, he started fucking with Shantelle."

Monte was still smacking hard as hell on those crackers and he was annoying the hell out of Starr. "She's pretty with a nice body and all but it's a workout body. You got that 'Donk.'" Monte was grinning hard as hell with cracker crumbs all over his mouth. He was trying to describe Starr's backside with a hand motion and it made her feel uncomfortable knowing that he thought of her that way.

"Monte, I didn't come here to talk about my ass."

"Okay, Trey fucked Shantelle."

"Yeah and he moved in with her."

"No way."

"Yes."

Suddenly, there was a loud-ass commotion. Monte and Starr looked in the direction of the vending machine. Six correctional officers were tackling an inmate between the machines. One of the officers was zipping the man's pants. The man was screaming and kicking as they dragged him out from between the machines.

Monte walked over to the vending machines and spoke with another inmate to find what all the commotion was about. He came back to the table and said, "You wouldn't believe what just happened?"

"Looks like they're about to beat the hell out that dude."

"Man, he was jerking off while looking over at you. The COs caught him and tackled him. This is the second time he's done this. My homie said he did the same thing a few months ago."

"Disgusting"

"Hey, that's life in here." Monte grinned. "Now where were we?"

"Long story short, she's gone and over a million dollars is gone."

"What the fuck?"

"Yeah."

"I don't understand? How can I help? I didn't even know that he was fucking with her."

"He wants to know whatever you know about her."

"She's from Olympia, Washington."

"She told Trey she was from Seattle."

"Well, it's not too far away."

"That's where her family is?"

"Yeah and she has a sister that lives in Miami."

"Really?"

"Yeah, teaches pole dancing." Monte was in deep thought. "I can't remember the name of the studio."

"She has her own studio?"

"Yes, I remember her name though. It's Hope."

"You sure?"

"Yeah. She used to call her all the time. Her and a girl named Lori."

"Lori?"

"Where does Lori live?"

"I want to say she still lives in Olympia but she visits Atlanta a lot."

"Who does she know in Atlanta?"

"She has an aunt that lives in Cascade Park."

"Where?"

"I don't know." Monte paused then he said. "I just remembered I have her aunt's number in my cell phone. Once on one of our trips to Houston, her phone conked out and she used my phone to call her auntie and I locked it in. I will call my mama and tell her to give you the phone. It's saved under Shantelle's aunt."

"Thank you, Monte. You've been a big help."

"You're not leaving, are you?"

"Well, I do have to be going."

"Stay fifteen more minutes. This is an escape for me. I don't want to have to go back there right now."

Starr said, "I suppose I could stay for a few more minutes."

"Cool."

Starr opened up to him about the break-up and how she'd started her new business.

"You were too good for him."

"Why do you say that?"

"Look, I loved Trey, but he wasn't ready for a woman like you. He didn't appreciate you when he had you."

"I've been told that before."

"That's because it's true. Shantelle don't compare to you. She comes from a decent family, has a college degree and all that, but she ain't a go-getter. You can't make someone become a go-getter. It's either in them or its not and it's not in her but it's in you."

Starr wanted to smile, but she didn't want Monte to think she wasn't used to compliments and she damn sure didn't want him to think he had a chance with her.

"Monte, I have to be going." She stood up from the table.

Monte stood and said, "I'll walk you to the door."

As they made their way to the door, Starr caused an uproar. Damn near every inmate in the visitation room beamed in on Starr's voluptuous ass. They were all pointing, shaking their heads, and gasping for air.

"Damn, you see that son?" one inmate said.

"She got a bubble butt," another said.

"Thick as fuck!"

CHAPTER 37

IT WAS AN HOUR BEFORE SUNDOWN AS BLACK DROVE RIGHT UP TO Sasha's building in a rented white Camry. Kyrie was in the passenger's side lusting after some Instagram model that resembled an ape in the face, but she had a massive ass. Kyrie had liked every last one of her ass poses that she had posted over the last six months.

Kyrie looked up from his cell phone for one second. "Man, you sure you want to take our shit over to this chick's house? You don't even know this woman."

Black wanted to backhand Kyrie. Who the fuck was he to question Black's judgment. After all, this was the same idiot whose six-year-old son took the dope to school.

"First of all, this ain't our shit. This is me and Shamari's and secondly you don't tell me what the fuck to do. Get it?"

"I'm just saying."

"Don't say shit unless you got somewhere we can take it. I told you this is temporary until I get a place to put it."

"I got you."

"Do you really?"

Black was about to pull into the garage of Sasha's building and was looking for the FOB. He'd thought he had put it over the mirror, but he didn't see it.

"Kyrie, look in the glove compartment, see if you see the FOB."

Kyrie looked into the glove compartment but there was no FOB. Then Black spotted the FOB lying on the backseat.

"The FOB is behind you in the backseat."

Kyrie reached back and grabbed the FOB and then passed it to Black. Black entered the gate of the building. He told Kyrie to wait in the car while he took the backpack full of dope into the building. Fifteen minutes later, he remerged.

Kyrie said, "She's cool, right?"

"Quit asking motherfucking questions."

• • •

Starr called Shantelle's aunt and pretended to be her friend Lori. She asked about Shantelle's whereabouts but her auntie hadn't heard from Shantelle in weeks and had no way of contacting her. Starr was able to find out the name of the studio that Shantelle's sister owned and she relayed the information to Trey who quickly booked a flight. As he was about to board, Trey got a call from T. J.

"It's mama. She's sick and is in the hospital. Daddy, you need to come up here."

"What hospital?"

"Northside."

"I'll be right there."

Trey left the airport in a hurry. Although he could care less about Jessica, he wanted to be there for his son. When Trey arrived at the hospital, he found out that Jessica was in room 606. He took the elevator to the sixth floor and a nurse pointed him in the direction of the room. When he entered the room, he saw Jessica lying in bed and little T. J. by her bedside along with Jessica's mother Mrs. Robinson. T. J. held his mother's hand.

T. J. said, "Daddy!"

"What happened?" Trey asked.

"Food poisoning. Mom ate some potato salad from this diner up the street and it must have been old," T. J. said.

Mrs. Robinson said, "Trey, can I speak to you outside." Then she turned to T. J. and said, "Stay in here with your mother. I have to talk to your father about something."

Jessica's mother stepped outside first and Trey followed. When the door closed, she said, "Trey, we got a big problem."

"What's wrong?"

"Jessica has been really depressed lately and she tried to kill herself."

"No."

"Yeah I told T. J. it was food poisoning but the truth was she took a bunch of pills. I had to explain to him that the pills were for the food poisoning. The doctors had to pump her stomach because she really didn't want to be here."

Trey sighed, thinking that he had to get custody of his son somehow, but he knew this wasn't going to be easy. As crazy as Jessica was, T. J. loved his mother.

"Trey, you know she has a bipolar disorder?"

"Yeah, she told me. She told me she was fine as long as she was taking her meds."

"She hasn't been taking her meds. Sometimes Jessica doesn't think she needs them."

"I remember."

"She's been really depressed lately."

"Why? What's wrong?"

"Well for starters, she just had another birthday."

"I don't get it."

"She said you didn't wish her a happy birthday."

"I forgot, but I never wish her a happy birthday."

"You know how she feels about you, Trey."

"I know, but I can't be with Jessica. I have someone," Trey lied. He didn't have anyone since Shantelle was no longer in the picture and Starr was not about to take him back.

"I know you can't be with her, but that doesn't mean that she can accept it."

"I haven't been with her in a long time."

Jessica's mother looked Trey directly in the eyes and said, "Trey, I know it's not your fault."

There was a long pause and Trey said, "I know you're not blaming me."

She took hold of Trey's hand and held it. Trey gave her a hug and said, "I want to take T. J."

"Well, he wants to be with his mother."

"Not right this moment. I'm talking about getting custody."

"I think that's a good idea, Trey, but I don't know if Jessica is going to go for it."

"She's not fit to take care of him right now."

"I know, but no mother wants to be without her child."

"You take him then."

Jessica's not going to give him up to anybody without a fight, but I'll talk to her and see if I can convince her to give you custody."

Trey looked at her with serious eyes and said, "I think you're right. She's not going to let him come with me."

CHAPTER 38

BLACK PULLED INTO A B. P. STATION TO GET SOME GUM AND SOME cigarettes. Black hopped out of his car and was about to go inside when he noticed a white Dodge Challenger. A man with dreadlocks was staring at him. Black didn't recognize the man. He was about to enter the store when the man said, "Black, can I talk to you for a moment?"

Black looked at the man again and said, "Do I know you?"

"No. Not yet."

Black reached for the gun on his waist.

The man said, "Relax, Black. Nothing is going to happen." He stared up at the camera that was hanging over their heads. "I just want to talk."

"Who the fuck are you?"

Black stared at the man who was at least two inches taller than him and looked like he was a regular at the gym. Black knew he would have to kill him if they ever got into a fight.

"I'm Shakur."

"Like as in Tupac?" Black stepped away from the entrance to get out of the way of the people walking in and out of the gas station.

"Yeah, like Tupac. But Shakur is my first name."

"Okay, Shakur. How you know me?"

"You know Lani?"

"Yeah, why?"

"I've been seeing her."

"Okay"

"And I want you to stay away from her or we going to have problems."

"I love problems."

"So I'm told, but see, there's no difference between me and you."

"So that means that you know by telling me to stay the fuck away from her, it's not going to happen."

"She doesn't want to see you."

"Let her tell me."

"I'm telling you."

"You can't tell me a motherfucking thang." Black pointed at Shakur, his finger touching the tip of Shakur's nose.

Shakur slapped Black's hand down. Black put his hand on his gun. Then he glanced above at the camera aimed directly at him.

He smiled and said, "It's your lucky day, Shakur."

"No, it's yours, nigga."

Black turned and stepped inside the grocery store. He felt like he'd been punked but he knew he would have to get over it. He had more important matters to handle. He would get back to Mr. Shakur later, but right now he had money to make.

• • •

Black was down in the lobby buzzing Lani and calling her cell phone at the same time. He'd tried to use the code to enter the building but it wasn't working. It had obviously been changed.

She picked up her cell. "What's up?"

"Let me in."

"What do you want?"

"Just let me in."

She buzzed him in and three minutes later he was inside her condo. She was standing there with her hands on her hips not really wanting to say shit to him, but she knew that if she didn't let him in, there was no way he would go away. She didn't need any drama and she damn sure didn't want any.

Black got straight down to business. "Who the fuck is Shakur?"

Lani just stared at his dumb ass and wondered who in the hell did he think he was thinking that she had to answer to him.

"Okay, so you want to tell me who this nigga is? Is he your boyfriend?"

"What difference does it make?"

Black sat on the love seat without being asked to.

"Look, Lani. I don't care who you're fucking but don't be telling them lame-ass dudes to confront me. You already know that I play for keeps. I'm not going to be threatened by this clown."

"What the hell are you talking about?"

"Your little boyfriend approached me tombout, 'stay away from Lani.' "

"And you think I put him up to this?"

"I don't know if you did or you didn't, but the fact of the matter is, the nigga approached me making threats."

"I don't know anything about that." She made her way in the living room and said, "Don't get too comfortable. Actually you should leave now. You made your point. Now go."

Black laughed at her but he stood and was making his way to the door. "One of these days, Lani, you're going to find out who really loves you."

"Black, I'm just hoping I don't go to jail."

"Jail? You're worried about jail? I got you one of the best attorneys in Atlanta. You ain't going to jail, prison or none of that shit."

"You don't know that."

"Are you locked up now?"

"No, not now, but it's just a matter of time." Lani stood up and made her way over to the window and stared down into the Atlanta streets. "I've got damn near every law enforcement agency in Atlanta wanting to speak with me because of yo' dumb ass."

She started tearing up, so Black stood up and approached her trying to console her. She pushed his hands away and said, "Don't touch me."

"Don't touch you or what?"

Black reached out for her hands but they struggled a bit before he took possession of her hands. He pushed her against the window and tried to kiss her but she was still struggling to get away. He ripped her shirt and he tried to suck her nipples while she was still pinned against the pane.

"You're going to break my goddamned window, asshole!" Lani said. She kicked him in the groin area, and although she didn't hit him in the balls, she was close enough. He released her.

"What the fuck are you doing!?" screamed Lani.

"You belong to me, Lani. You're going to be with me. Fuck that dude and fuck the police."

"Black, I don't want to be with you. It's to the point where it's just too much to even be friends with you."

"So I'm not your friend, Lani?"

"I wouldn't consider you a friend."

"Why not?"

"First of all, everything you've ever did for me, you've thrown back up in my goddamned face over and over."

Black was pissed off now. It was obvious that this Shakur dude was inside her head and he'd turned her against him. "I'm going to leave now."

"Yes, you do that."

Black made his way to the door and was about to leave when he turned and said to Lani, "You tell that bitch-ass Shakur, don't ever threaten me again and you better check his background. That beaded necklace makes me think he wants dick too."

"Goodbye, Black."

"I love you, Lani."
"Whatever."

•   •   •

Black was lying in the bed with Sharee, a stripper from the Pink Pony. Sharee was a pretty, light skinned woman with long natural hair and just a handful of tits. Although her ass was average, her hair was beautiful. But her best feature was her amazing dick-sucking full lips that turned Black the fuck on. She told him her father was Dominican and she believed that she looked exotic though nobody else did. Sharee was giving Black some of the best head he'd had in a very long time and he was giving her instructions on how he liked it.

"Lick the shaft."

She complied.

"Now hum on my balls."

She hummed on his balls.

"Lick the head like you're licking a lollipop."

She complied again.

"Okay, I want to fuck your mouth."

"Huh?"

"Just lay your head down. I'm going to fuck your mouth."

"Are you some type of pervert?"

"And you're some type of stripper that wants to get paid. Now do what the fuck I say."

Sharee smiled and propped her head up on the pillow and just when Black was about to put it in her mouth, the phone rang. He glanced at it. It was Kyrie but that nigga would have to wait.

He dropped his dick in Sharee's mouth and started to hump but the phone rang again and again. Kyrie.

He grabbed the phone off the nightstand. His dick swelling in Sharee's mouth.

"What the fuck do you want?"

"Watch the eleven o'clock news. "

"For what?"

"Just watch the news tonight. I don't want to say shit over the phone, but please watch the news."

"Ok." Black glanced at this phone. It was 10:20 p.m.

Sharee removed the dick from her mouth and caught her breath and then placed it back inside. Black humped her mouth until he exploded, sending a load of cum into her mouth.

She bounced from the bed, disappeared into the bathroom and spat it all down the toilet. "You ass! I told you I didn't want you to cum in my mouth, Black."

"But you want my money?"

"What does that mean?"

"That means that you are mine for the night."

"Fuck you, Black!"

"So this is the thanks I get? I help you with your bills and you talk shit to me?"

"Help me with my bills?" Sharee's hands rested on her hips like she was waiting for an explanation. "You asked me to come home with you and you would pay me."

"And you're going to use it for your bills."

"Ok. Now I get it, but you're talking like you give me loads of cash to pay my bills. Bottom line, Black, I've been knowing you for almost five years and you're not going to do shit if it don't benefit you."

Black threw a handful of bills and said, "Get the fuck out!"

"You don't tell me what the fuck to do." She kneeled down to scoop the bills up off the floor.

Black made his way to the other side of the bed and took hold of her arm. He picked up his pants and shirt that were lying on the floor and dragged her out of the room, kicking and screaming. Although, she was struggling to get away from him, he was too strong for her.

"I need to get my clothes, you black motherfucker!"

Black just ignored her ass and dragged her by that long beautiful head of hair
across his shiny hardwood floors.

"I didn't even get to pick up my money, Black! Let me go! Let me go!"

Finally he made his way to the door and pushed her outside. She stumbled down the steps and fell on her bare ass. She was wearing only a thong and it was cold enough outside that you could see your breath. He tossed her another fistful of bills and said, "You disrespectful bitch."

Black closed the door and went back inside. It was almost time for the eleven p.m. news. He hated watching the news. It killed his spirits and he hated to see other criminals getting arrested. Not that he particularly cared about them, but seeing them get arrested often made him second guess himself. He decided not to watch. He called Kyrie.

"Did you see the news?"

"No."

"Why not?"

"You know how I feel about the news. What's so goddamned important that I have to see?"

"Twylla McDonell OD'd."

"Who the fuck is that?"

"Twenty-eight-year-old movie star."

"Okay she OD'd. Rest in peace. What the fuck does that have to do with me?"

There was a long pause before Kyrie said, "She OD'd off some heroin called Pretty Hurts."

"Damn, that's fucked up."

Black wouldn't speak any further over the phone. He told Kyrie he would call him back. He terminated the call and then the doorbell rang. Black grabbed Sharee's shoes and marched to the front door. He'd throw the bitch her clothes and shoes and slam the door in her goddamned face. When he opened the door there were two cops standing outside.

"Officers, can I help you?" Black asked in his best white man's voice. At that moment he was no longer a big drug dealer, but a legitimate businessman and he would try his best to sound like one.

Sharee stood behind them barefoot, covered in a towel that one of the officer's had provided. She said, "That's his black ugly ass, officer."

One of the officers turned and said, "I'm going to need for you to keep quiet."

"Do you know this woman?"

"Yes."

"She said you assaulted her."

"All I did was grab her and showed her to the door."

"He dragged me across his floor, picked me up and threw me outside. I hurt my back and my
legs." Sharee pointed to some fresh scars and bruises on her legs.

"She's lying," Black said.

The officer said, "Maybe she is, but that will be for the court to decide."

"The court?"

"Yes, you're under arrest for domestic violence."

"What the fuck?"

"Put on your shoes and come with us."

"Can I call my lawyer?"

"You'll get to use the phone when you get downtown. We can do this one of two ways, Mr. Massey. You can go get your shoes or we can take you downtown without shoes."

"Take his black ass downtown without shoes. He didn't care if I had shoes on or not," Sharee said.

One of the officers turned to Sharee and said, "One more word out of you and you're going downtown too. Is that understood?"

Sharee was quiet.

Black said, "I'll go get my shoes."

He disappeared into the bedroom to get his shoes. He sent a text to Rashida: *On my way to jail. Nothing serious tho. Call you later.*

Black came back to the porch. The officers were still awaiting him.

"Man, you ain't gonna put them cuffs on me are you?" Black said.

"Afraid we have to do it, Mr. Massey. I won't put them on tightly though."

The officers cuffed Black and led him away in the patrol car.

CHAPTER 39

RASHIDA BONDED BLACK OUT AND DROVE HIM HOME FROM JAIL. HE kissed his sister and ran inside the house. He picked his cell phone up from the night stand and saw that he had twenty-four missed calls. Most of them were from Shamari and a few of them were from Kyrie. He called Shamari back right away.

"Damn man, why haven't you been picking up your phone?"

"I've been in jail."

"Jail?"

"Nothing serious though. I threw this chick out of my house and she said that I hit her."

"Look, I'm coming over."

"Alright."

The doorbell rang. Black ran to the door and looked outside and saw Kyrie's car. He looked through the peephole to confirm it was Kyrie and then opened the door.

"I came over after we spoke last night."

"I went to jail last night, bruh. Long story short, I had Sharee over from the Pink Pony and she said I assaulted her. I did throw her ass out butt naked but the police didn't want to hear shit I had to say."

"Look, man. No more fucking rat poison."

"Why?"

"Are you out of yo' goddamned mind? You know ever since that movie star died, that's all anyone has been talking about. We can't keep doing it, bruh. I won't be a part of it."

Black shot Kyrie a look of disgust. "You getting soft on me?"

"It's not about getting soft. It's about staying my ass out of prison. You know I already got a case. Have you forgotten about that?"

"You have one of the best attorneys in Atlanta, that's what he gets paid for."

"Easy for you to say. You're not the one that has a charge."

"Look, I don't give a fuck about a motherfucking drug charge. That's what I pay my lawyers for," Black said. He paused then sat on the sofa. The doorbell rang and Black said, "Open the door for Shamari."

When Kyrie opened the door, Shamari walked right past his ass as he spotted Black sitting on the sofa and punched him in his motherfucking jaw. "Nigga, you said no more rat poison."

Black scooped Shamari up and rammed him into the wall, knocking the wind out of him. Black was about to punch Shamari in the face when Shamari kneed Black in the stomach. Shamari and Black held each other—neither man having the clear advantage.

Shamari said, "What the fuck are you thinking, man? Are you that motherfucking greedy for money?"

Black said, "Get yo' goddamned hands off me before I kill you up in here, nigga."

Kyrie wedged himself between the two men. Black swung a wild haymaker and barely missed Shamari's head.

"Wait till I come back." Black was on his way to his bedroom when Shamari drew his gun. A silver .380. He cocked it and Black froze.

"Shoot me. I've been shot before. But I'm telling you now, Shamari, if you shoot me, you better kill me because I ain't playing no games with you."

Shamari's face was serious as hell. "Let's talk."

"Talk then."

Shamari lowered his gun.

"Man, I want out."

"I thought we said we were going to do one more run?"

Shamari laughed and said, "I thought we said that you weren't going to use rat poison again."

"I made a mistake."

"That wasn't a mistake, homie. You knew what the fuck you were doing."

"You want out?"

"That's what I said."

"We still have a lot of dope to sell."

"Well, as soon as you sell that shit, I want my cut and I want the fuck out."

Kyrie interjected, "I don't know how you're going to sell anything now anyway. Whoever sells anything with the Pretty Hurts stamp on it is going to get buried underneath the prison, now that Twyla McDonald has died."

Black said, "He's right. We're going to have to wait for a minute, but you'll get your money and we'll split your partner's money."

Kyrie looked confused. He never knew they had another partner and neither man wanted to let him in on it.

Shamari extended his hand and they shook. Black said, "You lucky I like yo' ass, or I would've killed you."

"We would have been two dead motherfuckers in here."

They all laughed.

•   •   •

Trey flew to Miami and met with Shantelle's sister. She'd told him that she hadn't seen or spoken to Shantelle in over a week. Trey had a feeling that the sister knew more than she was letting on, but there was no way he could prove it. Afterwards he flew to Houston to try to catch up with his connect, Q. Trey hadn't been in contact with Q since Trey had left Houston with the product he'd copped from Q last time. He showed up at Q's building unannounced.

When Q opened the door, he threw Trey a pair of shorts and said, "Put these on."

Trey looked at him like he was out of his fucking mind.

"I need to know that you're okay."

"You think I'm wired?"

"I don't know."

Trey was looking at Q like he wanted to slap the fuck out of him but finally he grabbed the shorts.

Q said, "I need you to leave your watch in the bathroom and take the battery out of your cell phone."

"What?"

"Look, Trey, do what I said or get the fuck out of my house."

Trey laughed at this silly motherfucker and disappeared into the bathroom. He returned wearing the shorts that Q had provided.

Q said. "What happened, Trey?"

"What do you mean?"

"How did you get pulled over with ten kilos and not go to jail?"

"You kidding, right?"

Q's face was serious as hell. Not a hint of a smile.

"You bragged about how good you can conceal dope in the car. How you don't put it in the door panels no more and how nobody can find the dope that you conceal and you question me about how I didn't go to jail? This means to me that you don't have faith in your own work."

"I'm just asking."

"He never searched the car."

"Why didn't he search the car? They search everything in Louisiana. How did you get away?"

"He took the money and let me go. That's the truth."

Q studied Trey's face, trying to decide if he was telling the truth. Finally, he said, "The same thing happened to my brother when he was headed to North Carolina."

"You believe me?"

"I do."

"Can I take these stupid-ass shorts off?"

Q laughed and Trey disappeared into the bathroom. He came back out to find Q outside on the balcony smoking a Cuban cigar. He offered Trey one but when Trey declined, Q offered him a drink.

Trey wasn't much of a drinker but he had a Hennessy and Coke.

They stood side by side looking out at the city of Houston.

"So what brings you here, Trey? Don't tell me you came all the way down here just to chat."

"I knew what you were thinking and I'm disappointed that you thought that about me. Man, we've known each other too long."

Q blew out a big cloud of cigar smoke. "You can't blame a man for being careful, can you?"

"No, I suppose not."

"Where is your girlfriend?"

"She ran off with a million dollars."

"So, she's dead?"

"No."

"What the fuck you mean no?"

"I don't know where she is."

"Don't you think you should be finding her?"

"I've been looking."

"Trey, let me tell you something about life that I learned a long time ago. You have to stick to your kind."

Trey looked at Q like he'd lost his mind. Did he think Shantelle was another race?

"What I mean by your own kind, Trey, is somebody from the street like yourself. The minute I laid eyes on that bitch, I knew she wouldn't be with you if you didn't have money. And that's fine if you're going to just stick your dick in her, but she was not meant to be with you."

"I know that now."

"That was a million dollar lesson." Q laughed.

Trey sipped his drink. He didn't respond to Q who had made him feel like a goddamned fool, but what he said was true. Shantelle was never his woman and it was unfortunate that he'd left Starr for essentially what amounted to be some average pussy.

"Where is Starr?"

"I told you that we're not together."

"You need to make that right. I've always told you Starr is a good woman. A real woman. You need her."

"I do need her and I need you."

Q turned and made eye contact with Trey. "You're not broke?"

"I'm not. I have money but I just lost a lot. I want to get back to work."

"Look, Trey, you need to slow it down right now. You just got pulled over by the police."

"A crooked officer."

"Who's to say he won't pull you over again?"

"I'll get somebody else to bring the work back to Atlanta."

"What if they pull them over?" Q turned to Trey and said, "Trey, you know I love you like a brother, but I think you should just chill for a while."

"Chill? That's easy for you to say, you're not the one going broke."

Q looked Trey directly in his eyes and said, "Now, tell me that you don't have at least a million dollars and I'll give you whatever you want."

Trey looked away.

Q said, "A million dollars is hardly broke."

"I see your point."

"You need to find the woman that took your money and most of all make things right with Starr." Q paused and said, "I wish I had a woman like Starr."

"I've seen some of the women you've been around. They are beautiful."

"So is Starr, but not only is Starr beautiful on the outside. She has a beautiful soul. It's easy for me to walk out of here and go to the Galleria and pick up ten gold diggers looking for a free ride, but it's hard for me to pick up somebody like Starr. Somebody that's got my back. If you went to prison, do you think Starr would leave you?"

"No."

"Do you think she would fuck somebody else?"

"Absolutely not."

"You see my point?"

"I do."

"Make things right with her, Trey. You need to get her back. You must get her back."

"She doesn't want to be with me."

"Trey, don't take no for an answer. This is a once in a lifetime woman. You will spend the rest of your life trying to find somebody like her."

"You sound like you've had a woman like that."

Q puffed his cigar. "I did and I absolutely did not do right by her."

"What happened?"

"Got a hoe pregnant with twins. I love my twins but I hate their mother."

"How do you stay faithful to one woman?"

"I haven't figured that out either. I'm not perfect. But I'll never disrespect home. Never. That means when I find my woman, I'll never get another woman pregnant and I'll always come home at night and treat her like a queen because she is."

Trey respected Q's opinion. Though Q was a couple of years older than

Trey, he was like a big brother to him and he loved him.

Q said, "Go back to Atlanta and get your woman back. Take her on a vacation and when you get back, I'll make it right. I'll send you thirty kilos and I will personally have them delivered to Atlanta."

• • •

It was six p.m. and Brooke had gone for the day. Starr was about to lock up the showroom when she heard tapping on the front door. She looked up to see Trey. She made her way over to the front door and let him in.

"Hey, what brings you here, I thought you were in Florida."

"I went to Florida then to Houston and now I'm here."

"You saw Q?"

"I did. He's doing good and told me to tell you hey. He likes you a lot."

"I like Q too. He's always been good people. He's about his business, but he's a good dude. A fair dude. Why did you go down there? Business?"

"Well, I got pulled over about a month ago with a gang of dope. The police took a hundred thousand dollars from me but didn't search the car."

"I didn't know that."

"Nobody knew."

"Why were you transporting cocaine?"

"Being stupid. I guess when you took that money to start your business and I'd lost some more money, it put me in panic mode."

"Why? You still had plenty of money."

"I don't know, Bae. Guess I was just greedy."

She noticed that he'd called her Bae. She didn't want to admit it, but she kind of liked it.

"Trey, that's just plain out greed. I took money to start my business and you lost another hundred thousand. You lost money with Monte and Shantelle ran off with a lot of money but you still have a lot of money by most people's standards. Is money all that's important to you?"

"No. This has made me realize that there's more to the world than money. I want to do right by my son, my mother, and most of all by you."

"Me?"

"Yeah, Starr." He dropped to his knees as if he was about to beg something of her and she said, "Trey, please get off your goddamned knees."

He stood and locked eyes with her. "I want to do right by you."

"I told you, Trey. There is no you and me."

He took her hand and said, "I know you did, but I'm willing to do whatever it is to make this right. I'll give you the codes to the phones. I'll let you keep my money. I'll come in every night at a certain time that you determine. I don't want to be without you, Starr. You're my once in a lifetime."

"Your once in a lifetime. Sounds like an R&B song." She was laughing her ass off.

"Can you say you don't miss me?"

She turned away from him. She couldn't look him in the eyes and admit she didn't miss him.

"So you miss me?"

"I miss you every day, Trey. I think about, what could have happened. What should have happened. I miss you so, so much."

"Look, I'm not asking you to accept me back. I know I gotta earn your trust."

She turned and faced him and said, "Trey, all these things—you've said them

before. What is going to make this time different?"

"Just give me an opportunity. Just keep an open mind."

"I'll try."

He approached her and put his hands around her and said, "Don't try! Do it. Let's go on a vacation."

She smiled and said, "Man, you've changed. Big time."

"Yeah, I'm not going to live forever and neither are you. I want to get married and have more kids."

"No more hustling?"

There was a long pause before he said, "I'm taking a break."

This is not the answer Starr wanted to hear. Though she didn't know if she would take Trey back, she knew she didn't want to bring children in this world with a man who was still hustling. She remembered when her father had gone to prison when she was just a little girl.

"Let's go on a two-week vacation."

"I can't get away for two weeks, I have to work. I can't even go for one week."

"Can we go somewhere for four days?"

"Yes. Where?"

"Mexico."

"When?"

"This weekend. We can leave Thursday and come back Monday."

"Make it Tuesday. I can get Brooke to run the place on Monday because it's slow."

Starr was smiling hard as hell. She still didn't know if she was going to take Trey back, but she liked the man he was becoming. She just wished he'd come to this realization a lot earlier. Years earlier.

CHAPTER 40

JADA WAS GULPING DOWN THE LAST OF HER WHITE WINE WHEN Shamari said, "I'm not giving him a goddamned thing."

Jada stood with her hands on her hips in disbelief. She couldn't believe that Shamari would say that he wasn't paying Craig.

"You do realize how bad it can get if we don't give the man the money you promised?"

"I'm wanted for conspiring to kill a federal informant. It can't get much worse than that for me."

"What about Imani's body? Have you forgotten about the goddamned body?"

"He killed her. Not me. I'm not a plastic surgeon."

'But he's white. He knows too much, Shamari. Who do you think they're going to believe?"

"I'm not giving him shit, Jada. Not a goddamned thing. Zilch."

"Shamari, he gave you a new face, remember?" She poured another glass of white zinfandel and sipped it. "He knows too much about it. We have to at least give him his money back."

"Jada, he owes us this money."

"Explain to me why he owes us any money, Shamari. Ok, he didn't tell us how he was getting the dope back and Imani died."

"He owes me for getting rid of the body."

"Ok."

"So he owes us."

"What I'm trying to tell you is, he'll bring us all down. He's a bitch, Shamari. He's not like us."

Shamari's face became serious. "Okay, well we kill him then."

"Okay, you want to kill everybody now, Black is rubbing off on you."

"I'm not responsible for Imani, Jada; your friend is."

"But you wanted Don dead and that's why you're on the run in the first place."

Jada poured more wine and thought about the day that Shamari had planned the hit on Don. How it didn't go right and one thing led to another and suddenly their nice little life had spiraled completely out of control.

"True."

Jada looked scared. She looked him dead in the eyes and said, "Bae, do it for me. I'm right in the middle of this shit."

Shamari was weak for Jada and she was the last person that he ever wanted anything to happen to.

"Jada, I'll give him back what he gave us but not a dime more."

She hugged him and they kissed as she grabbed his ass.

•　　•　　•

Lani received a call from her attorney and he told her to meet him at his office right away. Lani drove right over. The receptionist pointed her in the direction of Mr. Gilliam's office. Gilliam was on the phone when Lani walked in. He pointed to a chair right across from his desk then said to the person on the other end of the phone, "Hey, I have a client in my office, I'll call you back." He terminated the call and gave her a smile but the man was so goddamned serious looking, even his smiles were devoid of personality. "Hey, Ms. Miller, it's a pleasure to see you again."

"Same here."

"Homeland Security called me the other day inquiring about you."

"They came by my house a few weeks ago."

"Really?"

"Wanted to know about my ex."

"And you told them?"

"I didn't tell them anything."

"Good. I hear this ex is pretty dangerous and I don't want to put you in any kind of danger."

"Yeah, but he's done a lot for me and my family."

Gilliam nodded his head.

"So, what did they want?" Lani asked.

"They wanted to know if you would give a statement."

"No. Didn't you just say that you didn't want to put me in danger?"

"Well, it's not a statement that's going to implicate him."

"What kind of statement?"

"Chris Jones and Tyrann almost got into a fight at Philips Arena, right?"

"Yeah, how'd you know?"

"Somebody else is telling about their history."

"So what do you need from me?"

"They're going to ask you if they were about to fight, and you just say yes."

"That's it?"

"That's it."

"What do I get in return?"

"Freedom."

"So they're not going to ask me about drugs, guns or murder?"

"Do you know about drugs, guns, or murder?"

"No."

"Well, keep it that way."

"So what is this statement going to prove?"

"It's just going to prove that they were going to fight and that they didn't like each other."

"I don't know about this."

"Look, Tyrann's in trouble already, and it's just a matter of time before they get him."

"He's paying you for me."

"But you're my client. My obligation is to you."

"I make this one statement about the fight and I won't have to talk about anything else?"

"That's it."

"How did you get them to agree to this?"

"I'm the best attorney in Atlanta."

"I thought Joey Turch was?"

"I was Joey's professor."

"Interesting. So when do we meet with them?"

"Right now. You can ride over with me."

"Okay."

The Department of Homeland Security building was located in a medical business park in Marrietta. It was very discreet so no one would imagine that they were located there. Even though Lani was confirming a fight that they obviously already knew about, she felt disloyal to Black because she knew that the white man was trying to bring him down. The attorney, Gilliam, hopped out of the car first, but Lani was hesitant.

Finally he said to her, "I know this is hard."

"You can't even imagine."

"You loved him once."

"As crazy as this sounds, I still think I love him."

"Listen, it will be over before you know it, and you can go on with your life."

"And what's going to happen to Tyrann?"

"I don't know."

Lani finally forced herself to exit the car and follow Gilliam to the building entrance.

He turned to her and said, "They're on the sixth floor."

"Sounds like you've been here before."

"I have a time or two. The last time I was representing someone with Al-Qaeda ties."

"Wow. I guess I'm a small fish compared to him."

"Most clients are."

As they approached the elevator, Lani said, "I can't do it."

"What do you mean you can't do it?"

"I love Black. Not romantically, but I do have love for him."

The attorney took a deep breath and said, "Are you serious?"

"Yes, I'm sorry but I can't do it."

"You have to."

"Why do I have to?"

"They have a lot of information on Tyrann. They are going to get him and I just don't want you to get caught up in it. Do you want to do time?"

"No, of course not. Who would want to do time?"

"Listen, let's go up there and it will be over before you know it."

"I thought you were a good lawyer."

"I am."

"Well, a lawyer's job is to fight."

"I am fighting—for your life. You'll thank me in the end. I promise you."

Lani reluctantly boarded the elevator and they took it to the sixth floor and entered the office. Gilliam told the receptionist who they were and who they came to see. A moment later, they were escorted to an office in the back and Lani recognized the same two agents that were there before. David Carroll and Scott Chandler who was looking even more like a movie star. He was toned and tanned like he'd been vacationing and he'd had his teeth whitened. Lani thought goddamn this white man was fine. They offered her a seat.

David Carroll said, "Good to see you, Lani. I'm glad you changed your mind."

The movie star was smiling with those white-ass teeth said, "You're doing the right thing, that's for sure."

Lani was sitting there playing with her phone trying her best not to think about what was happening around her. She was on Instagram laughing at the thirsty-ass niggas' comments on Jada's pictures.

Gilliam said, "Can we start the interview?"

David Carroll retrieved a yellow legal pad and a voice recorder. He spoke into the recorder announcing the date and name of the interviewee.

Lani's heart was pounding so hard that she had to take a deep breath to calm herself down. She knew the recorder was rolling and everything that she said from that point on would be on record.

The movie star said, "How long have you know Tyrann?"

Lani said, "I don't know. Maybe eight or nine years."

David Carroll said, "And were you in a relationship with him the whole time?"

Lani said, "No."

Agent Carroll scribbled on that pad and this made her even more nervous. What if Black saw this interview? Besides she was there to tell about a fight. What the fuck did this have to do with a fight?

Chandler said, "So when did you realize he was a drug dealer?"

Lani turned to Gilliam who was staring at the ceiling like he didn't hear the goddamn question.

Lani nudged him with her elbow and he said, "Answer the question as truthful as possible."

Lani said, "I want to speak to my attorney alone."

Gilliam stood and excused himself as he exited into the hallway. Lani followed and when the door was closed, Lani said, "What the fuck was that about?"

"That was about saving your life."

"What do you mean, saving my life? You told me that they were going to ask about a fight."

"Well, they are going to ask you about the fight, among other things."

"Look, I'm not here to snitch on Black. I can't do it and I won't do it. As much as I hate him, I can't do that. Do you know I will get killed for doing something like that? I guess you don't give a fuck, do you, Mr. Gilliam?

"What are you saying, Ms. Miller?"

"I want to end this interview."

Gilliam shook his head. "Let me go in and tell them that we won't be doing the interview."

"Do whatever it is you need to do."

Lani took the elevator down to the lobby. It was a very nice day outside and she wanted to enjoy the sunshine. She leaned against the building when she shot Shakur a text message: *Hey.*

Shakur: *Hey, You.*

Lani: *Wyd?*

Shakur: *The gym.*

Lani: *Keeping that body tight for me?*

Shakur: *Of course.*

Lani: *:-) :-)*

Lani was about to shoot him another text when a very familiar face exited the building. She made eye contact with the man and he said, "Lani."

"Kyrie."

"What are you doing here?"

"Waiting on someone, and you?"

There was a long silence as Kyrie was trying to think of an excuse to be in the building. He was sure that she knew that he was there to talk to the Homeland Security investigators. Somehow he felt that she'd figured it out, but why in the hell was she there? He assumed that she was there to give an interview with the investigators as well. She had to be snitching too.

Finally he said, "I was in a car accident and I had to go see a chiropractor." He'd passed a chiropractor's office in the building on the way to the Department of Homeland Security's office.

"I hope you're okay."

"I am." Then he looked at his watch and said, "I have to go. Goodbye. Good seeing you, Lani."

"Same to you."

Kyrie hurried away really fast and Lani mumbled, "I can't believe Kyrie is snitching on Black."

● ● ●

Kyrie walked around the corner and then waited until he saw Lani leave. Once she was gone, he made his way back up to the Department of Homeland Security's building. When Kyrie marched into David Carroll's office, the first thing he said was, "Why in the hell did you ask me to come up here when you knew that Lani was going to be here."

The movie star said, "Her attorney didn't confirm she was coming until about an hour ago."

"Why didn't you let me know that she was coming?"

David Carroll said, "Is there a problem?"

Kyrie said, "You goddamned right there is a problem. If Black finds out that I'm snitching, I'm a dead man. He'll kill my family."

"If you do what we tell you to do, Black will never have a chance to kill anybody."

Kyrie said, "No way I'm testifying on him. I told you, no way I'm testifying before the grand jury. He'll kill me. I'm a dead man walking."

The movie star was grinning and Kyrie didn't see a goddamned thing funny. "If Lani tells Black that you were here, you're dead anyway. But don't worry, she's not going to say anything."

Kyrie said, "How can you be so sure of that?" His knee was trembling because he was nervous. He'd tried to stop it from moving but he couldn't. He made eye contact with both of the agents and said, "Is Lani cooperating?"

"Maybe. Maybe not."

Kyrie said, "That means that she is. Is that why she's here?"

"Look, we can't tell you what she is or isn't doing. That's confidential."

David Carroll said, "But what we can tell you is that the last one to the party is going to get the most time."

"What the hell is that supposed to mean?"

"It means that you need to be as helpful as you can, so you can get the lighter sentence. Perhaps no prison time at all."

Kyrie dropped his head. He knew that if Black ever caught a whiff that he was talking to the Feds, he'd be dead, his family, even his children. He'd hated that Lani had seen him. Even if she was cooperating, there was still a chance that Black would still find out that he was snitching.

"Fuck!" he said.

CHAPTER 41

SOFT R&B PLAYED AS LANI LAY TOPLESS ON THE SOFA. SHE WORE A white thong and her ass looked absolutely brilliant to Shakur. And she was poking it out as if she wanted him to dive on top of her. Her hair flowed midway down her back and he just stood there in awe.

"Don't just stand there. Come over, but before you come, go into the bathroom and get the baby oil from the sink so you can massage my ass."

"An ass massage?"

She laughed and said, "You've never done that before?"

"No, but I'm game for it." He disappeared into the bathroom and reemerged with the baby oil. He kept his eyes on her amazing ass until the blood had rushed to the head of his dick and it was hard for him to walk. His dick wanted to breathe. It needed to be unleashed. He dropped his pants and removed his shirt revealing his eight pack. He was still holding on to the baby oil. She looked up at him and she giggled when she saw how hard his dick was.

"Looks like we woke somebody up."

He glanced at his penis. "We did. You know he has a mind of his own."

"Do you have a name for him?"

"Actually I do."

"What's his name?"

"Tango."

"Tango? I don't like that name. It's not masculine enough. I like names like Rambo or Ram Rod or Big Pun."

He was laughing his ass off, "So you like it rough?"

"Depends."

"On what?"

She said, "I need you to quit talking and bring Tango over here and give me an ass massage. Can you do that, Mr. Shakur?"

"I can."

She admired that sexy-ass body and those lips as he made his way over to her. He poured oil on her calves and massaged it in and then he moved up to her thighs. She was moaning before he aimed the bottle at her ass cheeks and the oil spewed all over that luscious ass. He massaged it in, cupping her ass with both hands and pulling that thong further up her ass crack.

Tango was struggling free and she could feel it throbbing. She grabbed Shakur's cock and stroked him a little, but she stopped because her arm was in an awkward position.

Shakur unleashed Tango and she smiled. He smacked Tango against her ass cheeks. His stiff dick turned her the fuck on. There was a river of water between her legs and she could tell with each smack against her ass that it was turning him on too. Pre-cum seeped from Tango.

He kept cupping and palming her ass and more than that, admiring it. That shiny ass just looked wonderful. His cell phone was on the table and he grabbed it and took a picture of it.

She smiled and said, "No face shots or videos."

"I would never disrespect you like that, my queen."

She smiled. She was growing to like this man. He was too good to be true.

He set the phone back down and began massaging her ass again. Then he propped her ass up and wedged a pillow beneath her stomach and pulled her thong aside so he could lick her pussy from behind.

"Damn, baby. You feel so good," Lani said.

He sucked her pussy and she loved every minute of it. She just wished that she wasn't on her stomach, so she could see those sexy ass lips put in work.

"I love this," she said.

"You do?"

"Yes."

He kept licking and sucking her clit.

"Tell me where you like it," Shakur said as he licked her clit. "You like that?"

She didn't respond the way he wanted. He knew she liked it but it wasn't her spot. So he licked just above the vaginal opening. He knew from experience that some women liked the clitoris licked and others wanted the spot above the opening. He was a skilled lover and he planned to lick her entire body until he knew what was going to turn her on.

He kept licking above the opening and she said, "Right there, Daddy. Right motherfucking there."

"You like that?"

"I love this shit, Daddy. Keep licking."

He kept working. He prided himself on his oral abilities.

He kept squeezing that pretty ass of hers. He licked her ass crack and she tried to run but he yanked her back with one hand and kept licking her ass.

"Damn, Daddy. You are so good."

"I want to please you."

"I need Tango, Daddy."

"And Tango needs you."

He fingered her for a few moments before entering her from the back. They were now doggy-style and she was looking back at him as he drilled her pussy.

His hands were around her tiny-ass waist and she was trying her best to run from his dick but he said, "Don't you go nowhere. You said you were a big girl. Now you're going to have to sit there and take it."

"I want it."

"Well act like it."

"I love this dick."

"Tell me you love it."

"I love it."

"Call Tango by his first name."

"Oh, Tango, I love you."

"Say it again."

"I love you, Tango."

He thrust a few more time but he pulled out just before exploding in the crack of her ass.

An hour later, they were cuddling in her bed. *Real Housewives of Atlanta* was playing on Hulu. His arms wrapped around her and she felt safe. At that moment she didn't think anybody could harm her. Not Black, not Mike, not anybody. She turned and kissed him and said, "So, was it what you thought it would be?"

"What?"

"The sex."

"The sex was more than I thought it would be."

She smiled. "Really?"

"Yes."

"You didn't think I had the goods?"

"No, it's not that. I just didn't think you would be as freaky as you are."

"Well, I am for some people. Just depends if you know how to bring it out of me."

"Whatever! I think you're just a freak."

She laughed. "Maybe I am. Is that a bad thing?"

"Hell no!"

"You're so good at pleasing. How do you know so much about a woman's body?"

"I've had a few women in my day."

"I think you've had more than a few." She paused and then said, "You listen, and you ask me what I want and mean it."

"You've never had guys ask you what you wanted?"

"I have, but I can tell that they don't mean it. You were really concerned about pleasing me."

"I was."

She ran her fingers through his locks and said, "I want to thank you for being here. I was not feeling very good today. Too much on my mind."

"Tell me."

"Tell you what?"

"What's wrong? What's on your mind?"

She turned away from him and scooted her butt against him and he draped his arms back around her. Tango woke up again. He was poking her in her back. She wanted him back inside her.

"Tell me what's on your mind. What happened?"

"My lawyer called me today."

"And said what?"

"He said the Department of Homeland Security wanted to meet with me."

"The Feds?"

"Yeah"

"What did they want?"

"Well, it's what my lawyer called a sweetheart deal."

"They wanted you to talk?"

"Well, they didn't want me to testify on Black, but they wanted me to confirm that he'd been in a fight with Chris at the Hawks game."

"That's it?"

"That's it"

"Damn, they must have the evidence they need to get Black."

"I think they do. I'm sure they do."

"So did you go and confirm what they wanted you to confirm?"

She turned to him and said." I just couldn't bring myself to do it, besides they wanted to know a lot more about Black than a fight at the Hawk's game. I love Black."

Shakur looked sad.

She ran her fingers through his locks again. "I'm not in love with him. I will never be in love with him. I think I'm falling for you, but Black and I have history."

"Are you willing to cut him off if we get together?"

"As far as I am concerned, he's already cut off. I'm through with him."

Shakur smiled. There was a long silence. Lani stroked Tango and Shakur said, "Lani, you have a big heart. Bigger than most niggas."

Lani smiled and said, "You have a very big dick. Bigger than most niggas."

They laughed their asses off and she took Tango deep in her mouth.

CHAPTER 42

WHEN BLACK ENTERED SASHA'S APARTMENT, SHE WAS STANDING IN the kitchen with her hands on her hips. When she spotted him, she made her way into the living room.

"Hey, babe," she said as she leaned into him and kissed him.

"Looking good today."

She smiled. "You always say that."

Today she knew he was telling the truth. She wore a pencil skirt that made her waist look extra small though it mashed her ass in a bit. It was a fuchsia color and it looked amazing against her brown skin.

She said, "I've been waiting on you."

"Really? How did you know I would come today?"

"I didn't know, but I knew you would come eventually. I have something that belongs to you."

He laughed. "You got that right."

"So when are you going to get this apartment that you were talking about?"

"I need at least another week. Why? Are you putting me out?"

"No." She looked reflective.

"What's wrong?"

She turned and was making her way back into the kitchen. Black glanced at her ass and it looked good to him in that outfit, but it was her skinny heels that were really turning him on.

"Tell me what's wrong."

"I didn't know that I was storing deadly heroin in my house."

"Huh?"

"Pretty Hurts. The stuff Twyla McDonald OD'd off."

"You went into my package?"

"Look, I'm sorry, but I had to know what was in my house."

"Do you want me to find somewhere else to take it?"

"No. You can leave it here...No, get it out of my house. Oh, leave it here," she said. She took a seat at the bar and then said, "Oh my God. What do you want me to say? I mean somebody has OD'd off this stuff and my daddy is the mayor."

"I'll take it with me." He headed to the room where the work was but she bounced from the barstool and cut him off before he reached the bedroom door. She wrapped her arms around him and said, "Look, I want to help you."

He stared in her eyes and said, "You really don't have to do this."

"I know I don't, but I want to. You can leave it here as long as you want."

"Why are you doing this?"

"Like I said, I want to help you and in the process you can help me."

"The franchise."

"Look, this is going to help you too. How long do you think you can do this?"

"Not very long."

"Exactly. But we need to get moving. I need to meet with your sister and we need to establish this partnership. And you need to get out of the dope business."

"I know."

"It's not a problem. Not at all. Nobody knows it's here but me and you right?"

"Right." Black said thinking about Kyrie. Kyrie knew the building but he didn't know which apartment. Then Black said, "What about your boyfriend?"

"He's a non-factor."

"What the fuck is going on with you and your boyfriend? How can you let another dude have access to your home and you have a boyfriend?"

"Look, I can handle him and don't worry about him. I'm not asking you about your women."

"What women?"

"For starters, the woman that you assaulted the other day."

"How did you know about that? And I never assaulted anybody. I just kicked her out of my house. Again, how did you know about that?"

"Looked it up online."

"Damn! You got stalker tendencies."

"No. I wanted to know what was in my house, so I found out. And I wanted to know about the man that left the shit in my house, so I found out."

"Ok, fair enough. Now can you step aside, so I can get my stash?"

She stepped aside.

• • •

Las Ventanas Al Paraiso was an amazing resort with an incredible view of the Pacific Ocean. Starr and Trey lay in hammocks and sipped mixed drinks from coconuts. Starr wore a light pink bikini that looked amazing against her tanned skin. Trey had to tell a few of the locals to 'Fuck off' because they had been following her. Starr sipped her drink and said, "I could get used to this life."

"Me too."

She looked at him and said, "Trey, you never like to enjoy life."

"All that is about to change. I have three people I have to live for. That's you, my son, and my mother , in that order."

"I'm before your mother?"

"Before anybody else."

"I'm flattered. If only it were true."

"I'm serious. You're before everybody. I love you, Starr, and I want to spend the rest of my life with you."

"Trey, I love you too but I'm not willing to commit to you just yet."

"I can understand that."

"I need you to prove yourself."

"Look, I'm not going to say I fucked up. You know that, and I sound like a broken record saying it. But I'll prove myself."

"Why can't you just be with one woman?"

"Look, I never intended to get caught up with that woman."

"How about you should have never intended to cheat in the first place? You had everything at home."

"I never loved her."

"Is that supposed to make me feel better?"

Trey reached across the table, grabbed her hand and said, "We're on vacation. Let's not talk about the past. I know I got a lot of work to do and I intend to do it."

Later that evening, Trey and Starr were sitting in a restaurant. Trey looked at Starr and thought she looked fucking amazing. He reached out and grabbed her hand then he placed a ring on her finger.

"Trey, what are you doing?" Starr recognized the gigantic ring. This was the ring that he'd brought to the W that day he asked her to marry him. The one he'd gotten from Jesus. "I thought I told you to take this ring back?"

"I never took it back. I always felt that you were going to come around."

"What do you mean, come around?"

Trey kneeled and everybody in the restaurant turned their attention to them. Trey said, "Will you marry me?"

Starr covered her face and there was a long silence.

A white man at the next table said, "Don't just leave that man hanging. Say Yes."

She didn't want to embarrass him so she said, "Yes."

The restaurant went wild cheering and whistling.

The man who had yelled from the next table had the waitress bring them the most expensive bottle of champagne in the house.

CHAPTER 43

BLACK CALLED LANI. SHE DIDN'T PICK UP, SO HE DROVE OVER TO HER building and buzzed her. Her voice came over the speaker. "Who is it?"

"It's me. Open up, and let me in."

"Tyrann, you need to leave. I have a boyfriend now."

"Look, I know. I just want to talk to you."

"You need to leave before I call the police."

"The Po-lice? Okay, we've gotten to this point, have we?"

"Just leave."

Black drove back home thinking about Lani and how she said she was going to call the police on him if he didn't leave. His mind went back to the day when he'd been confronted at the convenience store by Shakur and how he wanted to fuck Shakur up, but he had other shit on his mind. More important obligations. More important missions. He had to sell the rest of his dope, and then get more to provide the finances for the franchise. Shakur would have to wait for now, but Black would not forget how that clown-ass nigga challenged him.

An hour later, Kyrie arrived at Black's home. Black led him into the living room, and after they were seated, Black said, "Lani is tripping, bruh. She has a new boyfriend and she won't even talk to me."

"I can believe that."

Black was surprised at Kyrie's reaction. "What do you mean?"

"Look, bruh, I didn't know how to tell you this, but Lani is an informant."

"Shut the fuck up, nigga. You are lying."

Kyrie made eye contact with Black and said, "I wish I was."

Black became furious. "Lani would never do nothing to hurt me!"

"That's why I didn't want to tell you."

"Why are you saying this?"

"Remember when I was interrogated?"

"Yeah, I remember when you ran your motherfuckin' mouth."

"I saw Lani."

"Where did you see Lani?"

"She was coming in to interview with the same Homeland Security officers that I had spoken with."

"You didn't tell me that you'd spoken with Homeland Security."

"I thought I did."

"You didn't."

"Well Lani was about to talk to them."

"Did she see you?"

"Yeah."

Black figured there must have been some truth to what Kyrie was saying. He remembered Lani mentioning Homeland Security to him. But he found it incredibly hard to believe that she would inform on him.

"Are you sure?"

"My lawyer said she was talking," Kyrie lied. He didn't know if Lani was cooperating or not, but he had to tell Black that she was cooperating before she told Black that he was talking. He knew that if Black found out that he was ratting, he'd be dead, and if he couldn't get to him, he'd kill his family.

Black was deep in thought. This was exactly the reason that she didn't want to see him.

Kyrie said, "You know she knows about Chris and everything."

"I know."

"If they find out about Chris, we're fucked."

Black looked at Kyrie for a long time then he said, "What do you mean we're fucked? You weren't there."

"I know I wasn't, but she don't need to run her mouth about that."

"I thought you said she was talking for sure."

"My lawyer said it."

"I didn't even know you had a lawyer."

"You didn't think I would interview without a lawyer, do you?"

"You're smarter than I gave you credit for."

"But the bitch is talking, bruh. Believe me. Why else would she be down there?"

Kyrie was right and he knew that Kyrie wasn't making this shit up. Damn, he would have to deal with her. But how?

•   •   •

Trey and Starr were lying in bed, ocean waves pounded hard against the shore. Outside it was dark but the beautiful Pacific was still visible and absolutely brilliant. Starr lay in Trey's arms. She felt like she belonged there. She felt protected. He was her man and she was glad to be back in his arms, but she still had some reservations about him. She turned and faced him. "You know I can't just let you off that easy?"

"Huh?"

"Trey, I said yes because I didn't want to embarrass your silly ass."

"Oh, I'm silly now?"

"No. I didn't mean it like that. It was a stupid thing to put me on the spot like that. If I said no, then everybody is looking at me like I'm a bad person."

"So that's why you said yes?"

"Absolutely."

"So you're going to give me my ring back?"

"Absolutely not."

He laughed. "Why not?"

"I'm going to put you on probation."

"Probation? I don't do well on probation. Never have."

"Well you have to prove to me that you can keep your dick out of other vaginas."

"That's easy."

"Boy, please."

He laughed a little before realizing that she didn't think that shit was funny.

"One thing about you, Trey. I can't tell what you like."

"What do you mean?"

"You have no type. I guess as long as they have a pussy, you're game."

"Whatever."

"Did Shantelle have a vagina?"

"Of course she did." He laughed. "Hey, the girl had some runner's legs."

"Those hard-ass legs."

Trey put his hands over Starr's mouth. "Let's not talk about her."

She removed his finger. "We don't have to talk about her, but you are still on probation, mister."

"Well, if I'm on probation, you're on probation too for trying to holla at my brother."

"You know me better than that."

"But was he trying to holla? Tell me the truth."

"No." Starr lied. This was something she would have to take to her grave because unfortunately, if she was going to deal with Trey, his brother would always be in the picture in some capacity. Though Trey and Troy didn't have a good relationship, she was sure that she would see him again.

"Really?"

"Really. I mean maybe his intentions were to try to get with me. You will have to ask him. But I never saw any signs of him wanting me."

"Damn. Maybe I should apologize for whooping his ass. On second thought, I don't think I will."

She leaned in and kissed him and he held her. Damn, she missed her man. She missed how he held her.

CHAPTER 44

BLACK HAD PUT MOST OF SHAMARI'S MONEY TOGETHER IN LARGE bills. There were some twenties, but mostly it was big bills—fifties and hundreds. He'd counted out two hundred and fifty thousand dollars and placed the money in two briefcases. When Shamari entered his home, Black passed him the briefcases. Shamari thanked Black and said, "I've been thinking."

Black looked very concerned as he waited to hear what Shamari had been thinking about.

"Look, I think we should at least give the doctor the money he invested."

"Why?"

"Well, he knows Jada and he can make it bad for her. You know what I mean?"

"How?"

"Well, he can go to the police. You know white people. They'll go to the police in a minute."

"You honestly think he's going to go to the police?"

"Let's give the man the money he invested. We don't have to give him a profit."

"Well, I just gave you two hundred and fifty thousand. You can give him your fifty thousand."

"He invested a hundred thousand."

"I'm not giving him shit, bruh. Have you forgotten we got rid of a body for him?"

"I understand how you feel, but we gotta give him the money that he gave us, man. It's just the right thing to do."

"Why is it the right thing to do?"

There was an awkward silence and Shamari couldn't think of one reason why it was the right thing to do. Craig had actually made more trouble for him; as if he wasn't already in enough shit.

"Look, man. He just knows too much about me and Jada. He knows that I'm on the run and he knows that Jada is my girlfriend."

"I'll give him the money back on one condition."

"What?"

"One more run."

"I told you no more runs for me."

"I wouldn't ask you if you didn't have the connect."

"I'm not going to put my money up. I have enough."

"Well, I don't have enough," said Black.

"I can't believe that."

"I'm always in need of money."

"Don't be greedy."

"That advice is coming a little too late," Black said. "Can you do it or not? We can cut it with whatever you want. Hell, I won't even cut it. You and Kyrie can cut it."

"This is it, brother."

Black shook his hand and said, "I'll put up all the money and we can still split the profit. I just need you to go get it for me."

"Now, can I get the other 50 thousand dollars to give our silent partner?"

Black said, "For sure, but if it was up to me, his ass would be real silent. Like silent in the ground."

They laughed.

• • •

It was just a little past seven when Starr, Lani, and Jada met at Shout for cocktails. It was crowded as usual. The ladies sat outside enjoying the beautiful Atlanta weather. Star and Jada ordered mojitos and Lani had a P-Diddy. Her new favorite drink. Starr reached for her glass and Jada noticed the ring on her finger.

"Damn girl! You got some news for us?"

Starr was smiling hard as hell.

Lani said, "That's a big-ass ring. Why didn't you tell me I was going to have to get ready for a wedding?"

"Not yet." Starr sipped her mojito.

Jada said, "You're back with Trey?"

"Well, not exactly."

"What do you mean, not exactly?"

"Well, we went on a little vacation to Cabo and he was saying and doing all the right things but I don't know if I trust his ass. You know what I mean?"

Lani said, "Trey loves you."

"That's obvious," Jada said then she asked, "Can I try that ring on?"

Starr slid the ring off and passed it to Jada. Jada examined the ring and said, "Goddamn, this ring must have cost at least a hundred thousand dollars."

"Not quite. Trey has a jewelry connection in New York, so he paid about eighty for it."

Jada passed it back to her and said, "That ring is more my style than yours."

"You're right. The first time he gave it to me and told me the cost, I told him to take it back. There was no way I was going to wear something that expensive."

"What changed your mind?" Lani asked.

"Well I'm still not sold on it. If I take him back, I want a little security besides my business. This is an asset, but to tell you the truth, he could have bought me a ring for a thousand dollars. I would have been just as happy."

"You love that man," Jada said.

"I do."

"Go ahead and set the date and marry him. And have some kids so I can be an auntie," Lani said.

"Only if you marry Black." Starr smiled.

"I ain't even speaking to Black, but that's a topic for another day."

Jada said, "Black loves you."

"I don't doubt that, but he's no good for me. But Mr. Shakur is good for me. Damn is he ever good for me."

Starr said, "When am I going to meet this Shakur dude? You know I need to approve of him first."

Jada said, "You will definitely approve of him in the looks department, unless you're blind."

"There must be more to it than looks?"

"Of course there is."

Starr said, "You look happy."

"I am."

"Well, I'm happy for you."

"Hopefully, I can get one of those rings. Damn, I want that ring so badly," Lani said.

Starr said, "I promise you're going to get your ring one day."

Jada said, "I'll just take some good dick and some good shopping. I don't need a ring."

"You'll get tired of the streets one day, Jada," Starr said.

"I know one day I will, but right now I'm having fun."

Starr sipped her drink and said, "Keep having your fun. You're still young. One day, you'll meet the right man."

"My feelings exactly," Jada said.

• • •

Later that night the girls wanted to go dancing, so they went to The Compound. Lani called Shakur and Shakur drove over with Big Papa and another guy from Arizona named Straight A. He was actually from New York, but had moved to Arizona. Straight A was a tall, lighter-skinned brother with wavy hair and a slight mustache. His skin was rugged and he looked much older than his twenty-eight years. After Lani sat next to Shakur and Jada sat on Big Papa's lap, Straight A sat next to Starr. Although she wasn't interested in him, she shook his hand to be polite.

Big Papa said, "So I finally get to meet Starr."

Starr smiled and said, "And I finally get to meet Big Papa."

"Who?" Ty said.

Jada rubbed his stomach and said, "That's the nickname I have for you, baby."

Big Papa laughed and tried to play it off and not get offended, but the truth was, he was self-conscious about his weight. "I never knew that you called me that."

Straight A and Shakur laughed and said, "Big Papa. I love it when they call me Big Papa."

Everybody laughed except Big Papa who was clearly offended. He was mad that he'd gained ten pounds since the last time Jada saw him. He'd lost three hundred thousand dollars in a deal gone bad and he'd binged on junk food to try to forget about his loss.

Jada kissed him on the cheek and said, "You're my big teddy bear and mama will always love you, no matter what size you are."

Big Papa grinned and looked dumb as hell.

Straight A said, "Why didn't y'all tell me Starr was so damn gorgeous?"

Starr was beaming. Though she was not interested in him, she always felt good when a man paid her compliments.

Big Papa said, "Didn't you just hear her say it was nice to meet up finally?"

"You all on Jada's Instagram. I'm sure there must be a picture of Starr on there."

"Damn dawg! You gonna put me out there like that, huh?" Big Papa said, clearly not wanting Jada to know that he was peeking in on her Instagram account.

Jada said, "It's okay, daddy. Look at me all you want on Instagram." The truth was that she already knew he was stalking her. Though he didn't follow her, she figured his clumsy ass accidentally liked one of her pictures. And the only reason she knew it was him was because his profile picture was a picture of his Bentley.

Lani said, "Starr is taken." She turned to Starr and said, "Show them your ring."

She held up the ring and Big Papa said, "Damn! He must love you. That ring must have cost at least a hundred bands."

"He cares a little about me."

"He cares a lot about you," Straight A said.

Lani tugged Shakur's arm. "I want that exact ring. That is my dream ring."

Jada said, "That ring is more my speed, though I wouldn't pick that exact ring."

Lani said, "I love that ring."

Shakur said, "I can take a hint."

Big Papa flagged the waitress over to their table and ordered five bottles of Ace of Spades at six hundred dollars a pop.

"Why so many bottles?"

Big Papa said, "We are celebrating Starr's engagement. I believe in everybody getting their own bottle."

The server dropped the champagne off at the table as rap music blasted through the club.

Starr grabbed Jada's hand and said, "Let's dance. I love this ratchet-ass song."

Jada said, "Me too, girl. This is my shit."

Seconds later, Lani joined in. All three girls were dancing and singing. Jada tried to get the guys to join them, but they were all too cool to dance. Fifteen songs later, some R&B was playing when Lani stumbled and busted her ass.

She was sitting there, flat on her ass and embarrassed as hell, when Shakur and Starr ran to her side to pick her silly ass up off the floor.

"Are you okay?" Shakur said.

"Are you hurt?" Starr said.

Lani slurred, "Damn right I'm hurt, but I'm having the best night of my life." Lani passed Straight A and asked him to take a picture of her and the girls.

Lani said, "You know, ya'll two are my best friends and we've never took a picture together before?"

Jada said, "We have plenty of pictures together."

"I'm talking about us three."

Starr said, "You're right."

"Starr, you get in the middle since you're the one that's getting married."

"No, Lani you get in the middle since you're the best friend of both of us."

Lani said, "How about we all get in the middle, since we're all special. We're all bad bitches."

What was supposed to be three pictures turned into a photo shoot with at least thirty pictures of the girls.

None of the guys wanted to take pictures. They were all D Boys and didn't want to give the Feds anything to investigate. Pictures of expensive champagne would not be the best thing for business.

Jada posted a picture of her, Lani, and Starr on Instagram with hash tags #badbitchnation, #Mygirlslookbetterthanyours, #Poppingbottlesandwedontpayforshit, #excusemybossiness, and #donthate. In a matter of minutes, they had over four hundred likes. Mostly from thirsty dudes and the comments were hilarious.

NYCBrian said: *You in the middle. I wanna dip that ass in gold.*

Bossman38 said: *That's fine ass, Starlito. That used to be my baby in the third grade.*

A-Town player said: *I'll make all three of them tap out.*

Thetoelicker89said: *You in the blue dress I want to lick your toes and I hope they are good and sweaty, so sweaty that it taste like salt. Yum.*

Batman134 said: *Pervert above*

Jada showed Starr the comment of the guy that said he remembered her from the third grade. Starr laughed and said, "Now how in the hell would I remember him from the third grade?"

Lani said to Shakur, "I want to take one picture with you, baby."

She passed Jada the phone and Jada snapped a picture of them kissing. Jada knew Lani was drunk because Lani would never have taken a picture of her kissing him had she not been drunk. At the end of the night, Lani said to Jada, "I need to talk to you. Alone."

"Okay. I'll take you home because you are too drunk to drive."

"I'm going home with Shakur."

'Walk me to my car then," Jada said.

"Okay."

Lani turned to Straight A and said, "Walk my girl, Starr, to her car."

Lani looked at Starr. "I don't know why yo' cheap ass didn't valet."

"I'm a big girl. I can walk myself and I didn't see the valet when I drove up."

"I don't mind," Straight A said.

When they were outside, Straight A escorted Starr to the parking lot.

Lani pulled Jada aside and said, "Look, I'm not going to talk to Black again for a while but I need you to tell Shamari to tell him something that's important."

"What?"

"Black has a friend named Kyrie and he's snitching. Tell Black, don't trust him."

"Why don't you tell him?"

"I've been through too much with him. Just pass this information to Shamari and tell Shamari to tell Black to stay away from Kyrie."

"Okay."

Lani hugged Jada and then hopped into Shakur's car and they drove away.

CHAPTER 45

SATURDAY MORNING AND TREY WAS LYING IN BED WITH STARR. SHE was snuggled close to him because she was naturally cold and his body was always warm, even in winter. She loved that about him. He was her electric blanket. It was eleven a.m. and neither of them wanted to get out of bed. They'd gone out last night for a dinner and a movie. They'd seen the late night show, so they had gotten in very late. Trey stared at the ceiling as Starr rubbed his chest. He looked troubled and she asked what was wrong.

"Nothing."

"Trey, come on. You know I know you better than anyone. Something is bothering you."

He faced to her and said, "I was thinking about Shantelle."

"Shantelle?!"

"No, babe, calm down. I'm thinking about my money. I have to get her for what she did to me."

"You have to or you choose to?"

"Look, baby. Now is not the time to try to be diplomatic. I'm going to get her if it's the last thing I do. I can't let this shit ride."

"If you had that money that she took, would you be happier?"

"That's not the point."

"What is the point, Trey?"

"The point is, it's my money and she shouldn't have taken it."

"Look, Trey, you have more money than you can spend. You don't need to get even with this woman."

"Fuck that!"

"She knows too much, way too much. That's the reason you are in the position you are in right now."

There was an awkward silence. Starr placed her legs between Trey's and rubbed his chest. Finally she said, "I know you don't want to let it go, but you must, Trey."

"What if I see her?"

"Well, if you run into her, that's a different story, but don't go looking for this woman. If you go looking for her, you are asking for trouble."

"You're right."

"You understand?"

"Yeah."

"Trey, look at me."

Trey turned his body to face her. Their legs still tangled. His arms wrapped around her waist.

"Promise me that you're going to let it go," Star said.

"I promise."

"Swear to God?"

Trey laughed and said, "I swear to God."

She leaned into him and kissed him.

Trey said, "You make me so much better."

"That's what a good woman is supposed to do."

"I love you so much, Starr."

"I love you too."

•   •   •

Shamari had given Jada the hundred grand that Craig had invested. It was seven p.m. on a Saturday night when she contacted Craig. They decided to meet at Cheetah's again. Jada was sitting in a section roped off from the other patrons. Not that she was special, but she would pay a little extra not to be near the stinking-ass cigarette smoke. She spotted Craig immediately when he entered the club wearing a god-awful green golf shirt that was the color of vomit. His hair was unkempt and he looked like he hadn't shaved or bathed for at least a week. The once handsome doctor looked like a certified crack head. Jada was ashamed that she'd actually fucked him. She ordered a waitress to bring him to the table. When he sat down she said, "You look like shit."

"Good to see you too, Jada."

She stared at him completely disgusted.

He said, "Look, you would look terrible too if you had as much going on as I do."

"Fill me in."

"Look, you know my wife is trying to take everything, right?"

"Ok, same old news."

"Well, I'm also not working anymore."

"Why?"

"My partner is trying to buy me out because of my malpractice suits. He wants to part ways. He says that the business insurance will be through the roof as long as I'm practicing. So he doesn't want me there."

"Damn."

"And on top of that, my wife has been questioning me about Imani."

"What? How did she know about Imani?"

"Well, Imani was one of the girls texting me and sending me naked pictures. When she saw on the news that she went missing, she started asking me all these goddamned questions about when was the last time I saw her."

"You're seeing your wife again?"

"Well, I have to see the kids."

"Damn." Jada said as she flagged the waitress. "I need a shot of Patron. Make that a double."

The waitress returned with a double. Jada downed it and ordered another.

"What happened to that skinny bitch that works in this club?" Jada asked.

"I haven't spoken to her since that night. I came here one day last week looking for her, and the girl at the door said she hadn't seen her in a while."

Jada sipped her liquor. "You don't think your wife thinks that you had anything to do with Imani's death, do you?"

Craig shrugged. "Who the fuck knows, but you can see why I look so bad."

"Yeah, you've been going through it."

"You think?"

Jada detected sarcasm in his voice and said, "Don't get smart with me, motherfucker."

"Not getting smart. Just letting you know why I look as bad as I do."

"You're a goddamned coke head."

"I didn't come here to argue. Did you bring my money?"

"Yes, I brought you your investment."

"When do I get my profit?"

"You won't be getting no profit."

"What?"

"Motherfucker, you put us all in a bad position. Nobody knew you were using these girls' bodies to smuggle drugs."

"What difference does that make?"

"Shamari had to get rid of a dead body for you. Have you forgotten about that?"

"No. I live with that every day of my life. I cared about that woman."

Jada wanted to smack the fuck out of his silly, lying ass. Thinking how in the hell could you care about somebody and risk their life at the same time.

"Look, I know that sounds crazy, but I loved her."

"You're right. It sounds crazy, and I don't believe you one bit. She was somebody that you knew had self-esteem issues and you wanted to mold her into your perfect little fuck toy. I know how sick you plastic surgeons can be, always in search of perfection. News flash doctor. There is no perfect woman."

"I don't want to talk about that. I want to talk about my money."

"Your money is out in the car. I will give it to you when the valet pulls my car up."

"I want my money now."

Jada downed her drink then tossed a hundred dollar bill on the table and they headed out to valet. Jada gave the valet guy her ticket. Broke-ass Craig had parked in a regular parking spot. He waited on the valet guy to retrieve Jada's car so she could pass him his investment money.

He turned to her and said, "Jada, the last thing you want to do is not pay me my money."

'I'm giving you your money in just one second."

"I'm talking about my profit." He paused and then said, "Now why would you leave my money in the car in the first place? That is just too goddamned much money to leave unattended."

Jada smiled and said, "It's your money, not mine."

"I want my profit."

"Not going to happen."

He leaned toward her and whispered in her ear. "Jada, you really don't want to try me. I'll go to the goddamn police and tell them everything. The trips to Cali, the dead body, the new face, everything."

"You killed that woman, not us."

"I did kill her...at gunpoint."

"What?"

"Shamari made me do it, at least that's what I'll tell the cops."

"You white piece of shit."

"Try me, Jada, and I swear I'll get even with you."

The valet pulled Jada's Benz to the front of the club. She handed the man a ten-dollar tip, retrieved the briefcase from the trunk, opened it and peeked inside to make sure the money was still there. Jada passed the briefcase to Craig.

"You think long and hard about what I said, Jada. Don't try me," Craig said.

"You have a good day, Craig." She made her way to the driver's side of the car. The valet was holding the car door for her and she said, "You don't have to hold the door for me, honey."

"Not a problem, ma'am," the man said as he stole a look at Jada's ass.

She got inside and the valet closed the door. She screeched out of the parking lot, tires smoking.

The valet said to Craig, "That's one gorgeous woman."

Craig said, "Man, do yourself a favor. Don't ever get involved with a woman like that."

CHAPTER 46

IT WAS 2:17 IN THE MORNING WHEN TREY'S CELL PHONE RANG. STARR heard it first and she nudged Trey. He didn't move, so she picked his phone up from the dresser and saw that it was Jessica. Starr answered the phone.

"Hello?"

"Starr, put Trey on the phone. It's an emergency. The ambulance has taken my mother to the hospital and I need him to come and get T. J."

"Right now?"

"Put Trey on the phone."

Starr shook Trey as hard as she could. Finally he said, "What?"

"Telephone."

"Who is it?"

"Jessica."

"Tell her I'll call her in the morning."

"She says it's an emergency."

She passed Trey the phone and he said, "What do you want?"

"Hey, I need you to come and get T. J. I have to go to the hospital with mama."

"What?" Trey glanced at the clock on the dresser. 2:19. "Are you serious?"

"I have to go to the hospital with mama."

"You know where we live. Drop him off." He glanced at Starr. "Is that okay?"

"Of course, baby," Starr said.

Jessica said over the phone, "I would but dropping him off is out of the way. Besides he's asleep and I don't want to wake him."

"But you gonna wake me?"

"Trey, I don't have time for this. Are you coming to get your son or not?"

Trey stared at the clock for another minute before saying, "Yeah, I'll come."

"Baby, I'll come with you," Starr said.

"I don't want Starr near my house," Jessica stated.

"What?" asked Trey.

"Don't bring Starr."

Starr heard her through the phone. "It's okay, baby. Go get your son. I'll be here when you get back."

Trey sprang from the bed, made his way to the closet, and slipped into a pair of sweatpants, a white polo-shirt and a pair of Jordans.

Starr said, "Call me if you need me."

She was comfortable in her bed and she really didn't want to get out. She was actually glad Jessica said that she didn't want her to come to her house. Though she didn't truly trust Trey yet, she'd be willing to bet any amount of money that he was done with that crazy bitch.

After he'd finished lacing up his shoes, he stood and leaned over to kiss Starr on the cheek. "I'll be right back, baby."

●　　●　　●

The porch light was on and so was every light in the house when Trey drove into the driveway. He would get T. J. some clothes and his toothbrush then scoop him up and carry him to the car. Nothing more. Very limited interaction with his crazy-ass mama. He was hoping that Starr and T. J. got along because he would definitely try to get custody of his son as soon as he and Starr were married. Trey rang Jessica's doorbell at 3:01. A minute later, she opened the door wearing a red leotard and six-inch stripper heels. Her huge boobs were spilling from her leotard. Her tanned skin looking delicious. Trey was absolutely turned on by her but he'd vowed to his lady that he would be faithful and what in the hell was this crazy bitch trying to prove?

"Obviously you think I got time for games," Trey said.

She tried to drag him into the house, but he was too strong. "Will you get the fuck away from me?!"

He shoved her and she stumbled back and crashed into the door. "What's the matter, Trey? You scared of pussy? I know damn well you ain't trying to be faithful now. That's not in your blood."

"You don't know what's in my blood."

"You're right. I don't know what's in your blood. But I know where your blood money is."

Trey turned to her and said, "What are you talking about?"

"Every fuckin' dime you've ever made is blood money. You didn't earn it and you don't deserve it. You're like a vampire sucking all the blood out of your community. You don't give a damn about the people who are putting that poison into their bodies. You don't care about the kids whose parents are on drugs. You don't give one flying fuck. That's why I took the money!"

Trey was walking to his car when Jessica kicked her heels off and sprinted into the house. Seconds later, she came out with wads of cash and tossed the money into the air. It was raining one hundred dollar bills.

Trey ran toward Jessica but she galloped into the house and was trying to close the door but he managed to wedge his foot between the door and the door jamb. He pushed the door open and when he got inside the house, he locked the door behind him.

"Tell me where the fuck my money is? First of all, where is my son?"

"No, you got the order right. Money comes before your son in your eyes."

"Where is T. J.?"

"He's with my mama. At my mama's house."

"And your mama is doing fine?"

She didn't answer.

Trey grabbed her by her throat and said, "Answer me."

"Yes. She's fine."

"So you made all this shit up, so you can see me?"

"Yes."

"Where the fuck is my money?" Trey tightened his grip.

She couldn't talk. She pointed in the direction of the upstairs bedroom. He loosened his grip and she said, "Upstairs in my closet."

He released her.

"Fuck you, Trey! You get out of my house before I call the police!"

Trey sprinted upstairs into Jessica's bedroom and opened the bedroom closet. A mountain of cash covered the floor. Jessica followed him into the bedroom. "So, you're never going to take me back?"

"Are you fucking serious?"

Trey grabbed a black silk pillowcase from one of the pillows on the foot of her bed and began loading the cash into the pillowcase then stared at Jessica who had slipped into a bathrobe.

"How much of this money did you spend?" he asked her.

"Not one penny, but that's only five hundred thousand."

"Where is the rest?"

"Shantelle has it. She has half and I got half."

"I see. How the fuck did ya'll get into the safe?"

"I had the combination."

"How did you get it?"

"T. J. came home with a notebook that you had in your bedroom at your mother's house. It had all the safe combinations. I gave one of them to Shantelle and she took the money. You just better be lucky I didn't give her all the combinations."

Trey said, "No, you better be glad."

"Whatever."

"Where the fuck is Shantelle?"

"I don't know where she is. And I don't care."

Trey finished loading the money into the pillowcase and slung it over his back. As he was about to exit the closet, Jessica approached him and attempted to kiss him. He pushed out his hand to stop her and then he walked past her. He was about to exit the bedroom when she drove a twelve-inch blade through his back.

Trey uttered the words, "What the fuck?" Those would be his last words before he crashed into the floor.

Jessica rolled his body over on his back and said, "What's a little blood money without blood?"

His eyes were open wide and he was staring at her. He wanted to say something to her, but he didn't have the strength.

She kissed him. "I love you, Trey." Then she stabbed him sixteen more times. She sat there, looking at Trey's body. "Love sealed in blood," she said before taking the knife and jabbing it straight through her own heart.

• • •

The alarm clock sounded at seven a.m. and Starr hit the snooze button. Her plan was to lie there five more minutes but then she realized Trey wasn't in bed. She'd forgotten that he had gone to Jessica's house. Her phone was charging as it sat on the nightstand next to the alarm clock and she snatched it from the stand. She dialed Trey's number. It rang eight times before going to voicemail.

She dialed Jessica's number but it went to voicemail as well. Starr sprang from the bed and headed to the bathroom. She stepped into the shower thinking that she was a goddamned fool for taking this man back. She'd only set herself up for more heartbreak. She would never learn, then she rationalized and thought there had to be an explanation to why he wasn't answering the phone. Maybe he'd gone to the hospital with Jessica and you have to have your phone turned off in a lot of hospitals. Maybe he left the phone in his car. But why in the fuck would he even be that concerned with Jessica's mother? Why would he go to the hospital without telling her or texting her? He knew his ass was on probation. He knew that she would be pissed if he didn't tell her what the fuck was going on. After she showered, she dried herself off, moisturized her body, and then called his number again. No answer. She dialed Jessica's number and she didn't pick up either.

She called Trey's mother. "Good Morning, Ms. Annie."

"Hey, Starr."

"Hey, I hate to call you so early."

"Chile, I've been up for two hours. What's the matter?"

"Have you heard from Trey?"

"No, I haven't spoken to him for a couple of days. Why? Is there something wrong?"

"Nothing. He left at 2:30 in the morning to go pick up T. J. and I haven't heard anything else from him."

Ms. Annie took a deep breath and said, "Oh Lord, I told Trey about that crazy white girl. I hope he don't get himself tied up with her again. Starr, you're the best thing that ever happened to him and I ain't never liked that girl from day one. I told him not to bring her crazy ass around me. When they had T. J., I felt so bad that Trey made me swear not to tell you about him. I swear, Starr, I never felt good about lying to you and I damn sure didn't feel good about Trey being with that crazy-ass woman."

"Ms. Annie, you ain't never lied to me."

"I lied by omission. In my book, that's worse."

"Well look, we can't change the past, we can only look forward to the future."

"True, but I haven't heard from Trey. I'll see if I can get him on the phone and I'll tell him that you're looking for him."

"Okay, thanks."

"Starr?"

"Yes, Ms. Annie."

"I'm so glad that you're going to be my daughter-in-law. I couldn't ask the Lord for a better daughter-in-law. I told Trey that you're like the daughter I never had."

"Thanks, Ms. Annie, and do call me if you hear from him."

Starr ended the call thinking that there would be no way in hell that Ms. Annie would be her mother-in-law if Trey's ass was cheating again.

She dialed Trey's number one more time. No answer. Strange.

●   ●   ●

Shamari gathered his belongings. He was moving out today. He'd found a small home for rent in Cascade Park where he could lay low for a while. Jada would keep most of his money just in case he was ever apprehended. He knew that he could trust her to do the right thing with his money. The attorney was paid in full, but he knew that attorneys could be greedy and they would often ask for more money depending on the difficulty of the case. Shamari was stuffing underwear and socks into a suitcase when Jada entered the bedroom.

"Baby, I hate that you're leaving," she said.

"I don't want to leave, but I have to go. You've done enough for me."

She made a sad face.

"It's not like we're not going to see each other," Shamari said. "You know I'll come by from time to time and you can come to my place. Well, at least for a little while longer."

"What happens after that?"

"I'm going to try to get the hell out of here. I need to go. I've been in Atlanta long enough. I don't want to keep pressing my luck."

"I know what you mean."

"A lot of shit has happened."

"A lot."

Jada made her way over to the bed wearing tight shorts that crept up her ass crack, and for a brief moment, Shamari wanted to yank those shorts down and give it to her doggy-style. Instead he continued to pack.

"Did you give the doctor his money back?"

"I did."

"What did he say?"

"He wants his profit."

"What? You're kidding, right?"

"No. He really thinks he deserves a profit," Jada said.

"Fuck no."

"That's what I said."

"I ain't giving him shit."

"Well, he said that he would go to the police and tell them that he was held at gunpoint by you and you made him give you a new face and that you told him that if he didn't insert the heroin in the women's breast implants that you would kill him."

"What?"

"That's what he said."

"You think he would do it?"

"I think we are dealing with a man who ain't got shit to lose now. He's lost his family and he's about to lose his business. You know that white people can't take pressure. Especially rich ones."

"He ain't rich."

"But he's used to a certain lifestyle, and he don't have shit."

"Look, I'm going to make one more run with Black, and I'll give him my profit."

Jada smiled, "I think that's the right thing to do."

"Black ain't going to give him shit, I'm telling you that right now."

"You can't worry about Black."

"You're right."

"Speaking of Black, Lani told me to tell him that somebody was snitching." Jada tried to remember what Lani said. They were all so goddamned drunk that night that she couldn't quite remember.

"Who's snitching?"

"I can't remember. I'll call Lani and ask her." She stood from the bed and Shamari smacked her on the ass.

She turned and smiled. "Boy, don't start nothing that you can't finish."

"Who said I couldn't finish?"

She dropped her shorts revealing some high-waisted bikini's that made her body look spectacular. Shamari kicked his shoes off and yanked her tiny-ass panties down.

CHAPTER 47

IT WAS 2:11 P.M. AND STARR WAS GIVING A TOUR OF HER SHOWROOM TO a client named Mr. Anderson when she received a call from Trey's mother. She turned to Mr. Anderson and said, "Sir, I'm so sorry but I really need to take this call. My assistant, Brooke, will finish showing you around."

Brooke came running from across the room and Starr disappeared into the back. When she heard Ms. Annie crying, she knew that it was bad news.

"What's wrong, Ms. Annie? Tell me what's wrong."

The woman simply could not gain her composure. Starr felt nauseous because she just had a feeling that it was all bad.

"What happened to Trey?"

No answer. Just more crying.

"Is Trey hurt?"

"Yes?"

"What happened? Calm down, Ms. Annie, and tell me what happened to Trey?"

"She killed him."

"Who?"

"That dirty little white bitch killed my son."

"Jessica?"

Ms. Annie finally gained her composure and said, "She stabbed him to death."

"Where is she now?"

"She's dead too. She killed herself too."

Starr yelled, "No! No! No! No! Please tell me this is a joke! A lie! He is not dead! I refuse to believe this!"

"He's gone, Starr. My son is gone."

"No. No. No. I don't believe it. I don't believe it."

Starr dropped the phone and flopped to the floor with her head between her legs sobbing. Brooke came running to the back where Starr sat on the floor.

"What's wrong? What's wrong?" Brook asked.

Starr continued to cry. She glanced at Brooke but then dropped her head again.

"What's wrong? Please tell me!" Brooke demanded.

Starr kept crying. Her cell phone was still connected to Ms. Annie on the other end. Starr scooped it up and smashed it hard on the floor, shattering the screen.

Brooke said, "I'm going to call Mr. Trey and tell him to come right over."

She attempted to grab the phone but Starr took hold of her wrist and said, "Mr. Trey is dead."

The young woman looked frightened. She didn't know what to do or to say. Finally she took a seat on the floor beside Starr and held her.

"It's going to be alright," Brooke said. It was exactly what Starr needed.

Trey's mother had attended Montclair AME Zion Baptist church faithfully for the past forty years and the church was filled to capacity for Trey's funeral. Trey was a well-traveled man and he knew people from all over the United States. People from Miami, New Orleans, Los Angeles, South Carolina, and North Carolina came. Q came all the way from Houston and Jesus the jeweler came from New York. Shamari and Black even strolled through and paid their respects. Lani avoided eye contact with Black. Starr sat with Trey's family along with her father, mother and sister, Meeka. Meeka's twin boys were there as well. Lani and Jada sat on the visitor's side.

Jessica's mother and little T. J. were also there. Ms. Annie and Jessica's mother had told T. J. that God needed Trey and Jessica in heaven to do some work for him. He'd cried at first and though he was still upset at God, he liked the idea that he had two angels watching over him. Jessica's mother had begged forgiveness from Ms. Annie, but Ms. Annie assured her that it wasn't her fault. There was no way she could hold what her daughter did against her. She'd come to terms that it was Trey's fault as much as it was Jessica's. After all, he'd slept with her and conceived little T. J.

Lani and Jada were there to support Starr in her time of grief. Starr had been there for Lani when Chris was murdered and she wanted to do the same for Starr.

Jada had grown to love Starr and though their relationship had gotten off to a rocky start, she loved her like a sister. Lani and Starr had become like sisters to her, even more than her own sister, and she was thankful for their friendship.

The preacher was very diplomatic with his message out of respect for Jessica's mother whom he knew was in attendance. His message was a message of forgiveness and living. He said that you had to live each day like it was your last day because one day, you'd be right. It was a saying that Starr had heard before and she could appreciate it.

After the preacher was done, Trey's mother asked if they could open the casket one more time. She wanted to see her son again. The request was granted and a few people who'd arrived late made their way to the casket to view the body.

A woman wearing a tight blue dress and very shapely legs made her way to the casket. Lani nudged Jada and asked, "Ain't that the woman that we confronted at Atlantic Station?"

Jada said, "Yes. The nerve of that fucking 'Thot' to show up at the funeral after she stole his money."

"Jada, you're cursing on church grounds."

"Look, I'm going to take that up with God later. Right now, I have some more important business to take care of."

The casket closed and the ushers picked up the casket and headed toward the exit.

Jada followed Shantelle outside to the church grounds. Lani was running behind her because she knew how bad Jada's temper could be.

Jada said to Shantelle, "Excuse me, ma'am, but I owe you something."

Shantelle turned and faced Jada. The woman looked very confused.

Jada said, "Yes, I owe you this ass whipping."

She removed one of her Louboutins and charged Shantelle. Jada grabbed Shantelle by her collar and beat blood out of her head with the shoe. "Bitch, you got some fuckin' nerve to show up at this man's funeral after you stole his money!"

Jada took hold of Shantelle's hair and slung her to the gravel parking lot then stomped on her.

Shantelle caught Jada's foot and lifted her leg from the ground. Jada knew that the chick was stronger than her from all the exercising and shit but she was not about to take an L. Not today. No way. Not Jada.

Jada was wobbling around on one leg as Shantelle held her leg. Jada spat a big glob of spit in Shantelle's face.

Shantelle released her leg and Jada charged her again with the shoes, smashing Shantelle's eye. By this time, Lani was trying to break up the fight.

The ushers were on the way with the body and Starr and Meeka were behind the ushers.

When they saw all the commotion, Starr realized that Jada and Shantelle had been fighting and it was obvious that Jada had beat Shantelle's ass. Two grown men were restraining Jada.

"Let me go! I'll beat that bitch's ass again. You didn't know I fight men like you," yelled Jada.

Shantelle, holding her bloody head, made her way to her car and drove away in a hurry.

● ● ●

Two days after Trey's funeral, Starr was lying in her bed crying when she received a text from Q: *Is everything ok?*

Starr: *Everything is not okay. How can it be okay, Q? I've lost the man I love. The man I wanted to spend the rest of my life with.*

Q: *I know. It's been hard for me too. You know I loved Trey like a brother. Always have, always will.*

Starr: *I know you loved him Q, and Trey loved you.*

Q: *I just hate that he was so hard headed.*

Starr: *Me and you both.*

Q: *I'm still in Atlanta. Do you want to meet for dinner or drinks?*

Starr: *Thanks Q, but I can't. I can't bring myself to get out of bed. I've been crying all day.*

Q: *Starr, you're a young woman. You have to get out. You can't live your life like this.*

Starr: *I know. I will be better in time. It's only been two days.*

Q: *I know. Well, I'm leaving in the morning. I wanted to see you before I left.*

Starr: *You can come here, but I'm really not in the mood to go out.*

Q: *Will call you in a few moments or text me your address.*

Starr: *Okay.*

Q arrived at Starr's place an hour later. Starr had thrown on a pair of jeans and her hair was in a ponytail. Starr looked cute but Q could tell she was still in pain over Trey's death. Q was wearing a blue pinstriped Armani suit, a thin tie and some designer shoes.

Q just stood and observed Starr's place before saying, "This place is incredible."

"Thanks."

"Trey told me that you'd started your own interior decorating business. How is it going?"

"It's been going okay. Could be better." Starr said, then she realized that she was being rude and asked him to have a seat.

"I won't be staying but a few minutes. I just wanted to see you before I went back to Houston. Like I said, Trey was like a brother to me and there's nothing I wouldn't do for Trey."

Starr nodded her head and said, "Well, would you like something to drink at least?"

"No, thanks."

She smiled slightly and said, "Well, I'm glad you came over. I know I didn't really get a chance to talk to you at the funeral. I wanted you to meet Trey's mother."

"You know, I met her a few years ago. She probably don't remember."

"Oh that woman remembers everything."

"Trey's son has grown so much."

Starr gave a faint smile. This brought back the unpleasant memory that everybody knew about T. J. except her.

Q noticed how quiet she'd become and said, "I'm sorry."

"It's okay. I'm worried about that boy. He has nobody. I've actually thought about adopting him."

"That would be nice. You have a really good heart, Starr."

"And it seems that this good heart of mine gets me in trouble over and over again."

"People like you struggle, but they always win in life."

"You think so?" Starr smiled and Q thought she was cute as hell.

"I know so."

"Again, thanks for coming."

He embraced her and held her for a long time and said, "Stay in touch, and if you need anything, don't hesitate to call me. What's mine is Trey's."

"Trey left enough money for me and Mama for a while. You know, I'm actually pretty frugal."

Q smiled. "I've heard."

●   ●   ●

It was 1:13 p.m. when Black entered Sasha's building to pick up the last thousand packets of heroin. His plan was to get the work, take it to his distributors, and collect the rest of the money by the weekend. He'd called Sasha but she didn't pick up. Not unusual because she worked this time of the day. He took the elevator up to her floor and entered the apartment. He thought he'd heard lovemaking sounds coming from Sasha's bedroom. He didn't care. She had told him she had a boyfriend. He guessed that the man finally came to get what was due to him.

Black moved closer and realized that what he thought were lovemaking noises were actually fucking sounds. She was moaning as she was being fucked. Black entered the other bedroom and retrieved the work. He was about to head out when he realized the door to Sasha's bedroom was open, so he peeked inside. Damn, her boyfriend was old as fuck, he thought.

The man was yanking Sasha's hair and smacking her ass while he fucked her doggy style. Black took in a side view of the man and thought the old man looked familiar. He tiptoed out of the apartment. He would call her later.

CHAPTER 48

ALL THE HEROIN WAS GONE AND BLACK HAD COLLECTED HIS PROFITS.
He drove to Shamari's new home for the first time. He looked around.
There was very little furniture. Black walked around the house and said,
"I like it. It's a nice, low key spot."

"Yeah, I like it."

There was a sofa in the living room and Black sat on one end while
Shamari sat on the other.

Shamari said, "I'm still tripping about what happened to Trey."

"Shit could happen to the best of us. That's what happens when you got
a crazy-ass baby mama. I got a few of them myself."

"Damn. But she didn't have to kill him."

"I know. Trey must have saw signs that the bitch was crazy. He just
ignored them."

"Yeah. Jada said that the chick was on some kind of bipolar meds."

"There you have it."

"She stole his money. She got the combination to one of his safes and
stole like a million in cash."

"See? He should have killed her ass."

"I don't think he knew until the night she killed him."

"How do they know she did it?"

"She told her mother what she'd done and the mother told her to give
it back."

"Damn. Fuck all this talk. We have to get busy. I know you want to get this last run out of the way."

"I do."

Black passed him a backpack full of money. "This is enough for four kilos."

"Damn, you're going for it, ain't you?"

"Why not? It's the last run."

Shamari's face got serious and said, "Jada told me that Lani said somebody from your circle is snitching."

"Huh? Who?"

"Jada couldn't remember who Lani said. She was supposed to call her but then we wound up fucking and forgot all about it."

"Lani is the one telling."

"No way."

"I didn't want to believe it either, but it's true."

"Who told you that?"

"My sources."

"'That's fucked up."

"It's true. I can tell just by the way she's been acting. She's not answering my calls and the other day at Trey's funeral, she wouldn't even look my way, bruh."

"Damn."

"I know. I've never seen her like this. I mean I know she's been getting some new dick, but Lani has never just cut me off. I'm telling you, bruh, something ain't right."

"Can she hurt you?"

"Maybe."

"You need to find out if it's true."

"No." He paused. "I need to go with my gut."

●   ●   ●

Sasha had called Black and asked him to meet up with her. She suggested Houston's but he preferred to meet at Spondivits since he was coming from Newnan and it would be quicker to meet up. Forty-five minutes later, they sat at a table eating lobster. Black was drinking a Heineken.

There was an awkward silence. She wanted to ask him about the money for the franchise. She'd spoken with the bank and they said they would loan her a portion of the money and now she needed his. She had asked him several times before, but there didn't seem to be a sense of urgency about the whole thing coming from him.

Black cracked open a crab leg and said, "So, how long have you been fucking your father?"

"What? Excuse me?"

"Look, I came into your place the other day to get the rest of my work and I heard the sound of two people fucking coming from your bedroom.

I figured it was your boyfriend. When I got what I'd come for, I was about to leave but your bedroom door was open and I saw your daddy, the Mayor, fucking you. I didn't realize it at first but then I thought that he looked familiar and I thought I knew him, but then I realized that I didn't know him at all but I'd seen him on TV before. He's the Mayor of Atlanta."

A single tear trickled down her face.

He reached across the table and took hold of her hand and said, "You don't have to be ashamed. I'm your friend."

She removed a napkin from the table and dabbed her eyes.

"You can talk to me," Black said.

"What do you want to know? I mean you seen it obviously."

"I did. Did he make you do it?"

"Well, I'm a grown woman."

"I know. So why are you doing this?"

"He's a very sick man. I want to expose him and let everybody know what he's been doing to me and my sisters for years."

"When did it start?"

"He started touching me as soon as I got my first period. I think I was about twelve."

"Disgusting motherfucker!"

"I know."

"Why do you keep letting him do this to you?"

"Right now, I'm dependent on him."

"I thought you had your own job and money."

"I do, but it's because of him. He got me the job. I make close to five hundred thousand dollars a year for a job that's supposed to pay seventy."

"How did that happen?"

"Well, he helps the company I work for get city contracts and they do him a favor by employing me."

"Kickbacks."

"Yeah.

"Five hundred thousand dollars a year is good money."

"Yes it is, if only I was getting it."

"I don't understand."

"He gives me about eighty thousand and he keeps the rest."

"Damn! This motherfucker is shady as fuck."

She kept dabbing her eyes. She'd never talked about her relationship with her father to anyone. She'd tried talking to her mother once but when she told her mother that he touched her, her mom cursed her out and told her not to ever say anything like that to her again.

"Look, this is the reason I keep asking you to help me to invest in the franchise. So I can get away from him. I don't want him to do shit for me. I want to make it on my own. I need your help."

Black kept eating his lobster, not wanting to believe what he'd just heard. She could tell he was deep in thought. She didn't know if he would help her or not but she felt relieved that another person knew what she'd been going through. Maybe she'd secretly hoped that Black would catch them in the act. She had been fucking her father for almost twenty years and it was time for it to stop.

They made eye contact and he said, "Is that why you're so freaky?"

She laughed and said, "Possibly. I've been having sex since I was twelve."

"Damn. I thought I started early at thirteen, but you got me beat."

"I guess so."

"Look, I want to help you. I'm going to help you."

"Thank you."

He dialed Rashida's number and told her about the business proposition. He put Sasha on the phone to speak with his sister and they agreed to meet later in the evening.

Sasha said to Black, "Thank you!"

"Just one thing you need to know about me."

"What's that?"

"I don't play about my goddamned money."

"I figured that."

CHAPTER 49

HIS NAME WAS LARRY HARRIS BUT IN THE STREETS HE WAS KNOWN as Big L. Big L was about 6'4" and weighed 280 pounds and muscular with a slight gut. L had no facial hair and wore his hair bald. There was a patch of bumps on the back of his head from ingrown hair. L was wearing a tight-ass Adidas windbreaker that was struggling to contain his huge muscles. Big L and Black had met in the state pen. Black and L had once argued over the TV but after Black witnessed L damn near knock a man's head off his shoulder for attempting to turn the channel from the *Young and the Restless*, Black thought it was better to be L's friend. Big L had done eighteen years for strangling his girlfriend to death after he'd found out she'd been running around on him.

Big L and Black met in a little hole in the wall spot called Handlebar on the west side of Atlanta. Nobody knew why it was called Handlebar, not even the people that worked there. The owner died and passed it along to his children and they didn't know why their dad chose to name it Handlebar either. It was a dimly lit place, but surprisingly very popular, especially on game nights. Handlebar was the kind of place where you could get some good greasy food and have a beer.

Black had chosen this place to meet Big L because Black didn't trust him. He knew that given the chance, Big L would rob him, so there was no way he was going to let that goon know where he lived. He also knew that Big L was the type of nigga that you would have to kill before he killed you and that was the exact reason Black needed him to do a job for him.

They sat in the back corner of Handlebar talking and eating greasy-ass cheeseburgers and drinking cold beer. They talked mostly about people that had been in state prison with them and the ones that had gone back to prison with new charges.

Black decided it was time to get down to business. "I need a favor from you."

"I'm listening."

"Somebody is out to get me and I need you to get them before they get me. You know what I mean?"

"It can be done."

"I know you can do it."

"How much is the job paying?"

"Ten grand."

Big L's eyes lit up as he thought about what he would buy with ten grand. He was forty-five years old but still acted like he was a little kid. Instead of investing the money, he thought about the rims he could put on his truck. He always wanted twenty-eights. He could get a new TV. He could go to the strip club and make it rain. He'd only done that once in his life. One time, he'd robbed a drug dealer with four other dudes. His share was thirteen thousand dollars and he blew it in a week on strippers and out-of-date Roc-A-Wear clothing.

"It has to be a clean job L. I got every law enforcement agency in Georgia already investigating my ass."

"It will be."

"And if you get caught."

"I'm not going to."

"But if you do."

Big L stared at Black like he wanted to slap the fuck out of him. "Black, are you saying that I'd tell on you?"

"No."

"Well, you don't have to tell me what to do if I get caught. If I get caught, you put money on my commissary and I'll do the time."

"Got ya."

"You got the information that I need to do the job? You know names and addresses? Where they hang out?"

Black passed Big L the information that he needed for the hit.

• • •

Black and Big L left the Handlebar and got into Black's Porsche. Black drove around with no particular destination in mind. They caught up some more on each other's life and Big L shared with Black that he'd been struggling to make ends meet. He was a father for the first time in his forties; something that he hadn't planned on. He had never wanted kids and it was a one night stand with a whore who had four other kids by four different men. He'd contested that the child was his in child support court though his mama had warned him the kid was his. She told him that the little girl looked just like him and the DNA test came back a 99.9 percent match. Big L had to accept it and he was trying to get used to fatherhood, but he needed money and he wanted Black to give him more jobs after this one.

Black looked at Big L and saw a man who was desperate for money right now. He'd be willing to take out anyone that Black wanted killed. Black thought he could always use another hit man, and perhaps a bodyguard, if this hit went well. Black's cell phone rang. He answered it without looking.

"Tyrann?"

"Hey, Ms. Carolyn." Lani's Mom was the last person that he wanted to talk to.

"Did I see you come through my neighborhood earlier?"

"No, I don't think so." Black lied. He and Big L had in fact ridden through her neighborhood, but she didn't need to know that.

"Now, you know I know you from anywhere and I know your car."

Black was thinking that if she knew for certain it was him, then why in the hell did she call?

"Look, Tyrann. I know that you and Lani haven't been speaking lately, but I want you to know that you're welcome to my house anytime you want."

"That's good to know, Ms. Carolyn. I already knew that."

"You're like a son to me. You hear me?"

"Yes, ma'am."

"And no matter what, I'll always love you. You hear me, boy?"

"Yes."

"Next time you in the neighborhood, I want you to stop by and get something to eat."

"I will."

"Take care of yourself, okay?"

"I will." He ended the call.

Big L said, "Damn, she was long winded as hell."

"I know." Then Black's face turned serious. "If you do this job right, I promise you that there will be more work for you."

Black gave Big L a pound.

•   •   •

Lani and Shakur lay naked in his bed and his strong arms were wrapped around her. His dick was still poking her in the side. He liked it cold in his home and she would have been freezing if she wasn't comfortable in his arms. She was so comfortable that she didn't even notice that it was freezing. She loved running her fingers through his well-kept dreadlocks and he liked palming her ass. This had become part of their regimen after sex. She looked at him and smiled.

He asked, "What are you thinking about?"

"You really want to know?"

"If I didn't want to know, I wouldn't have asked."

"Well, if you must know."

"I must know."

"I was just thinking I've never felt like this with a man before. I don't think I've ever been in love until now. I mean I loved Chris, and I love Black, but I've never felt like how you have me feeling."

"Describe what you're feeling."

"I feel like you got my back."

He smiled and said, "That's because I do."

"I believe that."

"You should."

"But I don't know how long this feeling is going to last. Whether it's just infatuation or what."

"It's not infatuation because I feel the same way."

She smiled then she became sad, and he wanted to know what was troubling her.

"I was just thinking about what's going to happen with me and Black."

"What do you mean?"

"I mean, clearly the Feds are after him and they want me to help them in their very active investigation on him, but I didn't help."

There was an awkward silence in the room and then he finally said, "You did the right thing. I know that you're done with him, but Black, for the most part, in his own little way, did a lot of good things for you."

"He did, but they are going to take him down. Now that I'm pretty sure his right-hand man is telling on him. It's just a matter of time."

"Did you tell him?"

"No, I haven't seen him. I sent word to him, and I know once he finds out, he's going to kill the snitch. That's how Black operates. I didn't tell him directly because if he kills Kyrie, I don't want that to lead back to me."

"You did the right thing."

"The right thing is the wrong thing for me. Right now I'm in love. I want to start a family and now this shit has come up."

He took hold of her hand. "Your hands are super cold."

"You think, Mr. Antarctica?"

"Oh, I didn't know you were cold." He stood up and made his way to the thermostat. Her eyes zeroed in on his dick swinging wildly. She kind of wished he was inside her but her mind was really somewhere else.

He climbed back into the bed and took his position. He grabbed her hand again. "I don't think you have anything to worry about."

"I do. When they came to my house, they brought up old stuff, including an old place I had in my name for Black."

"Did you have anything else in your name for him?"

"Just a couple of cars. Nothing expensive, though."

"They might try to get you for money laundering because you really didn't know about Chris's murder, did you?"

"Well, I knew that Black was out to get him back for shooting him, but no, I didn't know if or when he was going to kill Chris."

"I don't think that you have anything to worry about then. If they were going to pick you up, they would have already done that by now."

"I know."

He stroked her hand and said, "Lani, I have money. Lots of money, and I will help you fight this thing."

"Black has already paid an attorney for me. One of the best."

"What's his name?"

"Gilliam."

"Never heard of him."

"He says that he's one of the best in Atlanta."

"They all say that. But mine really is."

"Who do you have? Joey Turch?"

"Hell no! Joey Turch will sell your ass out."

"Black swears by him."

"I wouldn't use him or this guy that you have."

"I don't have any money."

"Didn't I say I have money? And what's mine is yours. I just need you to be true to me."

She leaned forward and kissed him.

●   ●   ●

It was raining semi-hard and Lani was driving to her mother's house. The wipers were operating loudly and so was the defogger in an attempt to provide more visibility. She noticed in the rearview mirror there was a blue minivan trailing her. It was very hard to see because of the rain, so she couldn't determine the make and model of the vehicle, but she could see two men wearing welding masks in the van.

She turned down one street and so did the van. She went around a curve and the van tailed behind closely. She called her mother. No answer. She remembered when she left Shakur's house that his phone was plugged into the wall and was still charging. She dialed 911.

"911 operator. How can I help you?"

"Yeah, yeah! There're two men following me, driving a blue minivan, wearing masks."

"Okay ma'am slow down. Do you know where you are?"

"I'm in my mama's neighborhood." Lani said, trying her best to remember the name of the subdivision. Her mother had lived there many years but right now the name of the subdivision slipped her mind.

"What's the name of the neighborhood?"

"I don't know."

"Can you tell what kind of minivan they are driving?"

Lani glanced over her shoulder trying to look at the minivan.

"I think it's a Ford."

"Ok ma'am. Stay on the phone, don't panic."

"Can you send somebody out here now?"

"Can you look for a street sign, ma'am. We need a street sign."

"Can't you find me by my phone? You are the goddamned 911! Come and help me!" She hung up and called Jada.

Jada picked up the phone.

"Hello?"

"Jada, it's Lani."

Lani was breathing heavy and Jada knew something was wrong with her friend. She'd never sounded like that.

"What's up?" asked Jada.

"There are two men wearing welding masks following me in a blue minivan."

"What? Where are you?"

"I'm in my mama's neighborhood. I don't want to go to her house because I don't want them to do anything to her."

"What did you say?"

"Can't you hear me?"

"I can barely hear you. Those windshield wipers are so damn loud and do you have the window open? I hear something blowing."

Lani lowered the pressure on the defogger.

"Stay on the phone," Jada said.

"Of course. Can you hear me now?" asked Lani.

"I hear you much better. If you turn those wipers off, I could hear you better."

"Then I can't see."

"I hear you, okay. Just relax."

"Relax?! Niggas with masks are following me."

"You should call 911."

"Already have but I wanted to talk to you. I wanted to tell you I think this has something to do with Mike."

"I'm going to call 911."

"No, stay on the phone with me."

"This don't make sense. You should call 911."

"I just called the dumb-ass operator. She was asking me all these stupid-ass questions. I want to talk to my friend. I want you on the phone with me."

Lani approached a stop sign but she ran right through it. So did the minivan.

She floored it and the minivan stayed right behind her. She went into the next subdivision and took them down two streets. She ran four stop signs until finally she came to a dead end.

Jada said, "You still there?"

"I'm here. I'm trapped in a dead end!"

"They still behind you?"

"Yeah."

"Get out the car and scream as loud as you can."

Lani shifted into park and attempted to exit the car but the minivan pulled up right beside her.

"They are going to kill me!"

Both of the men exited the van. Lani screamed before one of the men unloaded his 9 mm. Two shots ripped into Lani's mirror. The third, fourth and fifth bullets ripped right through Lani's chest and she collapsed in the driver seat, her hand still gripping the cell phone tightly. Jada could still hear those goddamned loud-ass windshield wipers. The men jumped in the minivan and fled the scene.

"You still there?" Jada called out.

Lani said to Jada, "I'm not going to make it."

Jada screamed into the phone, "Don't say that! Hang in there!"

"Tell my mother, I love her! Tell Starr, I love her. Tell Shakur..."

Jada yelled, "Lani! Lani! Lani!"

She didn't respond. Jada could only hear those loud-ass wipers. Wosh, Wosh, Wosh.

Lani was dead. Jada screamed uncontrollably. One of her worst nightmares just came true. She'd witnessed somebody that she loved take their last breath.

•   •   •

Jada and Starr were with Ms. Carolyn when she had to positively identify Lani's body although Ms. Carolyn already knew for certain that the body in question was Lani's. One of the police officers had brought her Lani's cell phone and driver's license and Jada had told her about the conversation that she and Lani had before Lani was gunned down. Ms. Carolyn became faint as soon as she laid eyes on her daughter's lifeless body. Starr and Jada quickly grabbed her and helped hold her up.

Ms. Carolyn screamed, "This is not how it's supposed to be! I'm not supposed to have to bury my daughter. My daughter is supposed to get married, have kids and bury me. Oh God! God, why did you take my one and only daughter? Jesus Christ!"

Starr held Ms. Carolyn's hand. "I'm going to be there for you. Lani was there for me when Trey died. I love you, Ms. Carolyn. Like my own mama."

Jada said, "That goes for me too. If you need me to stay the night with you, I'll stay with you as long as you want me to."

"That goes for the both of us."

Starr turned to Jada and said, "Did Lani describe who did this to her?"

"She said they were in a blue minivan. There were two men and they were wearing welding masks."

"Welding masks or ski masks?"

She said. "Welding masks."

"Damn."

"I know."

Ms. Carolyn gained her composure for a moment and said, "I think Tyrann had something to do with it."

"Black?" Jada said.

"Yes, I think his black ass had something to do with it."

Jada had known Ms. Carolyn for over twenty years and she'd never heard her utter one curse word before.

Starr said, "Are you sure?"

Jada said, "No disrespect, but I find that hard to believe."

"I saw him riding in my neighborhood yesterday, out of the blue. Now tell me what the hell was he doing there? And when I saw him, I called him and asked him if he rode by my house and he denied it. I know for a fact that it was his black ass."

"Damn."

Ms. Carolyn looked at Lani again and began sobbing. "God, why are you testing my faith like this?"

Lani and Starr held Ms. Carolyn's hands and Starr said a prayer hoping it would make them all feel better and it did for a few moments. Then all the women began crying again.

CHAPTER 50

"LANI WAS MURDERED THIS MORNING," SHAMARI SAID TO BLACK.
"What?"

"Lani got gunned down this morning. Jada said something about two men following her to a dead end and killing her in broad daylight."

"Nigga, quit playing. I don't believe that."

"Why would I play about something like that?" Shamari started pacing and said, "She called Jada before she got killed. Jada heard the whole thing. She was on the other end of the phone."

Black began to pace nervously. He removed his phone from his back pocket and dialed Ms. Carolyn's number. She picked up on the first ring.

"Hello?" she said.

"Is it true about Lani?"

"Don't ask me that bullshit, Tyrann. I know you know something about this, and I intend to prove it."

"You know I loved your daughter."

"Don't give me that love shit. The only person you loved, Tyrann, is you. You don't give a damn about nobody except yourself."

"Ms. Carolyn, I can't believe you're accusing me of this. I loved Lani."

"You don't have to prove nothing to me. You need to prove it in court."

"Court? What are you talking about?" Black's brown eyes filled with tears. "Please tell me you don't believe I would do something like that."

"Since you like killing everybody, kill me because I intend to tell everything I know about you to the police, Tyrann. This is the last straw."

"Huh?"

"Huh, my ass!" She terminated the call.

Black sat down on the edge of the sofa. His head between his legs with tears rolling down his face. He was bawling. "This can't be true. Please tell me this ain't true! God, you should have took me. Lani didn't deserve this. No way she deserved this!"

He turned to Shamari. There was an awkward silence and finally Shamari said, "Well, did you? I mean you did think she was ratting on you."

"You think I did it?"

"I'm just asking, bruh."

●   ●   ●

Shakur was at Ms. Carolyn's home for the first time. Jada and Starr were there as well. They both hugged Shakur. Ms. Carolyn offered him something to drink but he declined. They were sitting in the den and the girls were reminiscing about Lani and the good times they'd had with her. Jada was telling some elementary school stories about the two of them.

Ms. Carolyn said, "You sure are a handsome young man."

"Thank you," Shakur said. "Look, Ms. Carolyn, I loved your daughter. I know that you don't know me and I hate that we had to meet under these circumstances. But I loved your daughter more than any woman in my life. I know it sounds crazy since we hadn't known each other that long, but it's the truth."

"Lani had that effect on people," Starr said.

"She was a good girl that just got tied in with the wrong men," Ms. Carolyn said.

"Ms. Carolyn, I've done my share of dirt too."

Ms. Carolyn said, "I'm not a saint either. I'm not judging you, son. I just want whoever did this to my daughter to be brought to justice."

Shakur said, "They will be if it's the last thing that I do. I'm going to find the person that did this to Lani."

"Let the law handle it, son."

Jada said to Ms. Carolyn, "I'm with Shakur. Whoever did this to Lani needs to get theirs."

"And they will. The police will find them and prosecute them."

"If the police find them, they will be lucky. If I find them, not so lucky."

"I still think Tyrann had something to do with this."

"Who is Tyrann?" asked Shakur.

"Lani's ex-boyfriend, Black."

"Why do you think it was him?"

"Well, a few days ago, I'd seen him in the neighborhood. Just riding around looking suspicious. I called him and asked him if I'd just seen him and he denied it. I knew it was him. I know his black ass anywhere."

Lani and Starr were quiet. They didn't believe that Black would do something like that because he loved Lani, but they didn't want to say anything to Ms. Carolyn. She was grieving for her daughter.

"Is that so?" Shakur said.

"Yes."

"One thing for sure. It won't be long before we find out who done it. The streets talk. They always do."

• • •

Shakur trailed Mike's Camaro into a Publix parking lot on Piedmont Ave. When Mike was about to park, he noticed Shakur behind him. Mike sprang from his car. Lani was dead and Mike knew he would be a suspect. Not just with the law but in the streets. Shakur hopped out of his car and the two men drew guns. Mike with his Beretta 9 mm and Shakur had a Glock .45.

Shakur said, "Motherfucker, I know you had something to do with this!"

"What the fuck are you talking about?"

Shakur inched toward Mike with his weapon cocked and Mike was still pointing his gun at Shakur. Neither of the men wanted to shoot in a parking lot full of patrons. Nobody wanted to hit an innocent person, but both men wanted the other one dead.

People began screaming and somebody called for the police. Mike looked and saw security coming from the grocery store across the street. He jumped into his car and drove away. Shakur was right behind him. He tailed Mike for a few more streets until he decided to drive away.

• • •

Lani's funeral was even more crowded than Trey's. Trey's mother even attended. Even though she had never met Lani, she wanted to support Lani's mother. Chris's mother and stepfather were there as well. Black was noticeably absent, however his sister Rashida and his Nana were there. Lani looked like her old beautiful self and Starr had even placed her engagement ring on Lani's finger. Starr had so many things to remind her of the times she'd had with Trey that one little ring wasn't going to make a difference. Besides, Starr was young. She knew she'd get engaged again. Lani would never be married, but the least she could do as a friend was give her the ring that she had always admired.

Jada and Starr were crying as Lani was lowered into the ground. Both women had been strong for Ms. Carolyn but when they saw Lani's casket being lowered, reality set in. Their friend was gone. No more conversations with her. No laughing over drinks and no more late night phone calls. No more talking about men. Their friend was gone.

Jada screamed out. "No! No! Lani, don't leave me! God, don't leave me!"

Ms. Carolyn dropped to the ground crying, "My baby is gone. God, how could you do me like this?"

Jada regained her composure and she and Starr held Ms. Carolyn up and kept her from falling again.

Starr looked around. She was trying her best to keep her composure but everybody at the gravesite was in tears. She couldn't take it any longer, she broke down. Besides Trey's funeral, this was the saddest moment in her life. This had been the worst two months ever.

Later that night, in the pitch black dark at the graveyard, Black laid a flower on Lani's grave site.

"Even in death, I will love you," he said.

Black turned and was about to walk away when somebody punched the fuck out of him. Black stumbled to one knee and was about to stand up when another man kicked him in his ribs.

"What the fuck?" Black said. He glanced up and recognized one of the men. "Shakur," he said.

Shakur pointed his gun at Black's goddamned head.

Black reached for the gun that was on his waist but Shakur stomped on Black's arm so hard he almost broke his wrist.

"Don't even try it, nigga. If you reach for that gun again, I will blow your goddamned dome off. I swear it."

Shakur ordered Straight A to shake him down.

"Get that gun off him." Shakur then looked at Black. "Motherfucker, I will kill your bitch ass right now. I know you had something to do with Lani's killing."

Black had never been in such a vulnerable position, even when he'd been shot. But right now he was at the mercy at two motherfuckers who couldn't stand his black ass. He would have to beg for his life.

"I didn't have anything to do with Lani's death. I swear to God."

Straight A removed Black's gun and stood him up.

A light beamed through the night sky and the three men's eyes followed the direction of the light. It was security. An old white man with a pot belly wearing a blue uniform.

"What the hell is going on? What are you doing to that man?" the security guard called out.

"They're trying to kill me!" Black said.

Straight A let go of Black's arm and he and Shakur sprinted away.

There was no way the fifty-six-year-old white man could catch them and Black was too beat up to give him any help.

CHAPTER 51

SHAMARI SAID, "WHAT THE FUCK HAPPENED TO YOU, BRUH?" HE stared at Black's swollen eye.

"Got jumped by two niggas."

"Huh?"

"Yeah, they caught me coming out of the cemetery."

"What? Were they trying to rob you?"

"No. I think one of them was someone Lani used to fuck with."

"Why did he jump you? Lani is gone, bruh."

"I know. He thinks I killed her."

"Everybody does. It's just going to be a matter of time before the police come to ask you about the death."

"I ain't worrying about that."

"You should, and I should too."

Black said, "Oh my God, here comes more of your sentimental bullshit. Do you want to make this last move or not? If you don't want to do it, get the fuck out of my house."

"Look, I want to do it. But I deserve to know if you killed Lani."

"What if I told you no. Would you believe me?"

Shamari stared at him for a long time before saying, "I don't know."

"If you're not going to believe me, what difference does it make?"

"You're right. Give me the money and I'm on my way to get the work."

Black passed him a backpack with the money for the four kilos of heroin

Shamari left wondering if this crazy motherfucker had killed Lani, and if he killed Lani, would he kill him too?

• • •

Shamari and Jada had just finished making love and were lying naked between the sheets. They were cuddling as she ran her fingers through his hair. He'd just revealed that he was about to go to Cali for the last time, and when he returned, he would give Craig the rest of his money. Jada had begged him not to go. She was very concerned about him, especially after Lani had gotten murdered. There were just too many bad things going on.

"First, you tell me to pay Craig his money, now you're telling me not to go."

"I don't want you to leave me, Shamari." She turned to face him and they were so close that they could feel each other's breath."

"Think positive. Don't have bad thoughts, Jada."

"And what does that mean?"

"You have to believe everything is going to work out for the best."

"That's hard for me to believe."

Shamari stood up from the bed and walked across the room. His dick was swinging wildly. Jada said, "Wait, where are you going?"

"Look, I don't want to hear all this negative talk. You know I believe if you think negative, you will get negative."

She sprang from the bed and walked over to his dresser. She grabbed one of his t-shirts from the dresser. It swallowed her tiny body.

"Look, Shamari. I don't want to hear that philosophical bullshit. I'm talking real shit. I'm telling you not to go."

"What about Craig?"

"Fuck Craig!"

"So first you tell me that I need to give him all of the money I promised, and now, you tell me fuck him."

"Bae, you have enough money to give him. Just give him the money that you made already. Your lawyer is paid for. You have enough money."

"Look, right now, it ain't about Craig."

"Well, what is it about?"

He was silent for a while thinking that she had a point. He couldn't tell her what it was about, that he didn't trust Black anymore. Why the fuck was he doing this?

"Look, I don't know why I'm doing this."

"I know."

"Why do you think I'm doing this?"

"Because it's exciting to get away with and it's exciting being the bad guy."

"You are out of your fucking mind."

"Well then, tell Black you can't do it."

"I've called my connection to get the order together. They are waiting on me."

"So who is going with you to make the run?"

"My sister's boyfriend Hunch said he would do it."

"I don't trust him. He's not hard enough. He'll crack under pressure."

"I don't have anybody else to do it at this point."

She made her way over to him until she was inches away from him. They locked eyes and she said, "That's not true. You have me. I'll do it for you."

"No, Jada. You can't."

She leaned into him and kissed him and said, "I'm going to make the run and that's that. Who do you trust more than me?"

There was nothing else he could say. There was nobody that he would trust his life with except Jada. He embraced her and held her for a long time. His dick, now alive, poked her in her abdomen. They kissed again.

•   •   •

The doorbell rang and Shamari peeked through the blinds. He saw Jada's car. He opened the door for her and kissed her. She passed him the bag with the heroin in it.

"Thank you so much."

"I've been trying to call you for hours but your phone was off."

"I've been charging my phone, and I've been trying to call you too. Your phone says that I couldn't leave a message because your voicemail box is full. As a matter of fact, let me use your phone to call Black."

Jada passed the phone to Shamari and he dialed Black's number.

"Hello?"

"I'm on my way to you, black boy."

"I'm waiting."

He passed the phone back to Jada and kissed her again. She said, "Be careful. There's just so much going on right now. I don't know what I would do if something happened to you. You are my best friend."

"Nothing is going to happen. Don't think like that, Jada. Don't be negative."

She regained her composure and said, "You're right. I gotta think positive."

"Exactly, baby."

He retrieved his phone that was plugged into the wall in the bathroom. He would charge it in the car on the way to Black's place.

She kissed him again and said, "This is the last time you're going to deal with the devil, right?"

"The devil?"

"Black. Look, I'm not like everybody else around here thinking that he killed Lani. I actually don't think he did it. Lani's last words were that she thought that Mike had something to do with it, but what I do know is that something bad is always happening around him."

"I don't know if that's true."

"What's not true?"

"I don't know if Black killed Lani or not. It's a possibility."

"Why do you say that?"

"I told him that you said somebody was snitching. But I couldn't tell him who because you never told me who Lani said was talking." Shamari paused. "Then Black said Lani is the one snitching."

"I forgot what Lani said. We were all drunk that night and I forgot to ask her again."

"But Black thought Lani was talking. That's why I said it's a possibility that Black killed her or had her killed."

"I still don't believe it."

"Why?"

"Just the fact that Black loved her so much. He would never do anything to hurt Lani."

"Black loves Black more and if he thinks Lani or anybody else would jeopardize his freedom, believe me, he will take them out."

"I think it was Chris's brother, Mike. He thinks Lani showed Black where his parent's lived."

"I'm just saying it could have been Black. Anyway, I'm going to meet him. I will holla later."

He put the backpack on his shoulder and left. Jada followed him out the door.

•   •   •

Jada was glad that the trip was over and glad she'd made it home safely. They could finally give Craig the rest of his money, and he could quit whining like a bitch. She never meant to get herself this involved in the game. From now on, she would stick to what she knew best, dating hustlers or men with money. Now it was time to go home, take a long bath, and then she would visit Ms. Carolyn but first, she wanted to check her voice mail. She had twenty-four messages.

Craig-delete. Craig-delete. Her mother-save. Big Papa-delete. Big Papa-delete. Big Papa-delete. Big Papa-delete. Big Papa-delete. Big Papa-delete. Big Papa-delete.

Damn, this dude is thirsty she thought. Then there was a message from Lani. An old message that she'd never listened too. She debated with herself whether she wanted to listen to the message or not. She didn't know if she could take listening to it without breaking down. She wanted to hear her friend's voice again, even though she knew it would be eerie. She took a deep breath.

Lani's voice came through the phone. "Hey, baby girl. Just wanted to thank you for introducing me to Shakur. He's all I ever wanted in a man. Also just seeing what you are up to today and wondering if you got to tell Black what I told you about Kyrie."

She saved the message and called Shamari. Kyrie was the snitch. Shamari's number went straight to voicemail. She'd met Kyrie at Lani's mother's house, and she knew that Kyrie was Black's right-hand man. She had to reach Shamari and tell him what she knew. She called his phone again then she remembered that the phone was still charging. She had to reach him and reach him fast.

Jada jumped in her car and started the engine. Rain began to fall and this was the last thing she needed. Ever since Lani had died, she couldn't stand the sound of wiper blades. It made her re-live those final moments of Lani's life. On the way from California, it had rained and she had checked into a hotel to avoid listening to those wiper blades. They drove her insane.

She looked toward the sky and said, "God, why now?"

The rain was coming down so hard that there was no way she could drive without the assistance of wipers. She turned the blades on and she heard Lani say, "I'm going to die."

Those goddamned blades were driving her crazy. A tear trickled down her face. She wanted to cry thinking about her friend's horrible death, but there was no time for crying. She had to reach Shamari and reach him fast.

CHAPTER 52

THE FOUR KILOS OF HEROIN WERE GOING TO ALLOW BLACK TO WALK away from the game.

Black had called Kyrie to come over to help him cut the dope that Shamari was bringing and he arrived five minutes after Shamari. Kyrie pointed at Black and then in the direction the kitchen.

Black followed Kyrie to the kitchen. "What's up?" Black asked.

Kyrie placed his hands on his lips. Shhh.

Black was confused and he wondered what the hell was going on. What was Kyrie about to tell him? Kyrie scribbled on a piece of paper. *You know I wouldn't ever do anything to hurt you.*

Black looked at the paper wondering what in the hell he was talking about. What was going on? He looked very confused. Kyrie lifted his shirt revealing a recording device.

Kyrie whispered, "I'm sorry."

Black stood there dumbfounded. He couldn't believe this bitch-ass nigga. "Shamari needs to come with me," said Kyrie.

Kyrie left the kitchen and Black followed, feeling really fucked up and torn. He damn sure didn't want to speak. The gangster in him wanted to warn Shamari what was about to happen, but they had four kilos of heroin. He'd never get out of prison.

Kyrie said, "Shamari, we're going to go to my house and cut the dope."

Shamari looked at Black and he nodded in agreement. But something wasn't quite right with the way Black was looking at him. Shamari still believed in his heart that Black had killed Lani, and nobody could tell him otherwise.

"Why do you need me to cut the dope? I've never gone with you before."

"You complained about the rat poison. I want you to be there, so you can see what I'm cutting it with," Kyrie said.

"Look, I don't know anything about any of that."

"Just follow me to my house. I need you to take the dope. I mean, since we're not going to cut it here. I need you to carry it for me."

"I don't work for you."

"We're working together, homie. Don't be like that."

Kyrie left and Shamari was right behind him. Black followed them to the door, his face expressionless.

When they were outside in the driveway, Shamari sat in his car and Kyrie got into a black Ford pickup truck parked right behind him. Kyrie backed out first and Shamari was about to back out when Jada drove up and blocked him in. She bolted from the car.

"Where's the dope?" she asked.

"In the back seat? Why?"

"Give it to me. I gotta get rid of it."

"What are you talking about?"

"Just do what I say. You'll thank me later."

"No."

Jada tried to climb into the backseat, so Shamari triggered the automatic locks.

"Look, you need to listen to me, motherfucker!" Jada said.

"Why?"

"Kyrie is who Lani told me to warn Black about."

"Really?"

"I just listened to a voicemail. She was asking me if I had told Black about Kyrie."

Shamari opened the window and dropped the backpack on the ground beside Jada without Kyrie seeing what he'd done. Then he drove up beside Kyrie who was waiting on the side of the road. He trailed Kyrie for several traffic lights then Shamari veered away from him. There was no way he could get caught with this guy. What if he was wired? The Feds could be waiting at his house. His phone was fifty percent charged now. He powered it up and called Black to warn him. Black didn't pick up. He dialed his number again and there was no answer. The next time he called Black, the phone was off and it went straight to his voice mail. He didn't want to go home and he didn't want to go to Jada's house, just in case somebody was following him. Surely, if someone had followed them, they had seen him veer off. He called Jada's phone. She picked up on the first ring.

"Hello?"

"Don't go home."

"I'm not."

"Go to your mom's house or Lani—" He was about to say Lani's house. He still couldn't believe that Lani was dead.

"I know, it's hard for me to believe she's gone too."

"Jada, that motherfucker Black is not answering the phone. I think he might have known that Kyrie was with the Feds."

"Look, Shamari. I'll talk to you later. We don't need to talk right now."

"You're right."

He terminated the call. He hopped on I-20 going west toward Augusta. He didn't have a destination. He had to ride and think what was next. He was hoping like hell that Jada was getting rid of the dope. She had to get rid of it.

He pulled off on Candelor Road, near the mall. He remembered this is where he and Duke had been set up by Duke's cousin. He drove into the mall parking lot. He put the car in park and dialed Black's number one more time. Voicemail.

• • •

Shortly after ten p.m., the police accompanied by the FBI, the DEA and the Department of Homeland Security banged on Black's door. Black knew they were coming sooner or later and he'd cleaned up as much as he could. He'd gotten rid of the weed that he had been smoking. He had a hundred thousand dollars that he'd hid in the attic, and he hid several guns underneath the house. Black put up little resistance when they broke down the door. He was outnumbered and there was no way he could win against them all. They cuffed Black and sat him on the sofa.

Black said to one of the black officers, "Am I being indicted, bruh?"

"First of all, I'm not your brother and no you haven't been indicted. Yet."

"So why am I handcuffed? You ain't going to find nothing in here."

"We're serving you with a federal complaint and an arrest warrant."

"So I'm getting arrested, but not charged?"

"Not charged. Yet." Then the man smiled.

They continued to search the house and one of the officers found the hundred thousand dollars that Black had tried to hide. The guns weren't found, but they found a ledger with a list of names of people owing Black money.

Black was escorted to a windowless white van and driven to the jail.

• • •

Louise had started drinking again and had even allowed Charles to move back in. They were sitting in the living room with Jada when there was a knock on the door. Louise didn't take too kindly to someone knocking on her door.

"Who the fuck is at my door!" she yelled.

"The police, ma'am! Open up!"

"What do you want?"

"We want to see the person driving that Mercedes."

"Why?"

"Open up, ma'am or we're going to have to come in!"

Louise was drunk on Hennessey and she didn't know the seriousness of the situation. She paid the cost to be the boss in her home, even if it was against the police.

Louise said, "And if you come in here, I will put a ball in yo' ass!"

Jada realizing what was happening, peered outside and saw about thirteen cars outside parked on both sides of the road. Most of them were unmarked, but there were a few squad cars.

She approached her mother and said, "We're going to have to let them in, Ma."

"What the fuck have you done?"

"I can't explain it right now, but it was the right thing to do. Now, you have to open the door. I don't want nobody to die unnecessarily."

"Nobody is going to die in here."

Silly-ass Charles, repeating Louise, said, "Nobody is going to die in here."

Louise slapped the fuck out of him and said, "Shut the fuck up! Don't mock me!"

"I'm going to give you three minutes then we're kicking the door in!" the police called out.

Charles hollered, "Kick the motherfucker in then!"

Louise hocked spit at his silly ass.

Jada called out, "We're going to open the door in a minute!"

"Jada, what's going on, baby?"

"I have something that they want."

"What do you have?"

Jada stared her mother in the eyes and said, "I have some dope. They want the dope."

Louise, thinking of her other daughter who had been battling a drug addiction and her own demons with alcohol, looked at Jada. A single tear trickled down Louise face. "Baby, are you on drugs?"

"No, Mama. I'm not on drugs."

"What do they want with you then?"

"They want me because I have Shamari's stash."

"And where in the fuck is he?"

"I don't know."

"I swear to God I'm going to kill that red motherfucker if it's the last thing I do."

"It's not his fault mom. I swear to you. It's not his fault." She passed Louise her cell phone and said, "Call him when they take me."

"What kind of drugs do you have and how much?"

"A lot, Mama. A lot." She started crying. "Call Shamari and my friend Starr. They will know what to do. They'll get me out."

"Okay. I love you."

"Open up! Or we're coming in!" the police called out again.

Louise opened the door and two black Homeland Security officers and one DEA agent were at the door.

"Who drives this car?" one of the officers asked.

"Me."

"You want to open the trunk?"

"No. But I will."

Jada stepped outside and made her way to the trunk. She opened it and picked up the backpack. She passed it to the officers and they took her into custody.

Louise sat on the steps of her home crying as she watched her child get locked up for something serious.

She called Shamari. He answered on the first ring, "Hey, baby."

"Hey, Shamari, it's Louise."

"Where's Jada?"

"The police just picked her up from here."

"What?"

"Yeah, Jada told me that whatever it was, it wasn't your fault."

"It's not my fault, but it's my responsibility."

"What is that supposed to mean?"

"It means I'm going to get Jada out of jail. You know me, Louise. I know you've never cared for me, but you know that I'm a man and I'll get Jada out. I put that on everything."

"That's all I can ever ask for. And I believe you."

●   ●   ●

The next day Shamari stormed into Joey Turch's office. The receptionist asked him to have a seat because the attorney was on a conference call. She said that Mr. Turch would be with him right away.

Shamari looked at the receptionist. "No, I will not have a seat! I need to see him right away!"

The receptionist disappeared into Turch's office and the attorney came out a few moments later. Because of Shamari's extensive plastic surgery, Turch did not recognize him.

"What can I do for you?"

"I need to talk to you now."

Turch said, "I need you to fill out a questionnaire first. All my fees are listed on the questionnaire."

"Questionnaire, my ass! I've already given you a hundred thousand dollars!"

Turch ushered Shamari into his office and when the door was closed, he said, "You've already given me a hundred thousand dollars?"

"Yes."

"Who are you?"

"I'm Shamari Brooks."

"You don't look the same."

"That's a long story."

"The Feds got your boy, Tyrann, last night."

"I was with him last night."

"How did you get away?"

"My girlfriend saved me from the informant."

"Really? What happened?"

There was a long silence. Shamari was hesitant to tell him what had happened.

Turch recognized Shamari's reluctance and said, "Attorney client privilege. I couldn't discuss it even if I wanted to."

"Well, Tyrann's friend turned out to be an informant. My girl found out that I was about to meet with him and she basically came and took the dope from me. I got missing because I knew the Feds were probably trailing us."

"What happened to your girl?"

"They caught her with the dope."

Joey Turch remembered his girlfriend. Remembered the first time she'd come in his office. She was driving a Maserati and wore expensive jewelry. She had one of the nicest asses he'd seen in his life.

"But they're looking for you right?"

"More than likely."

"What do you mean more than likely? They were looking for you before all this shit even started."

"Well, if you knew that, why would you ask me something so goddamned stupid?"

"I'm just trying to get to the bottom of what happened. I have both you and Tyrann to worry about. I'm probably going to have to refer one of you to another attorney."

"Why?"

"Conflict of interest. But I'll worry about that later."

"I need my girlfriend released."

"What did she get caught with?"

"Four kilos of heroin."

"What?"

"Yeah."

"Damn."

"You're the best in Atlanta, right?"

"I am, but I ain't Jesus. This is a job for Jesus himself."

"Look, I'll wear the charges. I just want her out."

"You think she's talking?"

"I don't think so."

"I know you don't think so, but that is a shitload of dope. Most people will give their mamas up if they got caught with that much."

"Listen, it doesn't matter if she's talking or not. I want to turn myself in so she can go. Can you arrange that?"

"I think I might be able to do that. I need you to lay low and I'll make a few calls to the U.S. Attorney's Office and see what I can do."

Turch stood and peered outside the window. He was nervous and afraid that someone had been trailing Shamari. Then he said, "I need you to get a new phone number and call me."

"What about Tyrann?"

"Surprisingly, I don't think they have that much on him. I'll find out today."

Shamari wondered how that was possible. Unless, Tyrann knew that Kyrie was a snitch. He'd hoped to God that wasn't the case. He didn't want Black to be in trouble either, but here he was having to surrender himself and take responsibility for four kilos of heroin and there was a possibility that Black would walk away free.

"I will call you from my new number."

CHAPTER 53

JOEY TURCH ARRANGED FOR SHAMARI'S SURRENDER IN EXCHANGE for Jada's freedom. The U.S. Attorney's Office still charged Jada with aiding and abetting a fugitive because she knew that Shamari was on the run but Turch was trying his best to get those charges dropped. Shamari was assigned a new attorney because Turch decided he would represent Black since Black had retained him first. Turch visited Black in the county jail.

Black looked a little disheveled. He had a five-day-old beard, and he hadn't eaten in a week, so he'd lost some weight. He'd heard that Jada had been caught with the four kilos of heroin, and he was almost certain that his name would come up, even though snitch-ass Kyrie had spared him. Actually, this was even more of a reason for Jada and Shamari to turn on him. Why wouldn't they?

As soon as he sat down in the attorney's visitation room, Black said, "You've got to get me out of this, motherfucker."

"I'm trying."

"Trying ain't good enough. I need you to get me out of here. I paid you good money."

"Look, it's not about money. They want to know if you know something about the heroin this girl was caught with."

"Did they say I had something to do with it?"

"Surprisingly they didn't. She said nothing."

"Okay. Get me the fuck out of here then."

"Shamari has turned himself in and he's taking responsibility for the dope."

"Okay. Well, get me the fuck out of here then."

"It's not that simple."

"What's not simple about it?"

"Well, there is a matter of a few dead bodies."

"What?"

"Chris Stevens and Lani Miller and now the Feds think you and Shamari may know about Imani James."

"Imani who?"

"A girl that was supposedly bringing heroin back in her breast implants. The dope leaked into her blood stream and killed her."

"I don't know nothing about that."

"You want to tell them that?"

"I don't want to tell them shit. You know how I roll. I don't talk to the police."

"But you didn't tell Shamari that Kyrie was wired? Why not?" There was a long silence. Turch continued looking at Black before saying, "You know why? Because it was a matter of him or you and you would rather the cops get him, right?"

"Look, I wasn't wearing a goddamned wire. Kyrie was."

"But you could have saved Shamari."

Black looked away. "Maybe. Maybe not. If Kyrie was wearing a wire, I knew the cops were somewhere close by."

"And there we have it."

"So what are you saying?" asked Black.

"I'm saying, if you know anything about these bodies, you need to say something."

"What is Shamari saying?"

"I'm not his lawyer. I could only represent one of you. I had to get him and his girlfriend another attorney."

"Whatever I say, you're going to keep to yourself?"

"Yes.

"This girl Imani, I never meet her before, but Shamari called me one night and told me that she was dead. He said some doctor had stuffed dope in her body and she died, and we had to get rid of the body."

"Where is the body?"

"I can't tell you that?"

"Look, I'm your attorney"

"Why do you want to know?"

"The doctor has been arrested. His wife turned him in. She saw the girl on the news and knew the girl was one of his mistresses. She said she felt he had something to do with it and some stripper that works at Cheetah's verified the wife's story."

"And that's all it took?"

"No. His partner turned in Imani's breast implant. The doctor had left one of her implants on the counter and apparently those things have serial numbers on them."

"I've never met the doctor."

"And he's never met you, but he's saying that Shamari forced him to alter his face and to traffic cocaine."

"What?"

"Yes."

"But it'll be our word against his. Well, Shamari's word against his."

"Look, Shamari is screwed in another drug conspiracy, but if you're really his friend, you can save his life by telling us where the body is."

"How is this going to help me?"

"Believe it or not, nobody has anything on you. They were trying to bring kidnapping charges on you and conspiracy, but with Lani dead and your other friend taking the fall for Chris's murder and the fact that Kyrie set up Shamari instead of you, you're good."

"Did Lani say anything about me?"

"No. According to her attorney she was going to talk but she didn't. She said she couldn't."

Black broke down into tears. "Damn, I miss that girl so much."

Turch tried his best to console him. "So, you want to tell us where the body is?"

"And if I do. What happens next?"

"If you tell them where the body is, we make a deal for Shamari and he lives. If not, they are going to seek the death penalty. Here is your chance to make a wrong right."

"I'll do it. But I'm not getting on nobody's witness stand and I'm not talking about no dope."

"The doctor's blaming everything on your friend."

"You know I don't work with police."

"All they need is the body."

"When do I get out of here?"

"If they don't have charges to lay on you then in the next seventy-two hours. I'm taking you in front of the judge and demanding that they let you go."

"Get me the fuck out of here, man!"

●   ●   ●

Black was released from jail on a Thursday afternoon. He went to stay with Nana because he could no longer live at his house. The next day, he visited Ms. Carolyn's house. When Ms. Carolyn opened the door, she said to Black, "What the hell are you doing here?"

"I need to talk to you for one minute."

"Tyrann, you need to get away from here before I call the police."

"I just want to say one thing. I didn't kill Lani. I swear to God I loved that woman. I would never hurt her. You know that."

"Tyrann, even if you didn't kill her, I believe her involvement with you somehow led to her death. I believe that she indirectly died because of your bullshit."

Starr and Jada were in the den and when they heard Ms. Carolyn arguing with Black, they came out.

Black said, "What you're saying may be true. Lani's death may have something to do with me. I don't know."

"You do know. Deep down in your heart you know that if Lani hadn't been dealing with you, she would still be here."

"You're right. But I want to talk to you. I want to make it right."

Starr said, "Black, you heard the woman. You need to leave right now."

"Wait a minute. This is between me and Ms. Carolyn."

Jada flashed a pink .380 and said, "Black, you need to get the fuck away from here. I swear to God, I'll shoot your black ass right now."

Ms. Carolyn turned to Jada and said, "Put that gun away right now."

Jada placed the gun back in her purse and said, "Black, can't you see nobody wants you around? You're nothing but a bitch-ass snitch anyway."

"Is this how it is, Ms. Carolyn? After all I've done for your family?"

"You've done a lot, but there is one thing that I don't think I can forgive you for. At least right now. And that's for taking my only daughter away from me."

"I didn't do it and I intend to make it right."

"You can never make it right and you can never bring Lani back." She slammed the door in his face. Black stood on the porch for five more minutes and then he finally left.

● ● ●

The next day Black drove to Jada's townhome. She opened the door with her gun drawn.

He said, "Go ahead and kill me, Jada. But if you kill me, it's not going to help Shamari."

"You've already ruined Shamari's life."

"You don't believe that. Shamari was already on the run and you know it."

She lowered her gun.

"Look, Jada, I want to talk to you. Nobody wants to talk to me. I've done some fucked up shit. But I want to help. And I need your help."

"How can I help you?"

"Can I come in?"

She stepped aside and he came in, following her to the living room. She sat on the sofa and he sat on an armchair across from her. There was an awkward silence and she said, "Do you want something to drink?"

"No, I'm fine."

"Why did you pick me to help you out?"

"Everybody knows I'm not a good person, but you're no angel either."

"What the fuck ever, nigga"

He cut her off. "Look, I'm not judging you, Jada. I heard a lot of stuff about you fucking behind Shamari's back and I've never judged you. Ever. You know why? Because I knew that you had his back. No matter what anybody said, I knew you loved him."

"Still love him."

"I love that dude too. He told me to chill, but I didn't."

"You love him? Really?"

He looked her directly in the eye and said, "You find that hard to believe?"

"I find it hard to believe that you love anybody. Except for Lani."

There was a long silence and then he said, "I suppose you think I killed Lani too?"

"No, that's where you're wrong. I do believe you cared for Lani."

"Well, I didn't kill Lani."

"What do you want with me?"

"I need you to talk to Ms. Carolyn and get me back in her good graces."

"And what are you going to do for me?"

"I'm going to tell the Feds where that girl's body is and Shamari gets a life sentence instead of death."

"You know I'll do anything to help Shamari, but I don't think you'll ever get back in Ms. Carolyn's good graces. Why is this important to you?"

"I know this is hard to believe, but I do have a conscience. I wanna do what's right."

"Black, did you know that Kyrie was trying to set Shamari up?"

There was a long pause and he stared at the floor, trying to think of a diplomatic answer.

"You did, didn't you?"

"Look, he came into the house right after Shamari came in. He called me in the kitchen and showed me the wire he was wearing. At that point, I knew he was an informant, but I didn't know at first. I really didn't."

"Exactly what I thought."

"Look, Jada, Shamari had four kilos of heroin on him and I knew the Feds were somewhere around. What the fuck was I supposed to do? Go to prison for the rest of my life?"

"So you offered Shamari up as a sacrificial lamb?"

"I didn't offer anyone up. I didn't rat. It was Kyrie."

"It was Kyrie, but you could have warned my man."

"You're right, Jada, and I'm sorry for that, and I want to make it right. I'm going to make it right. If I take them to the body, Shamari gets life and not the death penalty."

"If you take them to the body? What are you talking about?"

"The Feds want to know where Imani is buried."

"And you know where the body is?"

"Well, my Daddy does. I'll get him to show me and I'll show them."

Jada burst into tears. "Please, do this! I don't want Shamari to die!"

"Look, Jada. I'll do that for him. I promise. I swear to you."

Black embraced her and held her tight. Tears were streaming down her face.

"Make it happen, and I'll work on Ms. Carolyn," she said.

•   •   •

Judge Henry Finnegan had a wrinkled face and a hanging jaw that looked like his mouth was always open even when it was closed. A few strands of gray surrounded his bald spot and he wore horn rimmed glasses. Although he was seventy-eight years old, he looked like he was about a hundred. Shamari knew he was fucked as soon as he heard Finnegan was assigned to his case. Shamari thought Finnegan looked like the type of old white man that wished slavery was still alive. The courtroom was fairly empty.

Jada, Tangie, and Hunch were sitting in the front row when they brought Shamari into the courtroom. He smiled and waved at his sister and Hunch. He blew a kiss at Jada. Jada blew a kiss back at him.

Judge Finnegan wasn't known for being lenient and he stuck to his script when he said, "I hereby sentence you, Shamari Brooks, to life in prison without the possibility of parole."

Jada and Tangie hugged one another. Both women wanted to cry, but Shamari's attorney had told them what to expect. Shamari's charges ranged from conspiracy to possess four kilos of heroin, conspiracy to kill a government witness and conspiracy to commit murder as well as attempted murder and he'd had a fugitive warrant in which they dropped. The U.S. Attorney had been asking for the death penalty but when Black had told them where to find Imani's body, Shamari was able to plead for a life sentence.

Shamari had wanted to go to trial because there was a possibility that he could beat the attempted murder and the conspiracy to murder charge since technically he didn't conspire to kill Imani. But there was a matter of the four kilos of heroin that he had admitted to possessing so that Jada could be free.

Judge Finnegan asked Shamari if there was anything that he would like to say.

"No, your honor."

"Court is adjourned."

Jada said, "Call me tonight, baby."

CHAPTER 54

JESSICA'S MOTHER HAD AGREED TO LET T. J. SPEND SOME TIME WITH Starr after they'd discussed Starr possibly adopting the boy. Mrs. Robinson knew she was simply too old to raise T. J. by herself. She didn't have the energy. Since Starr didn't have a child of her own and Trey was her best friend in the world, Starr figured she could take on parenting.

For the past couple of weeks, she and T. J. had gone to parks, movies, and plays. Starr's father even played football with T. J. He was holding up strong for a kid who'd lost both of his parents, but every now and then he would ask, "If there is a God, why did he have to take both my parents?"

A challenging answer to explain to a six-year-old and Starr would simply hold his hand and say, "God gives the biggest burdens to the strongest people and he knows that you're strong T. J." Then she would kiss him and he would smile and kiss her back and say, "I'm so glad God gave me you. I don't know what I would do if I didn't have you, Ms. Starr." She knew deep down inside that she had to do whatever it took to make this adoption a reality. There was no way she would let this beautiful child be alone in the world.

It was Saturday afternoon and Starr was winding down after a long day with T. J. at the park. They'd gone to see *Maleficent*. Starr was lying across her bed trying to catch her breath and T. J. was in the guest bedroom playing with his Wii when her phone rang. Someone was trying to get into the building.

"Hello?"

"Starr, its Q. Can I come up?"

"Q from Houston?"

"Yes."

Starr buzzed him in and moments later, he was knocking on her door.

She opened the door. She was dressed down in a pair of jeans and a white blouse. Nothing special, but she felt cute. Q smiled when he saw her and she invited him inside. Once inside, he said, "This is a nice building. Why don't they have a concierge?"

"I don't know. Maybe because it's a loft styled building. I really don't know."

"Yeah, maybe." Q marched past her and she shut the door.

"So what brings you here?"

"I came to tell you something."

"You came all the way from Houston to tell me something."

"I'm a face to face kind of person."

Starr looked very confused. "Is there something wrong?"

"Yes."

Starr stood there with her hands on her hips. "What's wrong, Q?"

"What's wrong is I'm not with you."

"Huh?" She studied his face and he looked very serious.

He walked over to the window, staring out into the Atlanta night. He didn't want to look her in the face. He couldn't. Not right now. He was going to pour his heart out to her.

"Look, Starr, Trey was like a brother to me and I always loved him, but I was always jealous of what you and he had. Particularly of what he had, and what he had was a real woman. I've never in my life had a real woman. Someone who had my back like you had his."

"What are you saying, Q? I don't understand."

He turned and faced her. "I love you, Starr. I've always loved you from afar, but I could never say anything out of respect for Trey. Plus, I wanted ya'll to be together. I told him the last time I saw him to go back and make everything right with you."

"You told him that?"

"Yes."

"But now you're telling me you want me?"

"Yes." Their eyes met and held.

She sat on the armchair, propping her feet underneath her butt as she watched Q. She'd always thought Q was attractive. He was tall with a nice body and he was a great businessman—both legal and illegal.

"I don't know what to say, Q."

"You don't have to say anything."

"But you are Trey—"

"Trey is gone."

He moved closer to Starr and finally he sat down in the chair across from her. A tear rolled down Starr's face.

"I know he's gone, and I don't want to disrespect his memory."

Q made his way to her armchair and sat on the arm. He took hold of her hand. "If Trey was here, never in a million years would I say to you what I'm saying. But he's not here, and he ain't coming back."

He massaged her hands and she continued to stare into his eyes. For the first time she noticed that his eyes were hazel and just beautiful to her. He caressed her hands.

She turned her head and he said, "I'm sorry if I offended you."

"You didn't offend me."

"It's just that I had to tell you how I felt. I wanted to tell you before you moved on with your life."

Little T. J. came running into the room with his Wii gaming console. Q stood up from the seat and said, "Hey, T. J. How you been, champ?"

T. J. looked at Q and then at Starr. Clearly the child was confused by the stranger talking to him. Finally, he said, "What's your name?"

"My name is Q. I met you when you were a baby. I'm your godfather."

T. J. looked at Starr for confirmation.

"Mr. Q was one of your father's best friends. He's your godfather," Starr said.

T. J. smiled and said, "I always wanted a godfather."

"Good, because I'll be moving to Atlanta in a few weeks."

Starr looked at Q and he was grinning as he brushed T. J.'s hair.

• • •

A few days after Black had showed the Feds where Imani was buried, he'd arranged a meeting with Sasha and his sister to form a partnership. Instead of opening one Wing King, he would open three. It was going to be a three way partnership, and Black would be a silent partner.

Several weeks later, Black had tracked Kyrie down. They met at one of Black's baby mother's house in College Park. They were sitting in the living room of her place when Black brandished a chrome .380. Kyrie stood up and scurried into the kitchen with Black right behind him. Kyrie was hoping to find a backdoor, but instead, all he found was a refrigerator and nowhere to run.

Black said, "Motherfucker, you take one more step, I will blow your goddamned back off!"

"What's wrong with you, man?"

"No, the question is what's wrong with you, man?"

"Look, is this about that Shamari shit? I had to do what I had to do. The important thing is that I spared you, Black. You know I would never, ever do anything to hurt you."

Black aimed the gun directly at his dome. "I wish I could say I felt the same way about you."

"No. Don't point that gun at me."

"Nigga, I will blow your whole block off."

Kyrie covered his face and Black slapped the fuck out of him with the butt of the gun.

"Move your goddamned hands. Because if you don't move your hands, I'll shoot you in your hands, and when you lower them, I'll shoot you in your motherfucking face."

Kyrie wouldn't lower his hands. He knew what Black was saying was the truth. He knew Black would kill him.

"Lower your goddamned hands, nigga."

He didn't lower them and Black slapped him with the butt of the gun again. Blood began oozing from his mouth.

"So you're not going to lower your hands?"

"Tell me why you're doing this?"

"You didn't think I was going to let you get away with the bullshit that you pulled, did you?"

"What?" Kyrie lowered his hands for one second. The blood was still oozing out of his mouth. With his t-shirt, he tried to wipe his mouth and Black slapped him in his goddamned ear and fired a shot at the same time.

"I want to know the truth, nigga. Let me know the truth."

"The truth about what?"

"Why did you do what you did?"

"Look, they made me do it. When my son went to school with that heroin and all those people were OD'ing, I told you we needed to use another cut. Shamari told you. Everybody told you. But all you wanted to do was make money."

"So it's my fault that you're a bitch-ass nigga?"

"Look, you could have warned Shamari. Why didn't you do it?"

Kyrie was indirectly calling Black a coward and Black didn't like the sound of that. He blasted a shot directly into Kyrie's balls and Kyrie crashed to the floor.

"Now tell me." Black put the gun up to Kyrie's motherfucking temple.

"'What do you want to know? I'll tell you anything. Please, Black, please don't kill me."

"Tell me what happened to Lani?"

"I don't know what happened to Lani."

"You telling a motherfucking lie! You do know what happened to Lani!"

"I swear, Black. I don't know what happened to Lani."

Black stood Kyrie up and shot him in the foot and Kyrie crashed back to the floor. Black stood him back up. Blood was coming from his left foot and his balls.

"You want to tell me what happened now?" Black said.

"Nothing. I don't know who killed Lani."

"Strip!"

"What?"

"Take off your clothes!"

"Huh?"

"Strip!"

Kyrie removed his clothes while he sat on the floor bleeding and wearing only a pair of blue boxing shorts.

Black ordered him to remove them as well.

After Kyrie was naked, Black said. "Lay on your stomach."

"What?"

"I said lay on your goddamned stomach!"

Kyrie was now butt naked on the floor and Black said. "I'm going to take this gun and ram it up your asshole if you don't tell me what happened to Lani!"

Tears rolling down Kyrie's face, he said. "I killed her! I killed her because she knew that I was helping the police and I knew she would tell you!"

"So you killed her and you lied?"

"But I never did anything to you."

"You know if you hurt Lani, you hurt me, motherfucker!"

"I know, but I never meant to hurt you. I would never do anything to hurt you."

Black said, "Today is your lucky day. I'm not going to kill you, since you told me what happened to Lani. Stand your ass up."

Kyrie struggled to rise to his feet. When he was barely standing, he said, "Thank you, Black. Thank you so much."

"I won't kill you. You're my friend. We've been friends since elementary school. Just like you wouldn't do anything to hurt me, I wouldn't want to hurt you. And I appreciate you telling me that you were wired."

Kyrie smiled. "Anything for you, my nigga."

"Well, I want to know who was with you when you killed Lani."

"My cousin, Avant."

"Now you know I'm going to have to kill him, don't you?"

"I'll give you his address. I'll even show you where he lives. Just don't kill me, Black. Please don't kill me. I spared you."

"Really? You spared me, motherfucker. Is that how you look at it?"

"Well, I could have—"

Black cut him off. "Shut the fuck up and give me Avant's address."

Black dug into a junk drawer and retrieved a pen and a piece of paper. He handed it to Kyrie and told him to scribble the address down.

"'Preciate it, bruh," said Kyrie after he finished writing the information.

Black gave him a pound. "Now get the fuck out!"

Kyrie stared at Black. He couldn't believe how fortunate he was to be able to leave relatively unharmed. He thanked Black immensely as he hopped out of the door.

As soon as the door slammed shut, Big L stepped from the back of the house and put a .357 magnum to Kyrie's head and fired a shot. The bullet ripped into his skull almost decapitating him.

Black looked out the blinds and said, "I promised that I wasn't going to kill you. I didn't say shit about somebody else."

• • •

To be continued.

GET A FREE eBOOK!

Enjoyed this book?

If you enjoyed this book please write a review and email it to me at kevinelliott3@gmail.com, and get a FREE ebook.

K. Elliott Book Order Form
PO Box 12714
Charlotte NC 28220

Book Name	Quantity	Price	Shipping/ Handling	Total
Dear Summer		X $14.95	+ $3.00 per book	
Dilemma		X $14.95	+ $3.00 per book	
Entangled		X $13.95	+ $3.00 per book	
Godsend Series 1–5		X $14.95	+ $3.00 per book	
Godsend Series 6–10		X $14.95	+ $3.00 per book	
Kingpin Wifeys Vol. 1		X $14.95	+ $3.00 per book	
Kingpin Wifeys Vol. 2		X $14.95	+ $3.00 per book	
Kingpin Wifeys Vol. 3		X $14.95	+ $3.00 per book	
Kingpin Wifeys Vol. 4		X $14.95	+ $3.00 per book	
Street Fame		X $14.95	+ $3.00 per book	
Treasure Hunter		X $15.00	+ $3.00 per book	
			TOTAL	

Mailing Address

Name:

Mailing Address:

City	State	Zip

Method Of Payment

[   ] Check [   ] Money Order

Thank you for your support

About the Author

K. Elliott, aka The Well Fed Black Writer, penned his first novel, Entangled, in 2003. Although he was offered multiple signing deals, Elliott decided to found his own publishing company, Urban Lifestyle Press.

Bookstore by bookstore, street vendor by street vendor, Elliott took to the road selling his story. He did not go unnoticed, selling 50,000 units in his first year and earning a spot on the Essence Magazine Bestsellers list.

Since Entangled, Elliott has published five titles of his own and two more on behalf of authors signed to Urban Lifestyle Press. For one book, The Ski Mask Way, Elliott was selected to co-author with hip-hop superstar 50 Cent. Along the way, he has continued to look for innovative ways to push his books to his fans while keeping down his overhead.

Elliott is passionate about sharing what he has learned with aspiring authors, and has conducted learning webinars filled with information on what works best for him. He is the author of numerous best-sellers including Dilemma, Street Fame, Treasure Hunter, Dear Summer, Entangled, The Godsend Series and the hugely intriguing Kingpin Wifeys Series.

CPSIA information can be obtained
at www.ICGtesting.com
Printed in the USA
LVHW011318060119
602928LV00017B/569/P